# Shadows on the Concert Stage

Vol. 4

by

Mary Visker

**Gotham Books**

30 N Gould St.
Ste. 20820, Sheridan, WY 82801
https://gothambooksinc.com/

Phone: 1 (307) 464-7800

© 2025 *Mary Visker*. All rights reserved.

No part of this book may be reproduced, stored in a retrieval system, or transmitted by any means without the written permission of the author.

Published by Gotham Books (February 19, 2025)

ISBN: 979-8-3482-6929-6 (P)
ISDN: 979-8-3482-6930-2 (E)

Because of the dynamic nature of the Internet, any web addresses or links contained in this book may have changed since publication and may no longer be valid.

The views expressed in this work are solely those of the author and do not necessarily reflect the views of the publisher, and the publisher hereby disclaims any responsibility for them.

# Table of Contents

CHAPTER 1 ...................................................................................... 1

CHAPTER 2 .................................................................................... 21

CHAPTER 3 .................................................................................... 35

CHAPTER 4 .................................................................................... 48

CHAPTER 5 .................................................................................... 65

CHAPTER 6 .................................................................................... 88

CHAPTER 7 .................................................................................. 102

CHAPTER 8 .................................................................................. 129

CHAPTER 9 .................................................................................. 138

CHAPTER 10 ................................................................................ 152

CHAPTER 11 ................................................................................ 176

CHAPTER 12 ................................................................................ 196

CHAPTER 13 ................................................................................ 211

CHAPTER 14 ................................................................................ 223

CHAPTER 15 ................................................................................ 227

CHAPTER 16 ................................................................................ 245

CHAPTER 17 ................................................................................ 263

CHAPTER 18 ................................................................................ 274

CHAPTER 19 ................................................................................ 297

CHAPTER 20 ................................................................................ 321

# CHAPTER 1

"Sorry for our manners, please come in," Evan says as he opens the door wide, and I lead Detective Douglas and Agent Fowler into the kitchen indicating they should sit at the table. Evan continues, "Now, what do you mean, Terry's the target?"

Agent Fowler tries speaking in a calming voice, "Terry, when Detective Douglas sent your testimony of the Mob Boss's sudden death to the FBI, it leaked quickly to the crime world and almost created a panic. When a Boss steps down, there is usually a staged accident to cover his disappearance, and Number One always moves in to take his place. With your testimony that both the Boss and Number One are dead, there is anarchy in the underworld. A large faction in the mob feels that if they eliminate you as the only witness, they can designate a Number One asserting he is the one the Boss chose."

Both Evan and I sit stunned; he is the first to speak, "Can anything be done?"

Fowler continues, "We think so if we act fast. We need to recover the bodies and flash their pictures in a media blitz. The mob will eventually reorganize, but it could save you and a blood bath taking out hundreds of innocent people. Will you help us?"

I answer instantly, "What do you want us to do?" There is no way I'm doing this without Evan.

"We want both of you to leave with us now to come down to the police station for your protection. As soon as the helicopter arrives, we want you to go with us to show us the avalanche site and approximately where the bodies are. I have arranged for large earth-moving vehicles from the closest open pit mine to meet us there. We should all arrive about the time it's getting light. We must recover those bodies before the mob does. We are also having a full National Guard unit set up a protective barrier."

Evan jumps to his feet, "Give us ten minutes to get on our winter survival gear and we're all yours." We're moving before we even get a reply.

Circling over the avalanche gives me the strangest feelings of anxiety and gratitude mixed together. The ugliest evil I have ever known lies beneath that snow heap, and I am safely flying above it. As we land and step onto the snow, we are approached by the supervisor of the mining company and the Lieutenant Colonel commanding the Guard Unit. Nothing is said, but all eyes expectantly rivet on me.

I move so that I can take in the whole panorama at once. I know that the cabin wasn't too far from where the road leveled. When Tommy and I came out of our tree snow cave the next morning, there were still traces of the cabin poking through the snow even though it had snowed most of the night. That helped me have a general idea of where the cabin rubble should be now. When Fake Fletcher and Number One parked their snowmobiles, they were on top of the demolished cabin. When I put that into perspective with the cliff high above us, I lift my arm to point in the general direction, "They should be somewhere in this general direction and on the down slope of this snow hill."

That's like the starting gun for a sprint. The snow is marked, and equipment begins to move at once. Two bulldozers with front loaders large enough to hold two full-sized vans start scooping up snow and pouring it into dump trucks that have tires twice my height. We are invited into the large tent that houses the command center. Stepping through the tent flap my nose discerns bacon, eggs, and hash browns. Evan and I are escorted to the front of the line and given plates overflowing with food. You can't imagine how good this food tastes. This is the first food other than venison I have had in almost a week. I'm almost ready to ask for seconds when I hear someone outside yell, "We found one of the snowmobiles."

I rush out of the tent to see where it is. I tell them they need to move about ten feet to the east. The message is relayed to the dozer drivers. They back up and move forward again scooping as they go. The other dozer picks up the second snowmobile. The snow machines are not dumped into the trucks but put to the side for a team to thoroughly gather evidence.

Two scoops later I hear, "We've got one of the bodies." The bulldozer is guided on where to put the frozen corpse. A team of FBI and police officers pull him out of the bucket and instantly began taking pictures. Within minutes there is an identification from the face photos and the fingerprint photos. Agent Fowler guides me to make a positive identification.

When we reach the deceased man, he looks more like he's sleeping. He still has all his color. Agent Fowler gives me the details, "This is Nicolas 'The Avenger' Night. He is the Boss of one of the largest mobs in the East. His fingerprints are all over the candy that almost killed you."

I look at him closely and shake my head, "His fingerprints may have been on the candy, but he is not the Boss. He is Number One."

"Terry, are you sure? This must be him."

I'm ready to assert myself when we hear another yell, "We've got the other body."

When it's placed beside the first, I move in for a close look, "Agent Fowler, this is the Boss. This is the Fake Fletcher we've been dealing with for a year. This is the man who told me he killed Roger Fletcher and made Roger's wife be his live-in slave for twenty years. This is the man that would kill an innocent baby for wounded pride."

While I've been talking, pictures were taken and sent for identification. When the ID is made and relayed back to Fowler, he shakes his head, "This is Earnest 'The Devil' Higbee. We closed the file on him years ago when we thought he died in a mining explosion. He has had his fingerprints removed, but the smudges are the same as those we found on his things at the Fletcher's residence. Terry, you have no idea how big this is."

I think he's going to say more when the air is pierced by a siren followed by a loudspeaker announcement, "Our perimeter is breached, the enemy is inside! Repeat the enemy is inside!"

I turn to Evan, "Down flat!" We both fall onto the snow. Our white winter survival suits blend perfectly. From the ground, I yell at Agent Flower, "Get those bodies on the chopper and get out of here."

"There isn't room for them and you on the chopper. Get in quick."

"Agent, we're safer here on our own than with you. Send the chopper back in three days. When you load the scum, throw the snowshoes out saying you don't need them anymore. I'll call you."

We slither backward over the lip of the snow that's been dumped and bury ourselves with loose snow. We can hear their shouts of disbelief, "Where did they go? Can't see them anywhere. Get those bodies in bags and loaded. I see them over on the avalanche back by the cliffs." I smile and silently thank Detective Douglas for giving us cover. We settle down to wait for the whole area to clear.

Fifteen minutes later there's no sound. It's an eerie silence. I'm getting nervous and am about to spring up to a sitting position. Evan must be able to feel my vibes. He puts his hand on my arm and whispers. "Terry let's give it a little more time. Something tells me all is not safe."

He barely has the words out when I start picking up the roar of a snowmobile. It's coming straight toward us, or maybe aiming for the road down the canyon. When it's right above us where the bodies had been, the engine is cut. I realize it's two snowmobiles with two riders each when I listen to their conversation, "I've been thinking, we're dumb to be out here in the open. That broad took out Number One and the Boss. We're sitting ducks." Another voice says, "Besides, with Number One gone, there's no one to pay any of the Boss's personal contracts. There's no prize money, and I have no loyalty to past mobsters." A deeper voice growls, "Let's get out of here before she finds a way to take care of us too." The engines start and fade away as they speedily make their way down the canyon.

We wait for what I think is another fifteen minutes but seems like an hour. Evan sits up shaking off his snow disguise but puts a hand on me to keep me down until he's sure all is safe. When he's convinced we're alone, he pulls me up to a sitting position, "Well my amazing wife, I think you succeeded in driving everyone away. What are we going to do for three days out here in the mountains all alone?"

"I was only trying to fill everyone's requests. Agent Fowler and Detective Douglas wanted us to disappear for a few days, and you wanted to have me to yourself until we start practicing with the OC to go to Carnegie Hall for Christmas. I thought we could have a short second honeymoon while practicing winter survival."

"That wouldn't happen to include a cave with a hot spring in it, would it?" He says with a sly grin.

I coyly answer, "It might."

On day three, Detective Douglas picks us up with the drop line from the helicopter on the top of the ridge where I was rescued with Tommy. When we're finally inside and buckled for the ride home, the detective is bursting with excitement, "There's chaos going on in the mob world, but we think you are out of the hot seat. Just to make sure Agent Fowler has found a safe house for both of you to stay in until school starts. He thinks things should be cooled off by then."

I focus on him with a shocked expression, "I know exactly where were going to be." He stares at me waiting for my next sentence, "We are going to be on the concert stage at Carnegie Hall the whole day of Christmas with Augustine's Oratorio Choir giving three maybe four concerts."

"Terry, you can't be serious. It's way too dangerous. You'll have to cancel."

"Sorry, Detective Douglas. You must understand there is no way I can cancel. I have signed a contract and more importantly, I can't let Pam and our students down. I will be there."

"I can't wait until Fowler hears this."

Evan and I are in bed talking about our trip to New York in four short hours. I don't think we'll even be able to sleep before it's time to get up and get ready. I'm so excited that Evan gets to be there with me this time. I am so startled that I almost drop my cell phone when it starts ringing. "Hello?"

"Terry, I'm sorry to bother you so late, but I wanted you to know that your grandfather has had a heart attack and is now having bypass surgery." I'm speechless for an instant then switch my phone to the speaker and ask him to repeat what he just said so Evan is part of the conversation. "Your grandfather, Dr. Martin, was having dinner with my family when he started having chest pains. We called an ambulance, and he was rushed to the hospital. He is now in surgery. I know you would like to be by his side, but I must ask you to go with the OC to New York. No one can take your place. I will take care of Albert here. I'll get him into a good nursing home." I'm speechless. I turn to Evan with tears running down my cheeks.

Evan wraps his arms around me, "Terry, he's as much my grandfather as he is yours. He belongs with us and not in a nursing home. Let me help you to fulfill your commitments. I'll stay here and be with grandfather every minute I'm allowed, and when he's ready I'll bring him home and take care of him."

Oh, sometimes life is so hard and complicated, but I feel at peace with Evan's plan. "Mark, did you hear Evan's plan?"

He answers, "Yes. I'll go with the choir and leave Martin in Evan's care.

"He was going to come with us as dean; will you be taking his place?"

After a short pause he answers, "If Evan will take care of Martin, I'll be there with you as dean."

"Dr. Rich, I'm dressed and on my way to the hospital. I'll keep you both updated. Take care of my wife, she'll explain the danger she's in."

While we are waiting to board our flight, Evan texts that Grandad is out of surgery, and the doctor says he's doing well. The three bypasses look good, and his heart is functioning well on its own. He is now getting more oxygen to his heart than he has for a long time. When he wakes up, he will want to get up and run. They will keep him pinned down in the cardiac critical care unit for three days. Then he can go home with a complete list of instructions for taking care of his new heart.

I silently whisper a prayer of thanksgiving. I feel like I just dropped 500 pounds from my shoulders. Now, I need to focus on putting my mind into this trip to Carnegie. I'm ready when the call to board our jet is announced. I'm surprised when I match the seat number on my ticket with the one above my seat. It's in first class. I'm even more shocked to see that Dr. Rich is sitting next to me. He motions for me to sit down, "I hope you don't mind. I had the seats rearranged a little so we could travel together. There are a few things I would like to discuss with you."

I start to sit down and am glad to see Tom and Pam taking the two seats in front of us. I smile and ask Dr. Rich, "How did we manage first-class seats? I like this idea."

"Terry, you have to remember that Carnegie is footing the bill for this trip, and they treat their performers with the best."

As soon as we're airborne, Dr. Rich turns to me. I know what his first question is going to be. We spend the next hour talking about the danger I'm in. He only ponders that a moment before he changes the subject, "What I need to discuss with you is the problem you and Pam have created for our college of music."

I know Pam has listened to our conversation, but now she turns her head to be involved, "Pam, why don't you come back here and squeeze in with me? This first-class seat is big enough for both of us for a while."

When Pam is settled, Dr. Rick begins, "Because of what you two have done, our enrollment for the middle of the year is way beyond anything we have ever experienced. We have both men and women wanting to transfer into our choirs. Some are already Augustine students, but most are transfers from other schools. We also have a large number of advanced piano students wanting to be admitted to our graduate programs. Since you're the cause, I'm hoping you're also the solution. Understand, I think this is a good problem, not a bad one. You two have done incredible things."

I know this is what Dr. Martin was working for, but I didn't think it would start quite so soon, maybe next fall. Pam and I look at each other, and she turns to Dr. Rich, "I've been thinking about this since last fall. I don't like taking new students directly into OC. They pull the quality down of the whole choir. It takes almost a semester to bring them up to speed. I wish there was kind of a prep choir to get them ready. Actually, I would want a men's and a women's choir to train separately. I would keep them in those choirs until they were ready for either the concert choir or the oratorio choir."

"I knew you would come up with the solutions."

Pam looks at me, "I would like to direct those new choirs, but half of our success depends on having an extremely competent accompanist."

"The music college can see we have underestimated the value of the accompanists in our choirs. Terry, do you have any ideas? You can't be the accompanist for all the choirs."

"Dr. Rich, the expectations I have for my doctoral students are that they become proficient enough to perform the masters on any concert stage with me or on their own, I expect that each of them will be able to accompany any individual or group and make them shine, in addition, they should be able to compose music at their level of performance. However, my highest goal for them is to be able to masterfully teach all the above.

"What do you think of this? Let's make Arundel an accompanist for the concert choir, Allen to accompany the men's choir, and Maria to take on the women's choir. We could also put Solomon in the men's choir to help tune them. He has a phenomenal ear for pitch. Celia took a conducting class last semester. If she went into the women's choir with you Pam, you could teach her more about directing. She and Jefferson seem bent on starting a children's choir in a poverty neighborhood after they graduate."

Both Dr. Rich and Pam stare at me. I patiently wait for all the ramifications to sink in. Pam nods her head in approval, but Dr. Rich still has a question, "What about the advanced piano students?"

I'm prepared, "Make Allen and Arundel part-time faculty, and they can teach privately to the incoming advanced students. I'll teach as many advanced technique sections as we need to get our new students moving down the road. I also want to teach a full semester of composition and one of accompanying for the doc candidates and those that just finished adv tec 2. That should keep us all busy,"

Dr. Rich shakes his head, "Martin told me to watch out for the whirlwind you two would create. He wasn't joking…Find out if Celia and Maria are excited about your suggestions. Let's meet with Allen and Arundel next week during the Christmas break."

I stand up quickly, "If you two would excuse me, I need to find a restroom." I make my way down the aisle muttering to myself, so far this pregnancy hasn't changed my life too much except for the constant trips to the bathroom. The one in first class is occupied, so I make my way down through the coach to the tail of the plane.

As I pass Celia and Jefferson, I say hi and casually add that I need to talk to Celia. She gives me a thumbs up and adds that she needs to talk to me too. On the way back down, Celia is sitting in the second seat and pats the aisle seat for me to join her. Jefferson is nowhere to be seen. When I'm settled, I look intently at her, "You first,"

"Terry, I want to talk to you about Dawn and Solomon."

"I passed them on the way. Looks to me like we have a wedding coming up, or they are already married."

"That's the problem. They're both madly in love with each other, but Solomon doesn't think it's fair for Dawn to be stuck with a blind man. I thought that since you had a similar problem when Evan came back from his mission missing a foot, you might talk to him."

"I'd be happy to do that, but I think there's someone more qualified. Since Cindy Jaconelli is married to AJ, she'd be the perfect person to talk to him. Why don't you arrange for Dawn and Solomon to sit at your table for dinner tonight and make sure there are at least three extra seats? I'll have AJ and his wife there with me. We'll do the best we can." I then tell her about the new women's choir class. She is ecstatic about the opportunity to work with Pam.

As soon as the wheels touch the pavement, I'm punching in Evan's phone number. He answers on the first ring, "Hi Terry, you must have just landed."

"How's Granddad? Did he make it through the surgery okay?"

"You don't need to worry about your venerable grandfather. He has years of fight still left in him. Says he hasn't felt this good for years and is ready to go home, now. The doctors say he needs to stay in the hospital for two days to make sure the incisions are not leaking. Here, he wants to talk to you."

Tears roll down my face as I hear his husky voice, "Terry, I'm so sorry I'm not in New York with you. It was going to be such a fantastic experience. See if they'll let you bring back a recording. Dr. Rich will take good care of you all."

"Granddad, I love you. When I get back, we are going to be more of a family."

"Terry, I love you with all my new heart. Wow them tomorrow, Merry Christmas…Here's Evan."

"Terry, I know you'll be back late tomorrow night. So, let's make our Christmas Dec. 26th. It really won't be Christmas until I'm holding you in my arms."

"Sounds wonderful to me…I've been thinking if you haven't already talked to Granddad about coming to live with us, wait until I can be there with you. I'm building my case. I love you. Talk to you tomorrow."

We're getting off the buses to enter Carnegie Hall for dinner. I'm blown away when we enter the reception hall which has been transformed into a banquet dining room. The decorations herald Christmas and round eight-seater tables are decked in magnificent red and green linens with beautiful decorations. I'm so glad our students are still clad in their forest-green university blazers and gray traveling slacks. They look so professional in all this grandeur. I'm glad Pam opted not to have a head-table but would rather we mingle with our students. This will work out perfectly for our discussion if all goes as planned. I pull AJ and Cindy aside to let our choir enter before we do. Once inside, I see Celia has done her job. We quickly move to their table.

As soon as we're seated, Owen Sterling, Carnegie Hall's director moves to a mic on a small stand by the food. "Augustine University, welcome to New York and The Hall. We are so honored to have you here for our Christmas Day Concert. It is with extreme pleasure that we honor your talents with dinner tonight. It is being served buffet style so you may pick your meal, and so you can eat as much as you like. Mrs. Masters, do you have anything to add before we begin?"

Pam stands where she is at her table, "It is alright with you if we sing one song for our supper and then have a blessing on our food?"

"Most certainly, the evening is yours."

Pam moves to the mic, and I hurry to the piano across the room wondering what song we're singing. She lifts her hands to stand the choir, "It feels like the acoustics are just right for us to sing 'Music Alone Shall Live'. Let's see if you can hold your parts standing where you are." She looks at me and I nod my head.

On signal, the high sopranos start singing and we're off in a swirl. Slowly we build to a twelve-part harmony and then fade to the basso's ending. I didn't hear one struggling part. As she lowers her arms, she looks around the room, "Calvin, would you offer a blessing of thanks on our food?" When Calvin finishes, the room starts moving toward the food tables since Pam did not seat the choir. Her mind is thinking faster and faster in this performing world.

Pam is closest to the food so, she's first in line. I get to her table just as she's sitting her plate down. I grab her in a huge bear hug, "Pam that was so ingenious. You nailed it right on."

"Terry, the Spirit just kept whispering for me to do that. I'm so excited they can sing scattered. We could even flash mob."

"Could you do that in your receptions after each concert tomorrow?" Mr. Sterling asks, standing behind us and looking as excited as we are.

Standing, Dr. Rich answers before we can, "Of course, they will." Then he hugs both of us.

I finally get a plate of food and make my way back to our table. As I'm finishing, I'm trying to decide the best way to begin this conversation about Solomon and Dawn. Before I can begin, Solomon turns his head toward the other side of the table, "Cindy, may I ask you a rather personal question? I know we are in a large group for sharing personal feelings, so you don't need to answer if you would rather not."

"Oh, Sol, my dearest friends are sitting at this table. Ask away."

He hesitates, seeming to gather courage, "Do you ever feel that it was unfair or too much of a burden to marry a man not completely whole, a blind man?"

Cindy breaks into a huge smile, "The only thing that would have been unfair was when he tried to use that argument on me to break our engagement after the accident. I love this man more today than I did when I said, 'I do'. The parts of me that he fills don't need his eyes to make me whole."

Solomon leans excitedly toward her, "What parts does he fill?"

"Mental, intellectual, emotional, social, and oh, did I mention physically?" Everyone at the table snickers. "Sol, we each have our strengths and our weaknesses, and we help each other. The more we become one, the more we individually become stronger. For your information, I have always and will always consider AJ a completely whole man." She looks at me, "Terry, didn't you have a similar experience with Evan after he lost his foot?"

"I surely did. It took everything I had to convince him we needed to be together. I'm complete now and so is he. You're right Cindy, the love continues to grow and deepen."

A new male voice enters our conversation, "Sol, Cindy's right. It was the best decision she ever helped me make. Our oneness makes me complete. A side benefit is that she's my eyes and watches out for everything I can't see."

Cindy breaks in, "And AJ has a vision for things I can't see with my eyes."

Solomon turns to Dawn, "Is this what you want, to be married to an incomplete, sightless man for the rest of your life?"

I know they are holding hands under the table and Dawn moves closer to lean on his arm as she looks into his eyes, "No, I want to be married to the most complete, intelligent, handsome man I have ever met. I love you Solomon Tune, and I want to marry you." She turns her head and kisses him on the cheek.

"Well, if that's how you honestly feel…" He hesitates, "We'll talk about it later, we're not in a very private place." I think I can see a blush on his dark skin.

It's after midnight when Dawn comes into our hotel room. I'm not asleep. My thoughts keep spiraling around Granddad, Evan, Dawn and Sol, the concert tomorrow, and Pam's brilliantness today. As she tiptoes around trying to get ready for bed in the dark, I need to ask, "Well, how did it go?"

I startle her so completely she falls on her bed breathing like she'd been shot, "Oh Terry, you scared me so badly I lost all control. I don't even know what you said, my mind was so far away."

"I ask how your evening went."

"We're engaged! He wants to get married next week before school starts. Can we do that?"

"You could get married tomorrow if you wanted, but it would be much easier next week."

"Could the bishop of your ward I've been going to marry us?"

"I think he probably would, and I think we could hold your wedding and reception at Pam and Tom's ranch house. You will need to get a marriage license first thing Monday morning. Now, I think you'll be awake all night, but I've got to get some sleep so I can think in the concert tomorrow or should I say this morning."

"Thanks, Terry, I can't even count how many times you've opened a door to a better life for me. I love you. Goodnight."

# CHAPTER 2

As the choir members make their way onto the stage, I notice there are many more men dressed like stage crew than I've seen before. I don't have time to speculate long when I spot two familiar faces smiling at me. "Good morning, Terry," Agent Fowler says. "This is a first for me, spending Christmas Day in Carnegie Hall."

"Can I say I'm not surprised to see you here. But Detective Douglas, aren't you a little far from your jurisdiction?"

"Who am I to turn down a free ticket to a Christmas Concert. Agent Fowler invited me to be a temporary part of his team."

I can see that Pam almost has the choir placed, and it will be time for me to start warm-ups. Agent Fowler gets serious. "Terry, trade me your diamond necklace for this one." He pulls a long thin jewelry box from his pocket. "They look close to the same, but with this one, we can monitor all conversations within a six-foot radius. You will have instant help if you need it. All these extra men will be behind the back curtains. If someone suspiciously approaches you, get them talking. You are so good at getting the criminal type to spill their guts. We're pretty sure the contract has been lifted off your head, but Pam is another story. We think someone may be tailing her in hopes she will lead them to Grandma. Stick to her like glue. If someone gets in your face, ask them who they are. My men will give you the name of one of the seven dwarfs. I have no women here. If a stage crew gives you their name, we will instantly check it out with a photo ID…Break a leg."

I smile and give him a thumbs up while heading to my home at the beautiful grand piano.

Our after-concert reception is bursting at the seams. There's hardly room to turn around with the number of people wanting to meet the choir. I think our performance was as good if not better than the Oratorio Concert last May. The score Pam wrote is priceless and delivers a powerful Christ-centered message. With eye contact from Pam, I start making my way to the piano in the back for our goodbye song.

I'm stopped abruptly when I spot one of our male singers entwined in the arm of a very sparsely clad woman. She has her arm around his neck running her fingers through his dark curly hair and is standing with her face less than three inches from his. At first, she appeared to be college-age, but on closer inspection, I can see she is probably about thirty with an excellent make-up job. I think Willie is being propositioned by a prostitute like Pam and I were in May.

When I reach the piano, Pam is already at the mike. She taps it twice and has the immediate attention of almost everyone in the room. She makes her announcement and raises her arms to begin. There is dead silence in the room except for giggling in the back corner. Pam lowers her arms and speaks into the mic, "Willie Johnson, could I please have your complete focused attention." All eyes turn to Willie and the woman. She whispers in his ear, and he quickly turns around.

Stammering, he blurts out, "Sorry Mrs. Masters," trying to focus on her. Pam lifts her arms again, and on her signal, I begin a short introduction. Two measures into the song she abruptly cuts the music. I have never heard such discord, and it all seems to be coming from Willie in the back corner.

Calvin places himself directly nose to nose with Willie and yells, "Don't sing!" Willie turns red but seems to take it as the opportunity to turn back into the arms of the wanton woman. Pam taps the mic again, lifts her arms and we begin.

Willie is quickly forgotten as the crowd is swallowed in live surround sound. With the last notes coming from the low bassos, the audience begins clapping and cheering, which evolves into hugs for everyone. When Pam steps into chaos, she is gathered into a giant bear hug by the older woman we had seen in the audience at the Oratorio Concert. The one that could be her older self. When I finally reach them through the crows, the gorgeous matronly woman turns and hugs me. "You two are something else. You will change the concert world." She squeezes both of our hands and hurries out the door.

Pam and I follow the crowd and the choir out the door. We will be back in this room in thirty minutes for lunch. I breathe a sigh of relief when we find Dr. Rich with his arm around Willie's shoulder anchoring him in place. Willie looks guiltily at Pam, "Mrs. Masters, I am so sorry. Nothing like that has ever happened to me before."

Pam puts her hand on his shoulder, "Do you know what that woman was trying to do to you?"

"Dr. Rich has been talking to me. Now I understand about prostitutes. I couldn't believe the feelings she aroused in me. I didn't even know I was capable of such sensations."

"Willie, I'm sorry you made that discovery on our choir tour. That should be saved for your wedding night. Now you will have more of a challenge to bridle your passions on your mission, but you can do it."

"Mrs. Masters, I don't think I can sing. You heard what happened when I tried."

Dr. Rich turns to look directly into his eyes, "Come with me, and we'll get you changed back into your traveling suit. I have my own spot backstage; we'll have a man-to-man talk. You'll be okay."

After the second concert and reception, I grab Pam's hand to rush her out the door, "I've got to find a restroom quick." When we get to the performers' women's room the line is coming out the door. I pull her again, "Let's go up a floor to a patron's restroom." There are no lines when we fly through the door.

I look up into the mirror as the door opens and am shocked to see Pam's look-a-like coming in. We both instantly turn around staring.

She walks gracefully toward us, "I am so thrilled to have the opportunity to speak to both of you. I was on the judging committee for the Oratorio Competition in April. When we listened to your submission recording, we knew who the winner would be in May. I have been a judge for years, and I had never heard anything like it. Mrs. Masters, I am so impressed with your composition skills. This Christmas Concert rivals the one you did in May."

She is about to say more when the entry door is pushed open so hard it crashes against the wall. The woman running in seems to be off balance and heading directly for us at top speed. I step close to our mystery woman, put my arm around her waist, and while pulling her close turn us both in a circle. The careening woman crashed into the sink hitting her head on the mirror shattering it. The three of us stare in shock at the seemingly stunned woman. I almost think she mumbles, "I thought I'd lost you." Then she moans loudly.

Medical Pam standing on the other side of her takes charge, "Are you okay? You hit your head awfully hard, but I don't see any blood. Maybe you need to sit down over here on this lounge." Pam says as she takes hold of her arm and tries to move her.

"No, I just need to use the toilet badly." She staggers toward a stall breaking Pam's grip and closes the door behind her. We all stare at the locked cubicle.

The older woman recovers first, "Dr. Timpson, you must be a dancer, that was quite a move. You saved me from being squished flat. I also need to tell you I think you are a brilliant pianist. Not only are you a talented concert pianist, but an accompanist extraordinaire. Together you two are an unbeatable duo…I do have a question for you. Did you write two different accompaniments for Pam's Christmas Cantata?"

Pam is now laughing, "No she never even writes one unless someone wants a printed copy. She always makes it up as we go along, but we always get the melody line for each part. You are right she is brilliant."

"I'm glad I got to chat with you a little. I need to get back to my seat before I'm crawling over everyone to get to it. I can't wait to hear what you're going to do during this last concert, Dr. Timpson. It's like attending three different concerts, amazing, absolutely amazing." She says as she walks unruffled out the door.

"Terry, I think it's about time for dinner," Pam says while pointing at the stall housing our intruder and indicating a question.

"I think we had better let housekeeping know about the mess in here and that one of their crew might be sick. Let's do that on the way to dinner. If we're late, there won't be any food left."

I bend down and pick up a little flat plastic box that I covered with my foot in the commotion. It's about a half-inch square and a quarter-inch thick. When I try to pick it up, I find it's stuck to the floor. I pry it up, put it in my pocket, and follow Pam out the door.

Entering the reception, now dining hall, we are hailed to a table where four men are seated, Tom, Dr. Rich, Agent Fowler, and Detective Douglas. Dr. Rich stands and holds a chair for me between him and Agent Fowler. As soon as I give the FBI agent eye contact, he speaks, "Terry…" I don't let him get any further. I put a finger to my closed lips and shake my head. I hold out my closed fist in front of him, and he looks puzzled. I point to him and hold out my other hand in a cup shape. When he finally understands, he holds out one hand palm up. I move my fist over his hand and drop the little plastic piece onto his palm. His mouth drops open, and he stares at me mouthing the words, "Where did you get this?" I grab my napkin and look around to see if anyone has something to write with. He reaches under his chair and puts his tablet in front of me. I quickly write an explanation. He notes back, "This is a listening device as well as a tracker, and it isn't one of ours."

Pam has followed every step of our silent conversation. She takes the tablet, "I think it was meant for the patron who was in the ladies' room with us. Why don't you give it to a female security guard and have her take a bus to Grand Central

Station, get on a train to the furthest point possible, stick it under a seat, and get off at the first stop to retrace her stops back here? If she chats with people along the way, the listener will think the plant was a success." Agent Fowler gives Pam a smug smile and a thumbs-up. He takes his tablet and the chip rushing out of the reception hall.

A few minutes later he returns with a triumphant expression. As he slides into his seat, he takes in Pam and me, "Alright, I want to know every detail." When we're finished, he says, "Now you know your adversary; you'll see her again. Get her to talk if you can and remember we're only feet away. I'm listening to every sound that's close to you."

I think our last concert is the best of the day. Maybe I'm just partial to hearing all our music in the Stem. We don't have a reception because of the time constraints of making our airline flight home. Mr. Sterling, Carnegie's manager, encouraged us to perform two encore numbers so the audience wouldn't feel short-changed. The "Music Alone Shall Live" round sounded even better than I thought it would. We ended with Pam's "Glory Hallelujah". It's stronger than it was in May. She dismisses the choir to change, then walks toward me. I stand to give her a big hug, "That was your best performance yet."

Her cheeks turn red in a rosy blush, "Oh Terry, I love composing Christ-centered music, but hearing my choir perform it is the greatest thrill I have ever had next to becoming a mother. We almost have everyone in the choir singing with their hearts and souls as well as their voices. I absolutely love it! Thank you for opening the doors to my music world." She gives me another hug.

I am about to comment when I catch a movement out of the corner of my eye. That crazy housekeeping woman is charging onto the stage toward us. I turn off the piano and lower the lid thinking I'll protect it. She yells stopping in front of us and pointing into the empty seats, "Who is that woman? You know her. You talked to her. Who is she?"

Pam and I turn to stare at a lone woman in the patron section waving a white handkerchief at us and wiping a tear. We both wave at her. She waves back and walks slowly down the aisle to the door. She never looks back.

"That was a prearranged sign, wasn't it? She's the Boss's old woman and Master's grandma. I know it. Her head's worth five mils." She lifts a small plastic box that's fixed to a chain around her neck and starts yelling, "A tall old woman is coming out—" I grab the box and yank it off the chain. I lift the lid of the grand piano just a little, set the box on the rim, and slam it down with a smashing crunch.

I am nosed to nose with this wild woman, "Who are you?"

She doesn't know whether to run or fight, but finally stammers, "I'm on the stage crew." Her eyes panic as they follow the stately woman out the door. "I have got to get to her. Maybe she'll come for her granddaughter."

She steps toward Pam with an outstretched arm going for her neck. I yell, "Pam drop!" sounding like one word. In a tennis replay, she instantly drops to all four. While that threatening arm is following Pam down, I jump into an aerial kick and smash it into the side of her ribs. I can feel at least three bones break while it pushes her away from Pam. I'm not surprised to see Tom pulling Pam into his arms. I move to guard the perp. Her breathing is increasing, and her eyes are going wild. She's working herself into berserk to block the pain.

She jumps to her feet in a karate stance coming at me, "I'll kill you!"

I wait until the last instant to take my stance, and a look of shock appears on her face. She tries to kick at the leg holding my weight, but I take out the knee of the leg she's standing on. I don't want to crippler her anymore, so I yell, "Hey, I could use some help in here."

Ten men instantly appear from behind a curtain dressed in hats, trench coats, and holding guns with silencers. I don't think this is my cavalry, so I ask, "Who are you?"

The answer comes from my disabled opponent on the floor, "Randy, I'm so glad to see you. Shoot her."

Randy looks down at the irate voice and then at me, "Who are you?"

"I'm Dr. Timpson, a concert pianist, and I just finished playing on this stage. You look like the mafia, are you the new Boss?"

I have caught him so completely off guard, that he can't tell if I'm a friend or an enemy, "No, I'm just Number One."

Before he can sort things out, I continue, "Good! You can explain to your lackey here that all contracts posted by the old Boss are no longer valid and will not be honored or paid."

Still lost Randy answers, "That's true. There is no money. When both The Boss and Number One went down, they took all the money with them. We know they had all the bills from our operations exchanged for gold bars. The main job of Number One is to always be close and guard the stash, but when they both died together, we have no idea where to continue to look… How come you know so much about us? Who are you anyway?"

"She's your worst nightmare Randy, and I'm your second," Agent Fowler says as the whole stage fills, circling us with FBI, police, and building security officers all pointing guns. "I suggest you lay your weapons carefully on the floor and then take a spread-eagle position on the deck. Now!"

Once they're down, he turns to us, "Mr. and Mrs. Masters and Dr. Timpson, I think you better hurry and change you have an airplane waiting for you."

I call back as we are hurrying off-stage, "Hope you enjoy your Christmas presents, Agent Flower."

"Merry Christmas to you too, Terry," he yells.

As soon as we have Dawn and Solomon's wedding planned with Tom and Pam, I slip into my seat and turn to my traveling companion, "Dr. Rich, can I talk to you about a problem?"

I can tell I've caught him just in time as he jerks to give me his attention, "Sure Terry. If it's about your up-and-coming motherhood, that's never a problem in our department."

Laughingly I say, "No, that's not the problem…It's about a university policy." Now I have his undivided attention. "It's the policy that piano teachers can't be concert pianists at the same time."

"Most universities have that policy. It's only reasonable. We want our teachers' main focus to be on teaching not flitting around the country performing."

"Yet you want your instructors to teach your students how to perform. You don't have one faculty member on your staff who can teach a piano student how to bridge into the prodigy music to become a concert pianist. I've given my whole heart and soul into teaching and accompanying, but occasionally it's great to be under the spotlight on center stage in a real concert hall. I know you've arranged it so your concert pianist in residence can perform at other schools, but it's just not the same. And, concert quality teachers need a place to advertise their wares."

"Terry, you need to understand how the concert circuit works. To get a venue anywhere, you need to have an agent. That agent makes his money by lining you up with as many concerts as possible. No agent is going to take you on if you only want two or three concerts a year. They want you in all the performances as they can arrange."

"Dr. Rich, do you understand why we are getting a flood of advanced piano students?"

"Obviously, it's because of you."

"They know they can learn how to bridge if they come to our school. We could become a choice instead of Juilliard. Allen and Arundel are now capable of teaching bridging. They would make excellent faculty members for our department, but I know they would both like to perform a little. What if we had an agent that worked for the university instead of the performer?"

"We'd never find someone that would do that. There's too much money in being an agent."

"Oh, I think I know the perfect person." He looks at me with a giant questioning expression. "You could retire Dr. Martin into that position. He needs a spot, knows the ins and outs of the concert performing world, and he would help us build our performing arts programs at Augustine."

Now I'm ready to drop my last bomb on him, "Are you aware that I have been invited to perform at a two-night venue on the Stem Stage at Carnegie in February? I have the whole evening including the preshow. I'm planning on my doctoral students performing as well as my small singing group."

He opens his mouth and closes it again, "I thought your mother was a whirlwind; you're a category 5 hurricane. We better get a policy change in place next week."

# CHAPTER 3

Granddad stands up with open arms as I rush through the door of his patient room in the cardiac care unit. I wrap my arms around him while crying try to get my words out, "Granddad, I'm so glad you're okay. I don't think I could stand losing you right now."

Granddad laughs a little, "I'm not going anywhere for a while. The doctors told me I still have years left if I stop making so many of those apple pies."

I can't let go of him, "I'm ecstatic you're going to come and live with us."

He pushes me back and holds me at arm's length, "Since I can't be alone for a while, it's either a rehab center or your home. The rehab center isn't even a choice. As much as I would like to stay with you permanently, I think it would damage your career."

"My career, what does my career have to do with you living with us?"

"Augustine University has some very strict rules regarding nepotism."

I'm aghast, then understanding begins to lighten my mind, "Is that why I didn't know you were my grandfather?"

He takes a deep breath, "Oh Terry when you were about ten years old, both your mother and I could see that you had the potential to be a world-class pianist. The university was having trouble with your mother's and my relationship. We decided to distance ourselves from one another, especially outside of school. That tore my heart apart, and it almost destroyed your grandmother. When your mother was killed in that accident, I think Kendra died of a broken heart, especially when she couldn't come to you with her comfort and love. I know now that we probably didn't do the right thing, but we thought we were doing the best for you."

I shake my head, "Oh Granddad, no career is worth losing your family for. Now that I've finally found you, I'm not sending you away. If Augustine has a problem with my family, we'll leave them behind, and the Lord will open a new door."

"We work to build family relations not to sever them. Grandpa, you're coming to live with us," Evan says. "We're going to need your help once Scott arrives for Terry to continue with her career. We have plenty of room for you, and if you need a little extra income on top of your retirement, we'll fix up your house to make it rental for university students."

Granddad can't say a thing. Tears roll down his cheeks as he hugs us both at the same time. Evan starts us moving, "Come on let's go home; we've got a Christmas to celebrate."

As we begin moving out of the hospital parking lot, Granddad jumps with a start, "What's happening? We're rolling. Are we going to crash?"

I chuckle, "I forget, Granddad, you've not been in an electric car before. There's no engine sound. It takes a little getting used to. This is the car that A.J. designed and Tom produces. It's neat."

"That's the strangest feeling I've had in a long time. It almost takes my breath away… Terry, tell us about the Christmas Concert in Carnegie." I spend the rest of the drive home bringing them up to speed on the whole New York adventure.

"Evan, it smells heavenly in here. What are we having for dinner?"

"Remember the sandhill cranes that wandered onto Tom's ranch three months ago? I talked him out of one for our Christmas dinner. It's poultry low in fat, but it has the taste of a rib-eye steak. Grandpa you're going to love this."

We are sitting in our music room enjoying the fire when Granddad's countenance begins to fall then tears start rolling down his cheeks. Finally, he mumbles, "What am I going to do? I know Dr. Rich has replaced me as dean of the College of

Music. I'll go crazy sitting around doing nothing. Your baby will not even be born until May. The only thing that saved me when your parents and Kendra died was that I had to go to work every day because someone needed me. Now no one needs me. Maybe I should have died from that heart attack."

Now it's time for my lawnmower, "Granddad when you ended your concert pianist career, did you ever miss performing on stage after you started teaching?"

He looks at me strangely; my question is so out of context with what he has just said, "I did Terry; I loved the teaching, but I did miss being on stage."

"If you could have performed three or four times a year, would it have satisfied you?"

"It would have been more than enough, but it's not the university policy. To get a concert venue, you need to have an agent, and no worthwhile agent is going to work for you if you only perform a few times a year."

Now I have him where I want him, "What if that agent worked for the university instead of the performer?"

He gives me a blank stare, but I know his mind is turning cartwheels, "That's an interesting thought… It has possibilities… You know it might work well."

I laugh at him, "Granddad, do you have any idea what's happening to the enrollment in the vocal and piano programs starting in January?"

He shakes his head, "No, Rich has been monitoring our student population."

"Well, let me bring you up to speed. We have enough advanced piano students coming that we need to hire two new part-time faculty to teach them. We don't have one current piano instructor skilled enough. They are coming here to bridge; we are moving Allen and Arundel in to fill that gap. By next fall they should both have their doctorate degrees. We need them to stay here at Augustine and be part of our faculty. They also need to be on a concert stage to keep advancing and to advertise their teaching skills. If we had a university agent, that all would be possible."

"Terry, this is what I envisioned for two or three years down the road but not next month."

"Oh, there's more. Pam has created two prep choirs with students trying to get into the Oratorio and Concert Choirs next week. The OC needs a place or two to be on a concert stage to advertise our vocal program. Pam and Tom need the chance to shine. I need an agent along with my doctoral students, my Knights of Ebony, and my ensemble, The Master's Touch. All our performing arts programs need a place for professionally sounding and acting students to get their feet wet. That way, when they leave us, they are professionally qualified to enter the real-world competition."

"Terry, you are so right. Now, all we must do is get the board of regents to change the policy. I don't know if that will ever work."

"It must change if we want our music program to be more than a feeder program for secondary school music departments. Dr. Rich is going to meet with the board of regents this week."

"How did you ever talk him into that?"

"I merely explained that I have a signed contract for a two-night venue in The Stem at Carnegie in February, and I'm taking my Knights of Ebony and The Master's Touch—When the policy is abolished, will you be the agent for Augustine?"

I get up before dawn with Evan when he rolls out to meet his survival classmates to go on a snowshoe rabbit hunt this morning. He invited me to go with them, but Scottie and I decided that we didn't want to tramp through the snow up the side of a mountain. He's starting to limit my activities. Instead, I leave Granddad sawing logs in his bed and come into my office to work on another melody swirling in my head. The organ captures me for an hour. Finally, this pesky melody lured me away to the recording keyboard.

Two hours later, I have most of the elusive notes seized on paper. I'm startled out of my trance when I hear tapping on my office window. I don't know how long they've been trying to get my attention. I smile and move to the locked door when I realize it's one of my doctoral students. "Hi Stephanie, I hardly expected to see you here on your Christmas break."

"You certainly do move into another world when you're playing, don't you? I've been trying to get your attention for ten minutes."

"Sorry Stephanie, I truly do get lost in my music world. That's the reason I have all the electronic gadgets to get my attention. Sometimes they work… What can I do for you?"

"I am so sorry to bother you, but is there any way I could talk to you?"

I can tell from her level of anxiety that this will be more than a casual conversation, "Absolutely. Let's go into my music room and turn on the teaching light so we won't be disturbed." On the way through my outer office, I casually ask, "Planning on coming to the New Year's Eve wedding tomorrow afternoon?"

I pull in an extra chair and close the door behind us. She quickly sits down to face me, "Yes, we're planning on being to Solomon's wedding. It's about time; Dawn is such a neat girl, and she loves him so much." She pauses, staring at me with almost pleading eyes.

I put one of my hands on her clenched fingers resting in her lap, "Stephanie, I am here for you, how can I help you?"

Tears begin rolling down her cheeks, "Doctor T., I trust you more than anyone I have ever known, and I must tell someone. Then, I desperately need your advice." I squeeze her hands with both of mine and nod my head for her to go on. I never lose eye contact with her and pray that she can feel the love I have for her.

I whisper, "Stephanie, you're safe with me." Then I wait.

"From the time I was ten until I was fourteen years old, I was abused by my mother's brother, Mike." I take a quick breath and feel like I'm going to be sick but encourage her to go on. "On my tenth birthday, he came to my party. He was such a funny guy, and everyone seemed to like him. When it got late, my dad invited him to spend the night so he wouldn't have to travel in the dark. In the middle of the night, he came and got into my small bed and hurt me like I had never been hurt before. The next morning my dad told him he could come to visit any time and could spend the night in our spare bedroom. He hurt me badly every time he came. I tried to tell my mom, but she wouldn't let me talk about it. Said if anything happened, it was my fault." She stops, hanging her head and sobbing.

I move to put my arm around her shoulder, "Never, ever is a child responsible for the abusive actions of any adult. You are not responsible, nor should you feel guilty for anything he did to you. Why did it end when you were fourteen?"

"I could see no way out of all that pain and shame, and I began to realize that I could get pregnant. I tried to kill myself. I heard that people take pills to end their life, so I swallowed a whole bottle of Tylenol. I was rushed to the hospital. Instead of dying, I had a tube put through my nose down into my stomach. The doctor pumped water into my stomach and then pumped everything out. They did that until my stomach stopped bleeding. The Tylenol only burned holes in my stomach lining. I didn't know how to kill myself.

"While I was still in the hospital after the tube was out, my grandmother, on my father's side came to see me. She wanted to know why I tried to commit suicide. I didn't want to give her details, but she finally got out of me that Uncle Mike was abusing me. Then it was a whirlwind. When I was released from the hospital, my grandparents picked me up and took me to live with them several states away. My grandmother was a concert pianist and taught me to play the piano. I lived with them until I went away to college to major in music.

"An hour before my grandparents picked me up from the hospital, Uncle Mike walked through my door with the grin he always wore before he attacked me. I started screaming, punching my call button, and throwing things at him. He laughed at me and said, 'I'll be back when you're older, and I'll really have some fun.' He ran out the door knocking people down who were coming to help me."

"I am so, so sorry. It makes me sick and angry that he would do that to you. No wonder you hurt inside." I hold her until she quits sobbing.

"You must think I'm the most despicable person you have ever met. If you want me to drop out of your doctoral program, I will. I won't blame you."

"Stephanie you are one of the most beautiful sensitive women I have ever known. The only place you are going to go is to complete healing. You have nothing to be ashamed of or to feel guilty for. You are doing phenomenal work on your doctorate." I squeeze her tighter, "I love you; everyone who knows you loves you. You are going to stay right here at Augustine and learn how to help others heal with your music." Stephanie turns and hugs me back.

We sit silently for a while, "Dr. Terry Masters Timpson, you will never know what you have done for me. You have given me a life again. You are right; I'm going to learn to heal myself and those like me with music…

"Now for the advice I need. I know I'll see my perverted uncle again. What do I do?"

"Seek the Lord every day in prayer for his direction and protection. When you see the pedophile, be aggressive in every way you can, especially with words."

"Next question. You haven't been married for very long. Every time you're together with your husband does he hurt you? Is that always a part of lovemaking?"

"No, no, no! What you experienced is pure abuse. Lovemaking is nothing like that. You marry to become one in every aspect of your life. It is to take care of each other, help each other develop their full potential, and to enjoy and be thrilled with every aspect of complete love. It's not a matter of enduring pain. There should never be partner abuse. I love being married and wouldn't trade it for anything. The plus is I also get to be a mother."

"You make it sound so wonderful."

"Oh, if only I could tell you how fantastic it is if you are with the right man."

"Last question. You have probably noticed that I've been spending a lot of time with Russel, the grad student in our technique class. When I was fourteen, I decided that I would never marry, so I dated very little. I have gotten to know Russel through our music, and he is so fun to be with. It's been so slow that I didn't realize I was developing deep feelings for him. We've spent every day of this Christmas break together, and last night he kissed me, and I felt fire run through me. I never felt any of these things when Mike was hurting me. Russell is hinting that we might get married. I think I am beginning to love him. Do I tell him about my past?"

"My answer to that is the truth is always the best policy. As you come together to function as one there should be no secrets between you. If either of you has a secret, you need to create lies to keep it safe. When it finally comes out, and it will come out, the hurt it will cause may be unrepairable. If Russell doesn't know, he can't help you heal. Let me give you a little scenario. You're married; it doesn't make any difference how long. You and your husband are at the piano and a knock comes on your door. You both go to answer it. To your horror, it's your Uncle Mike. He's all smiles and happily announces that he has come to town to visit his favorite niece.

You are speechless, but your husband warmly welcomes him as he would any member of your family. Your husband is cordial and even invites him to stay the night because he has far to travel. You can't say anything because it's your secret, but you know that you and your husband will probably die tonight.

"If you have told him, you can yell you're calling the police, and your husband has probably smashed his nose knocking him off the porch and landing him flat on his back.

"Think how different your life would have been if your mother had told her secret to your dad before they were married. Stephanie, I want you to ask our Heavenly Father if you should tell Russell. If the impression you get is yes, then ask Him to give you the opportunity and the strength to do it. If he walks away from you, it's better now than on your wedding night, or the night Uncle Mike shows up."

This wedding is quite a bit fancier than my first one was. I love Tom and Pam's great room. They can host almost any kind of event. This afternoon it looks almost like a small chapel. It even has an aisle for the bride to walk down. The best part for me is that I get to enjoy this wedding sitting by Evan. Pam is going to play prelude music and then the wedding march. I am so excited about her growing musical talents.

"Terry, I can see it didn't take you long to get in a motherly way," Coach Vickery says as he and his wife head down an aisle to find seats.

I laugh at his observation, "Only long enough to get married. I'm happy for Dawn and Solomon…How does your team look for this coming season?"

"Strongest full tennis team we've ever had. We miss you and Pam, but you certainly set us up for success. Thank you for your vision. We better find our seats."

A couple is making their way down my row to the two empty seats beside me, "Hi Russell. Glad you and Stephanie could make it."

He's whispering as the prelude changes to the wedding march, "I wanted to thank you for encouraging Stephanie to talk to me. I have issues of my own. With open communication between us, I think we will be able to help and take care of each other." I reach my hand over and squeeze both their interlocked hands resting in Russell's lap. The glowing Dawn now has my full attention as she floats down the aisle toward a stately Solomon who breaks into a broad smile when she touches his lifted elbow.

# CHAPTER 4

I'm almost finished with the syllabus for my new advanced technique 3 class. I look up from my computer when a man walks boldly through my door and sits in front of my desk. I haven't locked my door this morning because there has been a constant stream of people in and out of my office getting ready for school to start next week. I feel dark vibes coming from this overly confident almost familiar person. I'm uneasy enough that I flip on all the recording switches under my desk as I ask him how I can help him.

"You probably don't remember me, Dr. Timpson. I was the man who tried to get you to sign a contract the night of your senior recital. I was right about your prodigious talents. Look at how quickly you've jumped into the spotlight at Carnegie Hall, a double-night booking in February. I'm here today to offer you a deal you can't turn down."

There is something sinister about this creep, but I just let him keep talking. "I know you want to keep your appointment at Carnegie, and I'm here to offer you the insurance to protect your hands from any injury before your big night." He pushes a paper in front of me with a pen on top for me to sign. "If you'll sign right there on the bottom line, we'll make sure nothing happens to your hands." Both my hands are still under my desk, and my cell phone is in my pocket. If I can play the piano with my eyes closed, I can give him eye contact while I speed-dial Detective Douglas "911, in office".

"This paper says you'll take half of what I earn from the concerts in return for your protection. Do you have contracts with other pianists around the country or are you local?" Let's see if I can get him talking before, I burst his bubble.

"We have some of the top pianists in the country as our clients. It takes them suffering broken fingers or a hand, but eventually, they all come around."

"What happens to them when they can no longer pay your premiums?"

"Dr. Timpson, you need to look at it from our point of view. They kind of disappear. Now will you sign the contract, or do I have to use stronger arguments?"

I'm ready to play his game. I casually lay my left forearm on the desk with my fingers curled into a fist, "I'm sorry Mr. Derksin, but I'm not going to sign your contract now or ever."

Anger flashes in his eyes, and he instantly reaches for my left hand with both of his hands. As he makes contact, I draw my left hand back pulling him forward while standing at the same time. I come down with a hand-chop and feel both bones in his left arm splinter. While he's screaming and grabbing his injured arm, I round my desk and push him back into his chair. I yell in his face, "If you move, I'll break your neck." He looks up at me in horror, as campus security bursts through my office door. I yell at them, "Cuff his leg to the chair."

Dr. Rich and Detective Douglas reach my door at the same time. When they come through the door, Derksin yells at them, "She attacked me and broke my arm. She's dangerous; arrest her!"

Dr. Rich looks at him with disgust, "Apparently you have never tried to strong-arm anyone in a music college before. Everything you have said and done has been recorded on video. It's one of our best teaching tools."

Detective Douglas moves to face me, "Terry, what's up?" I fill him in with all the details then ask, "Can you get hold of Agent Fowler to see if he can get a search warrant to this scum's living quarters. We may be able to get a list of all the people his gang is extorting or selling insurance to under pain of injury or death."

He doesn't even answer me. While dialing his phone he gives orders to his men, "Search him for ID. Take his keys, find his car, and search it. We've got to find out where he lives."

"Hey, you can't do that. I have the right to make one phone call. I demand to make that call right now," Derksin yells panicking.

When Douglas gets off his cell, he smiles at the jerk while reading from his driver's license, "All in good time Mr. Derksin from Austin, Texas. All in good time. First, we need to get you to a hospital and patch up your arm. Then we'll take you downtown to my hotel. Once you've been formally booked into my jail, you may make your call."

The security guards put Derksin's arm in a sling, cuff his other wrist to an officer's, and help escort him out to the waiting patrol car. Douglas yells over his shoulder, "I'll be in touch as soon as Fowler gets back to me."

"Terry, I watched the video of you talking to the man. You got a complete statement from him while he was threatening to hurt or more you. You never let any fear show. Then that karate move was so smooth. I had no idea…"

Dr. Rich is cut short by laughter from Evan, Tom, and Pam who have silently come into my office behind him. Evan gains his composure first, "Quiet day at the office, dear?"

Pam gets in her comment, "Dr. Rich, you should see her aerial kick; it's breathtaking," followed by more gales of laughter."

"She's Godan you know," Tom finally says with a deadpan expression.

Dr. Rich is speechless. Finally, he stammers, "Terry, are you alright?" I nod my head. "I think we'll talk later about all this, but I thought you would like to know the board of regents changed the policy so piano instructors can perform on a concert stage up to four times a year' and they approved Martin to be the university's agent. If you all will excuse me, I'm late for my next meeting."

All our eyes follow him out the door and down the hall. Pam starts organizing, "Let's go get lunch, and Terry can give us a blow-by-blow account of all the drama this morning."

After returning to the university after lunch, I spend the afternoon with Dr. Rich. I share with him our year's experiences trying to keep Pam and her unborn child safe from the mob. I also assure him that my family was not laughing at him but trying to tease me. I need to have a positive working relationship with my new dean, and I know open honest communications work best.

"Terry, get a move on it. We don't want Scott to be late for his first filming."

"Settle down a little, we don't want to wait in the doctor's office for an hour before our ultrasound appointment. You can clean up the kitchen while I finish getting ready."

"You know Grandpa already has the kitchen spotless. There's nothing for me to do but give you a hard time."

We arrive a little early, but since we're the first appointment they take us right back to get started. They slather my growing abdomen with a type of gel for the sound head to glide in. After cruising around for five minutes, the tec begins giving us a guided tour, "He looks healthy and normal, has all his limbs and fingers and toes. His heart is beating strong, and the circulation looks complete including the kidneys." I can feel Scott starting to turn.

The tec goes silent with a gasp, "Mrs. Timpson, I am so sorry. Your baby has no eyes. His eye sockets are empty. What a tragedy." He seems surprised that Evan and I are not distraught with his heart-breaking news. He changes his objective, "He isn't very far along to consider an abortion. Blindness is at the top of the government's list of approved abortions. It will make your lives and his so much easier."

Now we are agitated and angry. Evan gets in his face, "No one is going to abort our baby."

The tec tries to take the offensive, "You have no idea how much this child will cost you and the government. Besides, most babies this frail don't survive the delivery."

I quickly dress and take Evan by the hand, "Come on, we're out of here. No one is going to destroy my baby."

"You can't leave before you visit your doctor. He's waiting for you through this door." The tech opens the door and runs through yelling, "Their baby is blind."

Dr. Trent stands and ushers us to seats in front of his desk. After he has closed both doors and takes his seat, I attack, "No government is going to mandate an abortion for a perfectly normal baby. I have blind friends, and they are phenomenal people. They have never cost the government a penny and neither will my son."

Dr. Trent holds up his hands to quiet me and puts his finger to his lips. Covers his ears with his hands and shakes his head. He points to his tablet and begins writing and speaking at the same time. He is telling us in a rote tone and manner all the reasons Scott should be aborted. He is writing, 'Do not abort your baby. He is strong, healthy, and will thrive. Never come back to this clinic. Find a midwife in a rural community to deliver your baby. You are my last patient at this clinic. God bless your growing family.' "Now, have you understood everything I said?" We nod our heads. "I'll walk you out to your car. I know you have a challenging time ahead of you." He goes to a third door which I had not noticed, and we walk outside together. He gets into the car next to ours as we slide into the panther. He gives us a thumbs up as we pull out of the parking lot at the same time. He may have just sacrificed his career to save Scott's life.

"That was the last thing I expected in our appointment this morning. I spent a whole year trying to protect Pam and her baby from the mob and now I need to shield mine from the government."

"Terry, I think their perverse actions are rooted in the drive for money. What about our unborn son? Do we need to find another doctor to deliver your baby?"

"I am the only person who can deliver our baby, and when he is ready, he will come out even if I'm all alone. Maybe you should help me." Evan looks like he's going to faint. "However, I do know a midwife, Grandma Sandy, in Red Rock. I'll give her a call. If we got into a serious bind, I think Pam could do it. I'm sure it was part of her paramedic training… Speaking of Pam. She invited the whole ensemble over Saturday afternoon for dinner and practice. We're singing in Tom and Pam's church on Sunday."

"Steaks are almost done, everyone start gathering to the table," Tom yells as Pam's phone rings. I wonder who could be calling her on a Saturday afternoon when most of her friends are here.

She listens for an instant then squeals, "Dad, are you calling me from your mission in South America." She listens again, "Dad's about an hour away from here, and he has Grandma Fletcher with him. They'll be here about the time we finish dinner." Shouting and clapping erupt from the group.

When the doorbell chimes, we're finished eating and Granddad Martin is dishing up his homemade apple pies. Pam starts for the door, but it is thrown open, and Dennis and Barbara Fletcher escort Pam's look-a-like from our concerts through the door.

"I knew it was you," Pam shirks and wraps her grandmother in a monstrous hug. They are both watering each other with their tears. Elder Fletcher and his wife are standing behind them, and he is beaming like a new father showing off his first baby. When they finally break their hug, they still have one arm wrapped around each other.

Pam begins to make introductions. Pointing, "This is Tom Masters, my husband, and he is holding our son, Tommy." Turning toward me, "Terry, you've met and that is her husband, Evan Timpson."

At that moment, Grandpa Martin joins the group from the back of the kitchen area looking stunned, "Dr. Hephzibah Flora McKracken!"

Grandma's expression changes from shock to childish delight, "Albert Francis Martin, Ph.D." He opens his arms wide, and she rushes into a giant bear hug.

Everyone else is stunned into silence. Finally, Pam's dad says the obvious, "I take it you two know each other." They both look a little embarrassed and laugh.

"Neither of us would have made it through our doctorate degrees if it were not for the help, we gave each other," Grandma says. "After we finally graduated, that was the greeting we gave each other whenever we met. Albert, this is like really coming home."

"Flora, I had no idea you were Pam's grandmother. But it does explain all the instant flashes of someone I should remember that comes at times when I look at Pam. Except for your ages, you could be identical twins...I am so sorry about Roger."

Flora looks searchingly around, "Where's Kendra, and that little prodigy piano player you adopted?"

"That little girl and her husband were killed in a car crash about ten years ago. Kendra died of a broken heart shortly after the accident. Terry is Lilly's little girl."

Pam breaks into their trip down memory lane, "Your Hephzibah Flora McKracken Ph.D.? I have all your voice training books and recordings. More than anyone else, you have taught me how to sing."

"I think I've given you more than the knowledge of how to sing; you have inherited my voice." Flora moves to take Pam in her arms again.

In his gruff impatient voice, Elder Fletcher takes charge, "All of this homecoming is very tender, but we're running out of time. Mother we've got to get you settled in your apartment."

"Dennis, I told you on the way here I came home to be with family, not to be stuck in some lonely apartment as soon as we arrived."

Tom wastes no words, "Grandma Fletcher, we want you to stay here with us. I've had a cottage built that you could move into right now."

"Dad, she isn't going anywhere. We have so many years to catch up on and she hasn't even held Tommy yet."

Dennis scowls, "Good luck with holding that screaming machine. Nobody can hold him but his mother and father.

Flora moves to stand glaring at her son, "Dennis, I am perfectly capable of taking care of myself, and I'm staying right here to get acquainted with my family. I want to hold a baby again. Bring my things in, and then you and Barbara fly off to wherever you're going." While he runs for the car, Flora hugs Barbara and asks, "Has he always been this controlling?"

Barbara laughingly shakes her head, "Yes, but he's better than he used to be. Pam learned how to get around him, and I'm still learning."

Flora kisses her on the cheek, "You have earned a mansion in heaven. I'll see you when you return."

Once they are out the door, Grandma Flora turns to us, "What's next?"

It's my turn, "Pam and I want an answer to the question we both have burning inside us."

"Terry, ask your question."

"It can't be answered with words come to the piano with me." Once I'm seated, I state my request. Pam would like to sing with you. After I warm you up, will you sing the aria from *LaBoheme*, 'Quando me n'vo'?"

"I can't turn that down, but I think Pam's tessitura is a few notes lower than mine."

Pam and I smile at each other then she turns to Tom, "Let me hold Tommy while I sing, he loves this song.

Once they're warmed up, I begin the introduction. Flora begins singing and two measures later Pam begins only she is singing in perfect harmony below her grandmother. While they are singing, Tommy looks at his great-grandmother and then holds out his arms to be held. She gathers him in her arms singing and crying at the same time. Finally, she is compelled to stop singing.

"What just happened? I have never in all my years felt like that when I've sung. Then when Tommy slid into my arms, I lost all control."

Dr. Martin puts his arm around her shoulder, "What you felt is celestial harmony. Pam indeed has your voice, and they blend perfectly. Tom, come and sing "Come Thou Fount" with them. Not only can you feel it, but so can every person in this room."

Tom places himself on the other side of Grandma Flora, and I begin. The harmony is electrifying and the most beautiful music I have ever heard. I am in a position where I can see Tommy. He wraps both of his little arms around Grandma's neck and places his ear as close to her throat as he can get it. I think he's even smiling.

When we finish the ensemble is wild with praise. When I finally have their attention, I ask, "Don't you think we could use Grandma's voice in the Master's Touch?" Again, I have difficulty getting everyone's attention. "Grandma Flora, would you consider being a member of our ensemble? Don't give me an answer yet. We are singing the song you just sang in church tomorrow. Sing with us and then decide. Stand in the back next to Pam." At first, she overpowers everyone, but she can hear and slowly reigns in her volume to blend perfectly. What a beautiful addition to our group.

"I would sing with this group anywhere in the world on any stage. You are magnificent. I can't believe my music career is starting over instead of ending."

Pam pulls her into a hug again, "Welcome home Grandma."

Pam, Tom, and their growing family are now at my home for dinner following our singing in church. Granddad has completely taken over the meal preparation in our kitchen. As we are finishing our heart-healthy meal, Pam asks, "How did you completely disguise yourself so the mob couldn't find you for all those years?"

Grandma Flora smiles to herself, "It took years of preparation. I knew I couldn't leave until Dennis was old enough to be on his own. Since the chump took over my house, I had all my personal documents and memories with me. I slowly started burning everything that had a clue to my earlier life. I knew I could replace the documents once I was free, but since Doggie had moved so fast, I didn't think he even knew my maiden name or any of my background. Every time he was in the shower, I filched two or three hundred-dollar bills from his wallet and hid my collection under a floorboard in our bedroom. He knew I was taking the money, but thought it was cute if I gave him what he wanted.

"After I got Dennis and Barbara off to start a new life, I stayed for six months so he would think splitting was Dennis's idea. They didn't get along very well. I think Doggie was at a point where he was either going to make him a mobster or kill him. Dennis never did know he wasn't his real father."

Pam can't resist, "Why do you call him Doggie?"

"He wanted me to call him whatever term of endearment I call Roger. I told him it was Doggie, and he seemed pleased with that. It was my way of fighting back... Once I was sure Dennis was safe, I stepped into my plan. Most of the time, Number One stayed with me when Doggie was off on mob business. We became pretty good friends. After Dennis was in junior high, No. 1, started leaving me by myself for hours. I seemed to be such an obedient hostage. Doggie never knew, and I never said a word. Four months after Dennis's disappearance, he started leaving me alone again. I charted his patterns and knew which day he would be away the longest, sometimes not coming back until after midnight and usually drunk.

"On my appointed day, I dressed as I usually did in jeans and a t-shirt, carried the shoulder bag I always carried but full of cash instead of empty, walked to my closest neighbor's house, and asked if she could drop me off at the mall two miles away. I told her that Nicholas would pick me up on his way home, but he was running late. I went into a clothing store and bought a dress, jacket, sandals, and a cute hat to stuff my long hair in. When I walked out of that clothing store, I don't think anyone would have recognized me. A cab took me to the train station, and I was off.

"After training around the country for three weeks, I finally returned to the university where I had worked part-time before marrying. They hired me back under my maiden name, and I've been there ever since teaching and giving voice lessons. I didn't dare walk onto a stage again."

Grandpa Martin puts his arm around her shoulder, "I'm so sorry you've had to go through such a despicable time. I am, however, amazed you were clever enough to survive, and thrilled you are here now, safe and sound." Grandma snuggles a little closer.

"Now my granddaughters, I want to hear all about how you took down the mighty mob." We spend the next hour detailing how we all tried to keep Pam and her baby safe, ending with mine and Tommy's kidnapping into the mountains in late December.

I express my concern, "Grandma Flora, I'm not completely sure that you're safe. After our run-in with the female mobster who hadn't received the word there's no contract money, you may still be in danger. Since you're going to be back on stage again, I'm wondering about your name. You can't be Pam's grandmother or Dr. M. Fletcher."

Dr. Martin has his lawnmower grin again, "I think I have a solution for that. How about changing it to Dr. M. Martin?" We all look at him with wide eyes and open mouths.

"Albert, are you serious?"

"Never been more serious Flora. It's the perfect way to protect you. No one will question who you are. I'll be with you most of the time. Together we can fight the horrid enemy of loneliness. And you'd have a built-in accompanist since you're going to keep singing. I tried to figure out how to make this happen all night."

Flora throws her arms around Grandpa's neck to look into his eyes, "Nothing would make me happier. I kept walking around my new home last night, and I could only picture it complete with you there. Let's do it."

"The sooner the better, so no one will learn any other name for you—Terry, are you okay with this, I did promise to help you with your new baby," Grampa Martin shyly says.

"Granddad, Scotty isn't due for five months, and once he's here, he isn't leaving my side until he can crawl. After that, we'll work something out. If my mom and dad did it, so can we."

"Albert, is tomorrow morning soon enough? I don't think the courthouse is open Sunday."

Grandpa Martin is all smiles, "I'll pick you up at 8:00 am. Now, all we need is a couple of witnesses."

"Granddad, Evan, and I both have appointments first thing in the morning. Why don't you follow me in your car, and Pam can take Grandma Flora in hers and meet you there at 9:00 am when it opens. After the ceremony, Flora's all yours.

"Since we're not letting any grass grow under our feet, I'll get the piano movers to be at your house at 11:00 am, and you can pack more things at the same time. You can follow your piano out to the ranch, and I'll head to my office," I say.

# CHAPTER 5

We had a productive meeting with my doc candidates yesterday afternoon. We set up the program for Carnegie Hall next month, and Allen gave us each our copy of his new composition for the five-piano choir. His composing skills are becoming professional. When we sight read through our parts, everyone is impressed. He had even transcribed Solomon's into brail. By the end of our practice session, we were starting to sound like a piano choir. I encouraged them to have their music memorized as quickly as possible, so we could tune it.

They begin gathering their things to leave, "I have one more thing to tell you; the policy has been changed, allowing faculty members to perform in a concert up to four times a year." Now I have their complete attention.

"You've got to be kidding, Doc. How did you ever swing that?" asks Allen.

"I simply presented them with facts. If you want to graduate concert-quality students, you must have concert-quality teachers. A concert performer needs to stay at their peak, even if they are mostly concentrating on teaching. Performing on stage three or four times a year would accomplish that end."

"But don't you need an agent to book concert venues?" Arundel asks.

"You do, that's why Dr. Martin is stepping down from his position as Dean of the College of Music and becoming the Music Agent for our university."

"Does that mean if I became a full-time faculty member with full benefits, I could still perform on a concert stage three or four times a year?"

"That's exactly what it means Allen. I have the authorization to offer you and Arundel full-time faculty positions for next fall after you receive your doctorate degrees this summer. Think about it." I so hope they will want to stay. I can tell all four minds are contemplating as they leave my piano lab.

Then I remember one more item on my list, "Solomon, you will have three new blind piano students this semester. None of them are beginners." I say hi to Dawn as he mumbles something to her on their way out the door.

I'm working hard this morning to get my new piece completed. I don't have appointments today, so I should have the rest of the day to finish it. I'm brought out of my deep concentration by red lights blinking on and off and finally a foghorn blaring. I move to my outer office to see who wants my attention. I'm totally surprised when I open the door, "Agent Fowler, you're the last person I expected to see so early this morning. Come in." He is followed by Detective Douglas; they quickly take their usual seats.

"Terry, I didn't think eleven o'clock was early in your world," Agent Flower laughs. I've lost track of time again. I've been working since 5:00 am.

"The FBI must have uncovered some information from the search of Derksin's apartment for you to be back so soon."

"Terry, you sure guessed that one right. We found all kinds of information to put him away for a long time. But no matter how hard we tried, he wouldn't lead us up his ladder to anyone above him. We did find this list of insured concert pianists who he is terrorizing. We want you to look at it and see if you know anyone well enough that we might be able to collaborate with them to crack open this scam." Fowler hands me the list.

I've heard of many of them, but none of them would know me enough to trust me. They seem to be in chronological order for how long they have been paying premiums. The amount they must pay also seems to increase with time. The last ten pianists on the list don't have a money amount behind their names, just the word disappeared. My stomach turns over; I think they couldn't afford to pay, and they must be dead. My eyes travel backs up the list to one woman I think I know. It's Matilda Bates.

"I think this woman, Matilda Bates, was a friend of my mother's. I went to several of her concerts with my mom and met her a few times. However, I was only twelve at the time, and I'm not sure she would remember me."

I am so engrossed in the list, that I don't notice people in the hall until my door opens and the Doctors Martin walk through. "Good morning, Terry. We thought we'd stop and say hi. See you've got company. We'll talk to you later."

My mind flashes to overdrive, "Wait Grandad, come in and sit down for a few minutes." I introduce my Grandparents to the law, then ask Granddad, "Did you know Matilda Bates, the friend of my mom?"

"Of course, I knew Matilda. She was and I think still is a fine pianist."

To my surprise, Grandma Flora also answers, "I know Matilda too. She gives her concerts in the area where I've been living. She isn't looking so good lately. She looks worn and stressed to the max. She's lost a lot of weight. I've been wondering if she has cancer."

Agent Fowler never misses an opportunity, "She's got cancer alright, but on the outside not on the inside. Would you two be willing to help us cure her?" We talk for almost an hour about building a snare we hope will save Matilda and catch more criminals. Finishing his phone call, he looks at us, "Alright, I have booked tickets for the four of us to travel next

Friday to visit with Matilda. I so hope she will let us help her. I don't want to see her name at the bottom of that list."

After the officers leave, Granddad has his lawnmower grin again, "Terry, we just thought we would stop and tell you we figured out how to get Flora into the Oratorio Choir this semester." I look at him with awe. "We visited with Dr. Rich this morning. He recognized Flora and knew she was a celebrated lyric coloratura. He reminded me that faculty can sing in either the concert or the oratorio choir. Dr. M. Martin is now a part-time faculty teaching voice. Pam will line her up with students. She is also going to collaborate with me as the Musical Agent for the university. We've got to run; talk to you later."

I think they gave him a new heart; he and Flora make such an awesome couple. I wonder what Evan will think about me running off with the FBI to help Matilda. I'd take him with us, but I know he has survival outings on Fridays every week.

During my musing, I notice my cell phone ringing. The collar ID doesn't show a source. I answer it anyway. I tentatively say hello, "Terry, this is Dr. Forest from the birthing center. I have replaced Dr. Trent as your OBGYN. He is no longer with us I want to talk to you about the problem you have with your baby."

"Sorry, Dr. Forest, I have already replaced my doctor and will not be using your birthing center." I'm ready to hang up.

"Mrs. Timpson, you must understand what a burden your blind child will be on you and our government. He will have an extremely difficult life. It will be best for all concerned if you terminate your pregnancy now. It is almost the number one government-approved abortion. The cost of doing nothing will be horrendous." I say nothing. "I know you're still there. Just understand, we can do this the easy way or the hard way." Now I hang up.

I'm so upset and angry I want to scream or throw something. That man's not a doctor, he's a cold-blooded butcher. The choice is mine, not his. I calm down a little, but my agitation is soaring. There's no way I can put my head into composing, what I need is a fast game of tennis. But I'm still not allowed to play tennis. I look across the hall and see that Pam is in her office. I can, however, swim. I wonder if their pool is heated today.

When I burst through her office door, she looks up in shock, "Terry, what's up? You look angry enough to take on the world?" I slump into one of her chairs and explain about our first visit to the birthing clinic.

"Terry, that's awful. He can't do that. It's your choice… Look at AJ and Solomon, neither of them is a burden on society or the government. I'll bet both pay plenty of taxes. Their wives don't even consider them a burden… Did that jerk actually threaten you?"

"He did. But what I came bursting into your office for was to ask if I might go swimming if your pool is heated. I need activity to get rid of my anxiety and agitation."

"Pool's heated. Go ahead and Tommy and I will join you when I finish with three more auditions. You should have heard my last one. He has a tenor voice to rival Tom's" I pass her next appointment as I'm heading out the door.

When I'm telling Evan about my day after dinner, I get upset again. It's kind of a mix of a little fear and tons of anger. "Evan, what if I'm not able to protect my baby or me?"

"You have more protection skills than any mother I've ever known." He thinks for a moment with his eyebrows furrowed, "Terry, when a mother lion conceives, she still needs to hunt every day to feed herself and in turn her growing cubs. She doesn't lose her strength or skills because she is pregnant. Her family's survival depends on her. I think it's time for a wife and father's blessing."

The first day of teaching, and my morning classes went well. I'm waiting for Evan to go to lunch. Our schedules work so we can eat in the university cafeteria on Wednesdays. Through our meal, he excitedly tells me about all the survival activities he gets to help teach this semester. I'm so thankful he's found a profession he can put his heart into. He will be awesome teaching youth in the media of survival.

We are returning to my office when a commotion occurs in front of us, and the students in the hall are pushed aside to accommodate a man running at full speed toward us. When we try to move to one side, he changes course to aim at us. When he gets two feet away, he doubles up his fist and starts a swing toward my stomach. I try to move but only succeed in bringing my hands in front of me to cover my baby. Just before impact. Even throws himself in front of me and puts his shoulder into the side of my assailant. The attacker is thrown to the side, but his agility puts him instantly on his feet running back the way he came knocking people down. I'm pushed backward to sit flat on the floor.

I begin to sob, "I don't have the skills to protect my baby. We're both going to be killed."

"Terry, Terry! Are you alright? Do we need to get you to a hospital?" Evan's yelling at me panicked.

I slowly regain my composure and realize I'm surrounded by concerned students. I finally have my sobbing under control, "I'm okay, just wounded pride. I may be a little sore tomorrow where I sat down."

Evan helps me up, "I think I need to take you home." He's still not sure I'm not hurt.

"I can't go home. I have a class to teach this afternoon. Besides you have a class you need to be in, just help me get back to my office."

Once we're inside my music room, he's shaking his head looking at me, "What happened to you?"

"When I started to move to protect me and Scott, I felt like I was off balance and all I could do was put my hands on my stomach. I can't protect us, Evan."

"Terry, I know you have the ability. I'm going to give you another blessing and see if I can get inspiration to help you cope with this problem." When he finishes, he kisses me and smiles, "Now I understand the problem; we'll work on it tonight. I've got to get to class but know you're going to be alright in every way." He runs out both doors without looking back.

I'm home first, so it's my turn to fix dinner. He walks in as I'm putting the finishing touches on grilled venison steaks. After the prayer, I blurt out, "Now are you going to tell me?"

With a mouthful he mumbles, "After dinner. I need to show you, not tell you." Our meals are usually relaxing and full of talk. Tonight, I rush everything, not talking at all except to tell him he'll have to wait for dessert until after he's shown me.

He slowly chews his last bite then quickly stands, grabs my hand, and starts leading me upstairs. We end up in our bathroom, "Okay Terry, put on your birthday suit." I just stare at him. "Take your clothes off, stand in front of the mirror, and tell me what you see."

I have no idea where this is going so I do as he asks, "I see me turning into an ugly duckling."

"You could never be an ugly anything. I see the most beautiful mother of our child. What I want you to see is what is happening to your body. What change do you see in your upper body?"

"An enlargement which converts to three larger sizes in my bras."

Even goes on. "What about in your abdominal area?"

"I think it sticks out about twelve inches."

"Terry, turn sideways. It's only about three to four inches right now. It may get to twelve. Now come out into our bedroom with me." I follow him out, but this feels so strange.

Standing in front of me he says, "Mirror me in a kata. Do you remember the first one?"

We begin. Three moves into the exercise I almost fall over. We begin again. This time I get halfway through the first kata before I do fall over. "Terry, why do we do katas?"

I feel like a small child being led on a trip, "To get centered. To get my mind to focus on every minute detail." I think I've answered right.

"It's also to center your body. Your center of gravity has changed, and all the karate movements pivot around your center of gravity. The katas are to help your body know where that center is."

Now the light comes on like I'm standing in the sun. "Of course, that makes so much sense. I stopped doing the katas when I got pregnant. Let's do some more; I can feel control coming back. I just need to put my karate gi on. Some parts of my body are a little too free. If I need to use my skills, I'm sure I'll be dressed."

"Oh, I really like your freedom."

"Later!"

"What about my dessert?"

"You go get your dessert. I'm going to finish the katas." I throw my arms around his neck and kiss him soundly, "I love you my dearest husband; you've given me my control and confidence back."

He comes upstairs a half hour later as I'm finishing my last kata. "The dessert was delicious, I cleaned up the kitchen, is it later yet?"

I throw my arms around his neck, "I think I need a shower." He picks me up and carries me into the bathroom.

I'm sitting at my desk pondering the added meaning of centering and waiting for Arundel to come for her lesson. She's right on time, but for the first time, she's walking with a good-looking guy taller than she is. They stop still chatting, then he turns into one of the practice rooms as she heads to my office.

She walks in with her usual, "Hi Doc."

"Hi, yourself. Who's the handsome guy you were walking with? Is he a music student? I've never seen him before."

"Oh, Doc. He is the most amazing tenor I have ever heard. He's stronger than Tom Masters."

Now she has my undivided attention, "Where did you find him?"

"He found me. I was practicing in my office during the Christmas break. He stuck his head in the door and about scared me to death when he spoke. He asked if he could talk with me. I was so taken aback by his appearance that I said yes without thinking. He came in and sat down. He wanted to know if I was head of the piano faculty because of how well I played. I told him I was a part-time faculty and a doctoral student. He wanted to know if he could hire me to be his accompanist. He needed to get ready for his audition to qualify for the master's program in vocal music. He wants to transfer to Augustine. I asked him if he had music with him, to which he pulled an operatic piece out of his backpack. We spent the next two hours with me playing and him singing. We have practiced together every day since. He is phenomenal; you need to hear him."

My wheels are turning at high speed, "I do need to hear him; can you get him?" She runs down the hall to the practice room he went into.

"Dr. Timpson, I would like you to meet Wallace Yates, an incredible tenor. Wallace this is Dr. Terry Masters Timpson, head of the piano department."

Wallace speaks first, "You must be quite a pianist if you play better than Arundel. No one at the school I'm transferring from can play or accompany me like she can."

Looking at Arundel I wink, "She is a very accomplished concert pianist, but she tells me I must hear you sing. Will you do that now?"

"Absolutely, I don't have to be bribed to sing." We move into my music room. I motion Arundel to the piano.

When he begins to sing, I'm blown away. Arundel didn't exaggerate at all. I hold up my hand to stop them. "Can you give me a few minutes I need to make a call."

I rush out of the room and return within with Grandma Flora in tow. "Well, Wallace, I see it didn't take long for you to come to Dr. Timpson's attention. He has quite the voice, doesn't he?"

I can hardly wait, "He does, and I want to hear what you two sound like together. What duet can you sing?"

They look at each other and then converse. Wallace pulls music from his pack and places it on the piano. Arundel frowns when she looks at the score. "I'll need a little practice to play this one. You better play it Doc," she says as she looks at me and moves from the piano. As I begin the introduction, they both move toward the back wall facing it. When they begin to sing, my heart soars. But I also understand why they are singing at the back wall, their voices are way too big for my small room. They could sing over a full orchestra.

When they finish, Arundel and I are both clapping and yelling bravo. I can hardly speak for my excitement. "You two are meant to sing with each other." Then I look at Arundel and Wallace, "Would you two be free to perform in a concert with me a week from Saturday if all our plans materialize? I will know for certain tomorrow evening."

"That would be perfect; live on stage. I can't wait." Grandma Flora yells as she runs out the door.

Staring wide-eyed Wallace stammers, "Are you for real?"

Arundel grins, "Wallace, everything Doctor T does is for real. I'm game whether you are or not. What do you say? Tell us a little more Doc."

I tell them about working with the FBI, and the opportunity to help Matilda.

Wallace punches the air, "Yes, I love this school already. The first week I'm here, I find the best accompanist I've ever had, I get to sing in a concert and have suspense and adventure at the same time. I'm all in. Tell us what we need to do Dr. Timpson." He hugs Arundel and quickly pulls back looking a little embarrassed. She kisses him on the cheek.

I'm looking out the jet window but seeing Evan and me last night. We went through the katas and then I practiced blocking all his aggressive moves. Finally, he put his arms around me pulling me tight to him, "Now, I feel better about sending you and my son off to be FBI agents. I think you can handle anything that's thrown at you."

"Oh Evan, you silly man. I'm not an agent, but I do promise to not take any unnecessary risks. I just pray that Matilda will let us help her. I hate to think of what will happen to her if she doesn't." It is so unfair when people prey on someone weaker to get gain.

Agent Fowler pulls me from my thoughts as he puts his computer away. "What do you think Terry, is Matilda going to let us help her? If she doesn't, I'm afraid she's next up on the list to silently disappear."

"My thoughts exactly. Probably following her concert next week."

The FBI Agent stands and pulls a box from his carry-on in the overhead rack. He hands it to me after he's seated, "I have a present for you Terry. Open it." I lift the lid to find what looks like a black wallet. The outside is soft leather, but it feels hard inside. I open it like a wallet, and my mouth falls open. I'm gaping at a bright shiny FBI badge on one side, and my name, number, and picture on the other half. I flip my head up to stare at him. "I had a meeting with my higher-ups, and we decided it would be better if you were an agent when you're working undercover with us. On top of that, you've brought in more criminals by yourself than my whole unit put together. Enough crooks have you on their hit list for later, we think you need the protection agents receive."

"I don't know what to say."

"Don't say anything. Just listen while I give you basic training. When you're under cover if there's any possibility of you being searched, don't wear your badge. Other than that, you must always have it with you but out of sight. You also need to have the codes for the week. It's how we check out other agents. This week is 'Candy's Apple Red' and 'Granny's Apple Green'. You need to get the s's in the right spot. It's a matter of life or death…" He continues with my training all the way to touchdown.

When we pull up in front of Matilda's small quaint house in his rental, Agent Fowler says, "You three go and invite her to lunch; I might be a bit intimidating. Introduce me as an old friend."

Granddad rings the bell, and we wait desperately hoping she will recognize one of us. When she opens the door, she looks startled to see me, "Lilly? No, you couldn't be Lilly, you are way too young."

That is my opening, "No, down one generation. I'm Lilly's daughter."

"The one who came with Lilly to my concerts." I nod my head. "You look just like your mother; you could be her twin."

Now she looks at Granddad and his new wife, "Albert? Albert Martin? Flora? What are you doing here? I haven't seen you for years. Please come in." She opens the door wider and stands back to allow us to enter.

Granddad hugs her before we can move, "Matilda, we are just visiting the area for the day and thought it would be wonderful to take you to lunch and catch up on old times. Will you come with us? Our car and driver are waiting."

"Oh, my goodness, I would love to spend the afternoon with old friends. Wait while I get my coat and purse."

As we reach the car, Agent Flower steps out and opens the back door, "Why don't you three beautiful women ride in the back seat, and Albert, you come up front with me."

As Flora starts to slide across the back seat, Fowler ducks his head inside and whispers to her, "Get her necklace, it's a bug." Matilda then slides in, and as I'm bending down, he whispers to me, "Necklace is a bug, drop it behind the back seat," Once he's buckled in, he turns to Dr. Martin, "Yes sir, where can I take you?"

"Take us to a nice restaurant where we can have a pleasant lunch and spend the afternoon talking."

"Yes sir."

Flora turns to look directly at Matilda, "I have been admiring your necklace; it is so unique. Can I get a closer look at it?"

Matilda reaches her arms up behind her neck to unfasten it, "I don't like wearing it much, but that insurance man said I need to wear it all the time." She drops it into Flora's outstretched hand.

I draw Matilda's attention my way, "Do you still play the Bumblebee as fast as you used to? I loved to watch your fingers." Flora puts her arm with a clenched fist behind Matilda on the back of the seat.

"Terry, you'll have to see her play. I went to one of her concerts just before I moved. She's still a grand pianist." Matilda flips her head back to look at Flora with a pleased look. Flora opens her fist and drops the necklace into my left hand, and I transfer it to my right. I quickly slide my hand down between the seat and the door squeezing the bug until I feel a crunch. I then tuck it behind the seat on the floor.

While we're unloading at the restaurant, Matilda suddenly remembers reaching to her neck, "My necklace." She looks at Flora.

"I must have dropped," she begins to hurriedly look in the car and on her clothes.

"Don't worry about it. I hated that thing being around my neck all the time. It was so cheap looking. I'll just tell them someone else lost it. I don't think they'll mind."

After giving our orders to the waiter, Dr. Martin turns to our guest, "Matilda, I would like to introduce you to FBI Agent Fowler."

"Oh my. Oh, dear! Am I in trouble?" She frantically says staring at him.

"Matilda, you know you're in trouble. I'm here with these folks to get you out of trouble and save your life. We would also like to put as many of these crooks behind bars as possible, but we need your help to do that. We'll do everything in our power to keep you safe."

"You mean I wouldn't have to have my fingers broken again or pay them any more money?"

"That's exactly what I mean. I'm so sorry that any of this has happened to you. Will you help us even if it means moving away, changing your name, and finding a new source of income for a while?"

"I'll do anything if I can get out of this nightmare. What do you want me to do?"

"First, we would like you to sign a new contract making Albert your new music agent, then we'll visit the concert hall and make a few changes to your concert next Saturday."

"Albert, are you a music agent now? What do you want to do at my concert?"

"I am a music agent, and we would like to set up the concert to be a trap to catch your tormentors. We're going to redo the contract to take it out of your name and bring in a top guest pianist to play with you. Dr. Timpson has agreed to be your guest artist."

"You mean the Dr. Timpson that's playing for two nights at Carnegie next month. Why would she ever consent to a low-caliber concert like mine?"

"We're hoping her name will bring the big fish from your insurance scam to the concert that night thinking they will get all the take. They will not know the contract will no longer be yours. All the money will be directly deposited into Dr. Timpson's bank and will then be given to you to start a new life."

"I still don't understand why she would even consider helping someone like me. She doesn't even know me."

Now it's my turn, "Matilda, see that piano over there. Would you play the Bumblebee with me as you did with my mom?" She looks at the piano hesitantly and then around the room. "Look there's no one here but us, and it would mean so much to me for my mom's sake. She walks to the piano I had rented for this very moment. She sits, and I sit beside her. I give her two measures into the song and begin playing. The more we play the more aggressive she gets, and so do I.

When we finish, she turns to gape at me, "Who are you? Are you really Lilly's daughter?

"I am Dr. Terry Masters Timpson, and yes Lilian Masters was my mother. I am doing this because I loved you as a little girl and still do now. It is also for the memory of my mother. It is what she would want me to do." Matilda throws her arms around my neck and sobs.

The negotiations with the concert hall went smother than I thought they would once they were convinced, I was Dr. Timpson. They tried every way they could to change it to a two-night venue, but one week is not long enough to get everyone ready. I told them we could consider it in the future.

Pulling up in front of Matilda's house, I notice more people milling around and more parked cars. Once we're inside, we engage in excited conversation about the concert. Fowler warned us there might be more bugs planted in the house. We are waiting for a female FBI agent who is going to stay with Matilda during the week until the concert.

Amid our banter, the front door bursts open and a girl about my age rushes in, "Grandma, where have you been, and who are all these people? Dad said I should drop by and give you a big hug."

I watch Matilda; she doesn't recognize this girl but doesn't know what to say.

I decide I can play the same game; I raise my voice, "Well who in the candy's apple red are you, and what are you trying to put over? I know for certain my Aunt Matilda has never been married, and she had no children."

The woman answers cooly but with no return code, "It's just a little joke we have between us. My dad is her agent and takes care of her needs. He just sent me by to check on her. She has short-term memory loss at times. I'll just hug her and be on my way."

I move quickly to stand between her and Matilda, keeping my eyes on the hand she has never taken from her jacket pocket. She is holding something. I become assertive, "You're not coming close to my aunt."

"Have it your way; I'll let Derksin know you're having one of your spells." She turns to leave and kind of trips brushing against an artificial potted tree going out the door.

I move quickly to the tree and reach down for what the woman dropped then think better of it. "Agent Fowler, you had better come take a look at this. It is a syringe dripping with fluid. He quickly produces a plastic bag and gathers up the weapon without putting his fingerprints.

He quickly opens his cell, "Apprehend the woman that just left and any car that's waiting for her. Book them on attempted murder and allow no outside contact. Matilda, we can't leave you here. Go pack two suitcases of your most prized possessions. Do the essentials on the clothes, we can always buy you more. When we come back for the concert, we will go directly from the plane to the stage dressed and ready to perform."

I noticed while Agent Fowler was working, Grandma Flora was on her phone. She hangs up with a satisfied look and announces, "The piano movers will be here in thirty minutes to package up her concert grand piano and store it under my name until she knows what to do with it." By the time we get to the airport, Matilda has a ticket with her mother's middle and maiden names on it, Ann Franklyn.

# CHAPTER 6

Here it is Tuesday, and I'm still having trouble dropping into my deep concentration. Matilda is staying with the Martins. If we hadn't signed a contract for the concert on Saturday, she would at least be out and somewhat safe. I don't have $15,000 to pay for a breach of contract, so we'll go back to fill our obligations. I need to look at the positive side if it can be called positive. Agent Fowler only captured two flunky crooks. The concert could create an opportunity to get higher-level scum. The other bright point is that Evan will be there by my side. He said he thought it would be okay for me to go alone to the set-up, but not to the sting.

I'm shocked out of my reverie when my lights start blinking, and my siren blares. Stephanie and Russell are at my office door trying to get my attention. "What brings you two to school at seven o'clock in the morning?"

"Dr. Timpson, we've decided we can't wait any longer. We want to be married this morning. Will you come and be a witness for us?"

Their excitement is contagious, "I would love to, but the city offices don't open until 9:00 am. You also need two witnesses; any other options?"

"Allen is in your piano teaching room. We'll go see if he will come."

"When you find a second witness, come back here and play some duets for me," I yell as they charge down the hall. Since Russell will be traveling to Carnegie with us, they could play a duet in the pre-show; I think.

This has not been my week for concentration. It's now Thursday, and I haven't made much progress on the new composition I'm hoping to have ready for Carnegie. The composition class I teach will be over in fifteen minutes. Their first composition is due at the end of class, and most of the students are printing their final scores. I'm anxious to see where they are in their composing skills. I tell them they are free to go when they give me their sheet music. Students begin filing out the door as they hand me their work.

I had planned to work a little more on my unfinished piece, but curiosity gets the best of me. I begin looking through the new compositions playing them in my head. When I get to Franklin's score something doesn't feel right. It's only one sheet of paper full of prodigy music. He is a very talented pianist, but he hasn't bridged yet. I don't think he could play this, let alone compose it. He's one of the new transfer students and is struggling at the bottom of my class. Then I play it through in my head again. I know what this is. It's part of Allen's piano choir music. I think it's out of the part I'm supposed to play. Now I have another problem to take care of, but this one will have to wait until Monday morning when I'm back from the Sting Concert.

"Hi Doctor T. Teacher hold you late after class." I didn't even hear Allen walk in the door.

"Something like that. Come here and look at this composition." I hold the sheet of music out to him.

His teasing expression changes to one of surprise then anger, "This is from my piano choir music. How did you get it? And why does it have Franklin's name on it?"

"It was just handed in for this week's composition assignment."

Allen's expression changes to one of disbelief, "Doc. I promise I agonized over every note on that page. Especially that page since I wanted to challenge you."

"Relax Allen, I know it's your work. Franklin could never have composed this. What we need to do is find out what going on with him."

"I'll tell you what's going on with him. I'm going to kill him. This is obvious plagiarism. I think he's even signed up to be one of my private students."

"Is this like when you accused me of blatant plagiarism?"

"…You're right; we need to learn more."

"I'm leaving town in the morning. Don't say anything to him. We'll have a meeting Monday morning in my office with him, Dr. Rich, you, and me. I think I'm sensing a larger problem here."

After another meeting with Agent Fowler, he changed our travel plans. We are flying the day before and staying in a hotel fifty miles from the concert venue. We will travel in an FBI van dressed in our concert attire arriving in time for our set up. We will go in the stage door directly onto the stage. Fowler isn't sure if they want to eliminate Matilda, the star witness, or go after the money. I think they'll try for both.

We begin with four hands on the Bumblebee. Matilda is quite nervous as we begin, but as a seasoned performer, she regains her concentration, and we play an exciting piece. The audience honors us with a standing ovation. We then play Liszt's "Hungarian Rhapsody #2". Matilda is a very good concert pianist. She stands and moves to the mic. "Thank you, ladies and gentlemen, for that warm welcome. I would like to turn the next few minutes over to our guest, Dr. Terry Timpson, pianist extraordinaire." She exits to a roaring round of applause. I'm praying the next few minutes will go as planned off-stage. The FBI should be sweeping her out the back door and into their waiting car. She is to be rushed off to a waiting plane at the airport. The FBI will take her to Tom and Pam's place when she lands. She is now in the Lord's hands.

The rest of the evening is my playing interspersed with pieces from Arundel, Wallace, and Flora. We end the evening with four hands accompanying Flora and Wallace performing Verdi's soprano/tenor duet from La Traviata. I would count this concert a huge success. Now I hope the rest of the evening goes as planned.

Most of the audience has left and the concert hall manager is raving about the successful concert. He is trying to get Dr. Martin to set him up a two-night stand. I move to the grand to do my usual take-down of the lid. I have just lifted it to take the weight off its leg when a man comes running, screaming and waving his hands. I quickly turn to Arundel and tell her to take Wallace and move to the lip of the stage and not to move for anything. Now the maniac is yelling in my face, and I can feel Evan behind me. I'm still holding the lid.

"Where is she!" the distraught man yells.

"Where is who?"

"You know, Matilda. She owes me big time."

"I have no idea. What does she owe you for?"

He is getting more frustrated as we speak, "I am her agent, and she owes me for this concert. The take must be huge, but the manager won't give me her earnings."

I look him in the eyes and answer as coolly as I can, "Oh, Matilda has a new manager. As for this concert, Matilda canceled, and I signed a new contract. Your name is not on that contract anywhere, whatever your name is."

He walks closer to get in my face which he needs to look up into. "I'm Derksin. I'm her insurance agent and her premiums are due."

"You mean the money she is forced to pay you, so you won't break her hand again or worse? She fired you too."

He looks at me in shocked disbelief, "Insurance is a legitimate business."

"It can be, but what you do is bully, assault, and demand extortion money. It's illegal no matter how many papers you get innocent people to sign by force."

He steps closer, "You will pay me what I deserve for this concert, or I'll break every bone in your body!"

Evan steps from behind me, "No one threatens my wife." Then he steps forward again and shoves him in the chest. Derksin stumbles backward and tries to stay upright by grabbing the side of the piano. Evan's movement throws me off balance sidewise, and I lose my hold on the lid. It smashed down on Derksin's hand and fingers. His scream is louder than any soprano that ever sang in this hall.

Agent Fowler rushes from behind the closest curtain to lift the lid from the screaming man's hand. He slumps to the floor with murder in his eyes. Fowler cuffs him to an agent while three more of the crook's team are rounded up. Once on his feet, he glares at me, "I'll send my representative to take care of you."

"Your son is already in jail with a broken arm; maybe you can share a cell."

"The big boss will never let you get away with this." With that, Agent Fowler and his men frog march the criminals out the door. We are rushed out into the waiting van and are driven to the closest airport.

I was able to get three hours of good practice this morning before we meet with Franklin. He's the first to arrive looking very nervous and Dr. Rich and Allen are right behind him, "I've asked you all to meet with me this morning to discuss a serious problem. I hand Franklin the music score he gave me which has his name on it. "Franklin, would you play this for us please?"

He hangs his head and tears start rolling down his cheeks, "I can't, I didn't write it."

I continue, "Where did you get it?"

"I found it in your piano lab on the floor just barely sticking out from under the piano. It didn't have a name on it, and I was panicked to turn in a composition. It's the dumbest thing I have ever done...I am so lost here at this school. I was the top pianist at my university, but no one there could teach me to bridge. Then I started hearing that students who came here were learning to bridge. I entered late and the Advanced

Piano Tec class I was supposed to take first was full. I thought as a master's seeking student I would do okay in advanced composition. I feel like everyone in the class is five years ahead of me, and I'm in kindergarten. No one in my school, including the faculty can play like the students in that class."

I hand the music to Allen, "Will you play this page for us." Allen moves into the piano in my music room and plays his composition.

Franklin moans louder, "I'm just burying myself deeper and deeper. Allen's my private teacher. Maybe the best thing for me to do is forget about piano altogether." I look at Allen, and I think he is finally thinking this through.

"Doctor T, Franklin is where I was a year ago when I made such a fool of myself." I nod my head to agree. "He needs to be in the advanced piano tec one class." I nod my head again. "I think I could teach the things you taught in that class. I have a couple of empty hours in my schedule, one on Tuesday and one on Thursday while you're accompanying the Oratorio Choir. I could use your piano lab then."

"That's exactly what I'm thinking. We've encouraged students to come to our school to learn to bridge but can't offer them the class to begin. Three more advanced students need to be in that class. What do you think Dr. Rich?"

"I think Dr. Timpson, that you are a very wise teacher. I thought I was coming here to discipline a student, but it appears we may have created most of his problems. Allen, I'm good with you teaching that class. I can see it's sorely needed... Franklin, you do understand that plagiarism is a very serious offense?"

"Yes Sir, I do. I will never do anything like that again. I have agonized and cried over turning in work that was not mine all weekend. All I want to do is learn to play like Allen." Allen reaches over and shakes Franklin's hand.

"Franklin, I'm sorry we let you down at the start of your music program at Augustine. For your information, you're only two semesters behind Allen. Take only that one class this semester and give it everything you've got, and you'll be on track with him."

"Doctor Timpson, are you serious? Only two semesters and he plays like that and composes prodigy music. I'd give anything to do that."

Allen puts his hand on Franklin's shoulder, "She's absolutely right man, two semesters and a summer in between. And just so you know, she doesn't require anything; she requires everything! Come on let's go find your classmates and get started." I give them a thumbs-up as they walk out the door.

I didn't realize how many little details there would be to put together our two nights at Carnegie. We're a week out and I think almost everything is in place. All the guest numbers are concert-ready, my new composition finally sounds like I want it to, and all the logistics are in place. Carnegie said they are taking care of us from the moment we walk off our airplane until we get back on, so I won't worry about our time there.

I'm trying to decide if there are any loose ends when Granddad Martin walks through the door. "I haven't seen you for a while. What have you done with Matilda? Is she still with you out at the ranch?"

"This new job of being an agent is keeping me busier than I thought it would. I've been out checking concert possibilities across the country. I could book you any place, but our students don't have credibility yet. I think that will change after the Carnegie Concert next week… The manager of Matilda's concert hall is very persistent. He talks to me every other day. I finally have him convinced that you can't come for a couple of years. Now he's after someone of the same caliber as those who performed with you. Anyone ready for you to send?"

I think over my growing crew; then I smile, "Yes, Solomon is ready, and he needs a little boost. I'll talk to him during his lesson this afternoon. What about Matilda?"

"I searched and searched for an obscure college needing a piano teacher with a Ph.D. I finally found one in the Pacific Northwest. They were excited to be hiring someone with her concert experience and her educational credentials. She is excited to enter the world of teaching. She doesn't even have to change her name. Since Matilda is her stage name, she will start using her real name, Dr. Ellen Frankel. She's leaving tomorrow, so we thought we'd have a little going away party for her tonight at the ranch house. She would like you and Evan to come. She wants to play four hands with you again…

"Terry, I need to share a concern Flora has. When she tried to give Wallace his first voice lesson, he was unteachable. She tried to get him to back off the loudness and try blending more. She said it is like he has moved into another world. All he could talk about was how he was going to fill the Stem with his marvelous voice. He's pushing so hard, he's yelling and becoming strident. She wanted you to know." I tell him we'll be there for the party, and panic starts gripping my heart that I may have made a mistake inviting Wallace to Carnegie.

My alarm goes off when Solomon and Dawn try to get into my office for his lesson. I ask them to sit in front of my desk instead of going straight to my music room. They look expectantly at me, "Solomon, are you ready for a concert?"

He looks confused, "You heard me play. You said I sounded good for next week."

"Oh, I'm sorry. I've shifted gears. How do you feel about doing a concert on your own near the end of March?"

"You mean a real concert in a real concert hall?"

"That's what I mean. How do you feel about it?"

His reaction is not what I expected. He looks deeply concerned, "Dr. Timpson, does this mean you want me to leave the college world and go out into the concert world?"

"Absolutely not! I want you to stay right here at Augustine and develop a department for teaching blind piano students. But I also want to build your credibility as a concert pianist so prospective students will know you are fully capable of teaching them."

"I'm sorry Doc. I thought you might be trying to get rid of me. Yes, I'm ready to be on a concert stage, but I'm not sure I could manage a whole evening by myself. What if Allen and I did it together? To me, he sounds as good as any concert pianist I have ever heard except for you. I also love playing his new composition for the piano choir."

"Good choice Solomon. I'll see if he's available" I text and tell Solomon he will join us in five minutes.

Solomon's head turns in my direction, "Doc, I have a confession to make. When I came to work on my doctorate it was with the intent that I would work hard to learn the improv skills and then head to the concert world. When you said I had to teach students, I doubted that would ever work. But using your method, I found my students improved as much as anyone else's, and I was proud of their successes. When you gave me the three blind students, my whole world changed. I am finding that I would rather teach than perform."

"Oh, Solomon, I was hoping that would happen. You have insight into the blind world that a seeing pianist could never have. But it is also important that you perform. Getting ready for a concert is what stretches us to improve. That's why all my piano teachers must be performing concert pianists… I also have a selfish reason for wanting you to stay. My baby will be born without eyes, and he needs an uncle who can give him visions I never could."

We all have tears in our eyes when Allen rushes through the door. He looks around, "What's happening? Is someone dying?"

Solomon wipes his eyes under his dark glasses, "No Allen, someone is just being born… How would you like to do a concert with me in a real concert hall at the end of March." Now Allen is speechless. Dawn pulls up another chair for Allen. "Yah man, it's for real. You and me on stage by ourselves. The boss says she's going to build our credibility, and this is part of the process."

Allen looks at me, "What's he talking about?" I spend the next ten minutes explaining the invitation, and then we begin developing a program. When I suggest they play the piano choir cantata, Allen objects, "It won't work without the part I wrote for you. You could leave out any or all the parts but not that one."

"Allen, you wrote it. You can play it. You have between now and March to put it together. You play the prodigy music and Solomon can play his part or any other. It will be phenomenal. If you have it ready for my Augustine concert in March, you can play it there to practice."

Allen grabs Solomon's hand, "Can you believe it? The two of us headed out into the music world on our own. It's a dream come true."

I burst their bubble, "Not the two of you, the four of you. Your wives will be going with you. The concert world will not break up our families. Two good-looking male concert pianists out on their own for the first time would make them the target for every immoral activity possible. No wives, no concert. Besides, they will be your escorts onto the stage and dressed as formally as you are. They are to be part of your world, not your audience." Everyone laughs, especially Dawn.

# CHAPTER 7

We are on our way to New York, and I still haven't decided what to do with Wallace. I talked to him about blending, but I felt like he was laughing at me when he said he had it all under control. I'm pulled out of my trance when Arundel puts her hand on my shoulder and leans over whispering, "Doc, can I talk to you?" Evan looks at us and says he needs to stretch his legs. She slips into the aisle seat beside me.

"I'm sorry to bother you, but I'm so worried about this trip." I wonder if she's getting stage fright, but I don't think that's it. But I do see fear. "I am more concerned about Wallace by the minute. I think he will ruin your whole show and me as well." I encourage her to go on. "He's been acting funny lately; like he's the star of the show and people should be paying him homage. He's also becoming extremely possessive of me. After the pilot turned off the seatbelt sign, he came and kicked Marie out of her seat. He said it was his place to sit beside his accompanist. He said very crude racial things to her. Then he started talking to me about how I was going to come to his room tonight and sleep with him. He's also been talking about how he's going to flood the Stem with his magnificent voice which will stand out above everyone else. The last time we practiced, his volume was increased, but it is now just yelling. I'm afraid he'll ruin the whole show. I'm even more afraid he'll ruin me."

I put my arm around her shoulder as her tears flow, "Arundel, we aren't going to let him ruin a thing, especially you." I get up as Evan is coming down the aisle. "Move over to my seat, and we'll get your traveling companion back." I tell Evan the problem as we walk toward the back of the plane. When we pass Marie, I tell her to go up and sit with Arundel.

We stop when we get to Wallace. He looks up surprised to see us, "Wallace, I believe you are in the wrong seat."

"Oh no, Doctor Timpson, this is my seat beside my accompanists."

"She is no longer your accompanist. If anyone accompanies you, it will be me. Now move to your seat. My husband and I are going to sit here, and you will sit right behind us so we can keep an eye on you. If you make one more racial slur to Marie, we'll throw you out the door without a parachute." Evan's looking like he's itching to yank him up out of his seat and move him.

He slowly begins to stand when a large burley steward comes up behind us, "Doctor Timpson is there a problem here?"

I take advantage of the moment, "Yes, this rude young man is sitting in the wrong seat and is refusing to move. My husband and I are going to sit here." We move out of the way. Wallace looks up into the set jaw of the steward and quickly moves to the seat behind.

Evan and I talk all the way to New York about my tenor problem. I have decided he will not perform, but I don't quite know what to do with him. I even stroll up the aisle to talk with Dr. Rich about him, and we decide to watch as the evening develops. He promises to keep him away from Arundel.

Everything appears to be going smoothly as we are picked up by a shuttle bus and deposited at the hotel's entrance. We each pick up our bags and everyone follows me to the front desk. "You must be Dr. Timpson and this your company. We are honored that you have chosen us to host your group." He looks us over and a scowl creeps into his forehead. He looks at me with dismay. "Dr. Timpson, we may have a little problem here." He takes two of the room keys and hands them to his assistant, "Change these for two rooms in the basement." Then he asks me, "Are you aware of our hotel policies."

I have a bad feeling that this is not going to end well. I answer, "No I am not. Carnegie made all the billeting arrangements for us. What's the problem?"

He doesn't quite know how to start, "People of Color don't usually stay in our facility. We can, however, put them in rooms in the basement, but they are not allowed to mingle with our other guests or use the front doors. They will need to find dining facilities outside of our hotel. I'm sorry you were not aware of our policy."

Celia moves up behind me to whisper in my ear that it's okay; they're used to it. They will go to the basement.

Now I'm angry, but I talk as matter-of-factly and calmly as I can, "Now, let me share my policy with you. I need my company in the same place where I am so I can have access to them at any time. I want them to be with me while we are eating in case there are changes in the program that everyone needs to be aware of. I want a piano available in the dining area that can be used if necessary. And for your information, I'm color blind and every person in my group is of equal value and has the same color of heart. I am canceling our reservation. We'll go where we are all wanted. Come on group, we're out on the street." I'm surprised to hear shouts, cheers, and clapping coming from the entire group including Dr. Rich and his wife. We bust through the doors rushing onto the sidewalk in front of the hotel, luggage and all.

Now that I've made my stand, I'm wondering what to do next. Feeling a tap on my shoulder, I turn around to look up into the face of a smiling immaculately dressed Black Man. "Pardon me, mam, maybe I can help you with your problem. I am Emmerson Daniels, and I own the hotel just down the street on the opposite corner."

I'm still a little miffed, "Does your hotel participate in discriminatory practices as well… Your grapevine is even quicker than the one at our university. You seem to be waiting for us."

"Dr. Timpson, you are very big news, especially in this part of town. My hotel will accommodate your entire group in our very best rooms. We only have one dining room, but I can put up partitions so you can have some privacy. If you decide to practice or perform, I hope you will allow us to remove the barrier so all of our guests can enjoy your music. I have heard you play. In my book, you're number one. I do need to make you aware that the majority of our guests are People of Color, but I don't know of one of them who wouldn't be proud to have you there. We'll deal with Carnegie and our prices will be more than competitive."

I don't know what else to say, "Lead the way." We all bend down to pick up our luggage.

"Dr. Timpson, leave your luggage where it is. We'll take care of everything. Please, follow me." We haven't gotten far when ten or more bellhops in bright uniforms rush past us and then rush past again with all our luggage in tow. Emmerson leads me to the desk and gives me papers to fill out. He asks, "Would you like all your rooms in the same area on the same floor? We will of course put you in the penthouse."

"If it's okay with you, I would like my room to be on the same floor and area as the rest of my company. I would also like to arrange the room assignments. I have one possible renegade; I need to keep a close eye on him."

"I understand completely. Your rooms will be ready in ten minutes. Carnegie has been contacted and contracted with. We will supply anything you need. Just call the front desk. The dining room will begin serving in thirty minutes and the back section has been cordoned off for your group."

"Alright group," I call to get their attention. "We are on the third floor in the north wing. The dining room will be open in thirty minutes. We will be sitting in the back section behind the screens. Take your luggage to your rooms, and clean up a little, but please come to dinner in your traveling clothes. No matter where we are we represent Augustine. It's getting late, so after dinner, I expect everyone to be in their rooms for the night. Please get a good night's sleep. Tomorrow will be a very demanding day." I look at Emmerson, "Breakfast at 10:00 am in this dining room?"

"Breakfast will be at 10:00 am. There are snacks in your rooms, but if you need more, there's a menu by your phone. You can order anything at any time, and it will be brought to your rooms. We will even bring you ice if needed. However, alcoholic, and carbonated beverages have been outlawed by your leader." Everyone snickers at the last comment. I smile as I hand everyone their key, and we head to our rooms. That rule is for one person only.

Arundel and Marie go into the last room in the hall. Our room is right next to theirs. The girls are totally surprised when we appear through the adjoining doors and inform them, we are trading rooms. I investigate their confused faces, "We're doing everything we can to keep you safe. I'm sure you haven't seen the last of your tormentor. I'm going to be the one he sees when he tries to get into your room tonight, and Evan will be right behind me."

"Doctor T, I'm so sorry I've caused you so many problems. I probably shouldn't have come."

"Arundel, you haven't caused me one problem. It's all coming from one slightly unbalanced young man. I have a feeling his problems are larger than we realize, and we are going to keep you safe. When you're ready, we'll go down to dinner together." She hugs me, and they hurry to freshen up.

Once we're in our dining area, I sit the girls at a table with Evan and move to check out the piano. I can tell we are a hungry group because within five minutes everyone is seated. Emmerson looks at me and I nod my head. Servers quickly take all our orders. While we wait, I need to work. Moving to the piano, I ask for Flora and Wallace to join me. When I'm ready, I look at them, "I want to hear your duet." Flora nods her head in understanding; Wallace looks shocked. "I want to hear exactly what it's going to sound like tomorrow in the concert." I begin the intro, and Flora begins to sing beautifully. Wallace waits for four measures then enters with a resounding double forte scream. I stop instantly and so does he.

"That's what I'm going to sound like tomorrow in the stem. I will out sing everyone. It will be my night."

"Wallace, I think you have built too many delusions of grandeur. You are not singing in this concert. Go back and sit with Dr. Rich if you want dinner." He obediently goes back to his seat. I think we have a real mental problem on our hands. "Pam, will you come up and sing with Dr. Martin." They sing a few lines calming my wounded musical spirit. I stop and ask Maria and Celia to join them. "What can the four of you sing together?

Maria timidly calls out, "A Poor Wayfaring Man of Grief?"

I think about it. It might work, "Let's try it." I begin with an introduction. They are so magnificent together. I don't know why I haven't put them together before. I hear a scraping sound behind me and then realize they are moving the dividing curtains. I have no idea how large our audience is, but it is completely attentive. There is not a sound. When we finish, there is roaring applause and a standing ovation. I turn to see the dining room is packed with a standing-room-only crowd. This number will replace Wallace. Now what to do with him?

I see Emerson raise his hand and our food is delivered to our tables. I turn to the crowd, "I know we should sing for our supper, but it's been a very long day. If you will give us thirty minutes to inhale our food, we'll share some more of our music with you." I am greeted with cheers, clapping, and laughter. I move to my table to eat. I motion for Emmerson to join us. "You don't happen to have four electronic keyboards stashed in a closet, do you?"

"We don't, but they'll be here by the time you finish eating." I give him a thumbs-up and dive into my dinner; I'm famished.

Our impromptu concert lasted way longer than it should have. They were such a responsive audience we just wanted to give more. By the time we had given everyone a last hug and got to our rooms, it is midnight. I'm ready to fall into bed, but I know I have one more problem to deal with. Evan and I are sitting on the bed when our problem rears its head.

There's a loud pounding on our door, "Arundel, my room is already. It's time for you to come with me. Open this door, or I'll break it down…"

I let him go on for about five minutes. I'm sure everyone in our wing is awake and in the hall. I slowly open the door with Evan right beside me but out of sight. In an angry voice I yell, "Wallace, you are supposed to be in your room. Arundel wants nothing to do with you. Go to bed." I step into the hall in my not-so-loose-fitting t-shirt and my most baggy sweats. "If you don't go to bed, I'll have hotel security lock you in your room."

He looks wide-eyed at me taking everything in, "Oh, Doctor Timpson, maybe I made a mistake, maybe the leading man should spend the night with the leading woman. I'll take you instead."

"I'm not going anyplace with you, especially to bed. I already have a bed partner."

"You just need a little gentle persuasion. All women do you know. I'll just put my hand around your neck, and you'll come more than willingly. They all do."

As his hand touches my face, I grab his wrist with both hands, duck under, and wrench his arm high up behind his back. Now he's screaming like a wounded pig. I calmly ask, "You mean this point right here deep in your neck behind your muscle which causes you to blackout." I push my thumb into it with all my strength. He's screaming "No" all the way to the floor, where he finally passes out.

Evan is now standing over him in case he's faking. I turn to my boss, "Dr. Rich, can we get him on a plane and fly him out of here? Evan, will you pack his things? I want no trace of him left at all."

Evan and Emmerson reach his door at the same time. It's not latched, and swings open easily. They stop short when they look in. "Terry, call Agent Fowler! This man's a maniac." They close the door so it locks, and no one can look inside.

Emmerson runs off and returns quickly with a large roll of athletic tape. He soon has Wallace looking like a mummy. I don't ever want to know what was in that room, and Arundel will never know.

When Fowler has everything wrapped up, he finds me, "Terry, I think you have a guardian angel that follows you and your bunch around. We know who this perp is and his MO. He's known as the Phantom of the Opera, but we've never been able to give him a real identity. You get a giant gold star for this one Agent Timpson."

"I don't want a gold star; I just want to put me and my baby to bed. We have a concert tomorrow. Emmerson, let's make breakfast lunch, and do it at noon." I hear a cheer from every one of my company who are crowded in the hall.

The concert went amazingly well. I was proud of everyone. I think my entire company must be as tired as I am. I planned with Emmerson to have dinner ready when we get back to the hotel by serving it buffet style. Only a couple more patrons in the reception hall, and we're on our way. As the crowd thins out, I notice one young man who keeps looking at me. I think he wants to talk but doesn't quite know how to approach me. My curiosity and the teacher in me reach out, and I motion for him to come to me.

The tall handsome man dressed in a tux moves to me, "Young man you look like you have a question. Can I help you?"

He hesitates looking at the floor, "I want to know more about your university."

"What would you like to know?"

He finally looks at me, "I am most interested in your vocal music program. Do you have a master's program? And if I were in it, could I try out for your Oratorio Choir?"

Now he has my interest, "Have you heard our choir?"

"I was at the May concert when you took first place. I had never heard anything like that before. I was able to get a ticket to your Christmas Concert at Carnegie. I was even more impressed. As soon as this concert was announced I bought a ticket. I would like to learn how to teach students to sing like yours do. This is the best concert I have ever been to, and I realized that all of you are affiliated with a university. It sounds more professional than most concerts I've attended. My name is David Russo."

"A little Italian blood to go with your darker skin?" He nods his head in confirmation. "Are you a singer?" He nods again. Sing something for me, Mr. Russo.

He has no hesitation about singing. He opens his mouth and begins "Come Thou Fount of Every Blessing." Now all my tiredness is swept away, and I'm filled with excitement. Here's the second tenor I've been looking for. I hold up my hand to stop him and at the same time call Tom and Jefferson to join us. David looks deflated.

"Tom, start the song again; David when you can feel a harmony join him, then jump in, Jefferson." Now David looks confused.

Tom begins singing, and in five measures, I signal for David to start. When understanding sinks in he joins with beautiful harmony. Jefferson is one measure behind him. I'm entranced with the harmony they make. I let them sing the whole verse. My stomach then growls loud enough to be heard, and I remember that everyone is waiting in the shuttle for us.

"David, are you hungry?" Now he's really lost.

"I'm always hungry."

"Good. Come join my company for dinner. We need to get better acquainted." I grab his arm with one hand and Evan's with the other. "Let's go before our dinner gets cold." Everyone cheers when we get on the bus. It starts moving before we even get seated. We have a blessing on the food before we exit the shuttle, and Allen and his wife lead us straight to the buffet tables in the dining hall.

As we start through the line David is between Evan and me. He tries to get my attention as I start loading a plate, "Dr. Timpson, I don't mean to intrude on your dinner."

I turn to him, "Eat. You can sing for your dinner later, and don't be shy about getting full." I lead us to a table to join the Doctors Martin, Dr. Rich and his wife, and Pam and Tom. I know everyone but Tom and Pam are curious about our new guest, but eating takes precedence.

When our eating slows enough to have a conversation, I introduce David to the people at our table. When we get to the Martins, he looks long at Flora, "I know who you are. You're Dr. Hephzibah Flora McCracken. I've studied all your works to train my voice. It's such a pleasure to meet you. I was so impressed with the women's quartet you were in tonight. You can sing on any opera stage over a full orchestra, and yet you blend perfectly into your foursome. That takes extensive voice training."

"Thank you, young man. You have quite a musical ear to take all that in. That's who I was, and now I've added a new last name. This is my new husband, Dr. Albert Martin, past concert pianist, past dean of the music college, and now the music agent for Augustine University.

We are about to explain more when I see Solomon standing. "Solomon, are you ready to play a little?" He turns toward my voice and raises his thumb. "Dawn, will you escort him to the piano?" I get another thumbs-up, and they are on their way. As piano music fills the air, the dividers are swept away. We are on to our next concert of sorts.

David looks around as chairs in the forward dining room are positioned our way, "What's happening? Are you having another concert? Man, you're going to make a haul tonight; this place is packed."

Evan slaps him on the shoulder, "David, look closely at those people, especially the ones standing. Do you think they could afford to buy a ticket at any price? My dear wife feels that they should have the opportunity to hear quality music as well as those who can afford Carnegie."

I think their conversation is cut short when I call the men in the ensemble to the piano after Solomon finishes his exciting jazz piece. I trade places with Solomon and begin the intro to "Come Thou Fount". The sound almost takes my breath away. Our audience is as excited as I am. Now I ask the women to join the men. On their way to the piano, Flora whispers in my ear, "You've struck gold." Now I need to figure out a way to take the gold home to Augustine. David enhances the whole ensemble as much as he did the men but doesn't stand out at all.

"Knights of Ebony, let's do Allen's concerto." I must do this since Emmerson went to the trouble to bring in four piano keyboards, and they are all hooked into the sound system. It's accepted as well as Solomon's Jazz. When we're through I set up all the individual and duet piano numbers. This gives me a little break.

David follows me back to our table and looks longingly at the serving table still holding food. I send him to fill his plate again. With his mouth still full of food he asks, "What do I have to do to be part of all this? It's what I've dreamed music education should be."

Dr. Rich looks at me and I nod my head. He then looks at David. "Say yes, enroll online, and be there Monday morning."

"I'd leave with you tomorrow, but I have one little problem. I can only go to school every other semester. I must work for a semester to get the money to go the next semester. It's taken a while, but I finally got my BA degree, 'and now I'm in my work track."

Everyone's surprised when Evan enters the conversation, "Terry, tell him about the haul you made tonight."

Now I know what their conversation was about, "All of our earnings tonight go directly into a university account set up for the music department. Each performer will receive a stipend, but the other half of the earnings go into a scholarship fund."

"Therefore, Mr. David Russo," Dr. Rich breaks in, "We are offering you a full-ride scholarship to earn your doctorate at Augustine University starting now. We will leave straight from the concert tomorrow night, and we even have a seat for you on our plane. What do you say?"

"Are you for real? That would be the answer to all my prayers and dreams. The only reason I'm here is for Dr. Timpson's concert. Nothing else is holding on to me; I haven't found a job yet."

I signal to Emmerson, "Do you have a room that this young man could use for the night? It's rather late for him to be out by himself in New York City?"

"Yes, Dr. Timpson, you still have an empty room on your reservation," I look skeptical, but he says, "Don't worry it's a different room. Would you like your breakfast/lunch at noon again tomorrow? There's still plenty of food here if any of your company would like more." I have noticed that everyone has made more than one trip back for food.

He is about to leave when Flora calls him over to her. "Emmerson, were you able to see our show tonight?"

He hangs his head a little, "I make a fair wage owning this place, but I also have a rather large family with many needs.

There's not much left for a night at Carnegie. This was such an honor that you would share your music with us. It's almost like being in the Stem."

Grandma Flora reaches inside her blouse and pulls out a ticket. "I want you to use this ticked tomorrow night. Wear your tux. You'll be right in the center of the dress circle." She takes the pen out of his pocket and writes on the back of the ticked. 'Given to Emmerson Daniels for five-star service. Flora McKracken Martin.' If anyone gives you a bad time, show them the back of your ticket." When he bends down to take the ticket, she touches his cheeks with two fingers. I don't know how many times he says thank you as he's bowing and backing away. Everyone at our table is staring at her, "What? It's my seat, and since I won't be using it, that deserving person should." I can see that Grandma Flora is as soft as the rest of us.

We finish the night with everyone doing the Alleluia and The Prayer. David watches from our table with tears in his eyes.

"Arundel, three more numbers, and our first concert at Carnegie will be over. Has it met your expectations?" We are standing in the wings ready to move on stage for "Moonlight".

"Oh Dr. Timpson, it is even more exciting than I thought it would be. It could get addicting, but also very tiring. I want to thank you for the gift you gave me on our first night. Normally when something happens like the Wallace incident, I would spend the rest of the night conjuring up thoughts of what might or could have happened. By morning I would be in a total panic and not able to play a note. Between your husband's blessing and you advising me to thank the Lord for what actually happened, I felt at peace all night. I think I have played the best I ever have."

"Your playing has been superb. You are a concert pianist. I think you play better than my mom did…"

"Terry Masters Timpson, what are you saying?"

"Mom, what are you doing here?" She suddenly appeared beside Arundel and me out of nowhere. "I've come to play 'Moonlight' with you in Carnegie. Remember our dream? And Arundel, you do play better than I do."

"Dr. Masters, if you are going to play with Dr. Timpson, I'll just watch."

"You'll do no such thing. I'm going to sit between the two of you and play the melody. My improvisations are nonexistent. We'll just get two piano benches. Arundel, you start on the top, and Terry you on the bottom. Halfway through, trade places looking like you are keeping one hand on the piano. The audience will hear all the notes, some will catch glimpses of my white gown, and a few like Pam and Tom will see me. It all depends on their spiritual eyes. Let's go." Mom leads us onto the stage.

The audience is spellbound as ethereal music fills the Stem. It would seem impossible that the two of us could produce such a sound, but there we are, and the music is out of this world. It's breathtaking to be in the middle of it all. When we finish the audience goes wild. It takes the whole time we are setting up for the last two numbers with everyone on stage for the crowd to regain their composure. We finish the night with the Alleluia and The Prayer.

Arundel takes my arm as we move to the reception room, "That was the most exciting music I have ever played. What do I say when people ask about all the extra notes?"

"That was my problem when Mom joined me before. I finally decided to be honest and tell them I was joined by an angel. They didn't believe me, but it put an end to the questions. I think we'll do the same tonight. You played superbly; you truly are a concert pianist."

In the reception room, I watch Emmerson thank Grandma Martin over and over again for his ticket. Then he heads straight for me, "Dr. Timpson, who was the third pianist dressed in dazzling white when you played 'Moonlight'?"

"Emmerson, you do have spiritual eyes. That was my mom, an angel from the other side. I'm so glad you could see her."

"That's what I thought. I can feel the Spirit radiating from you and your group. When you come back to our town, I hope you will come and stay with us again. We loved having you… Sack dinners are waiting for you on your airport shuttle. God bless you." I hug Emmerson, and so does Evan.

It feels good to be on our way home. I think our concert went exceptionally well. I wanted to showcase the talent we have at Augustine, and we did just that. Everyone performed at concert quality. Owen Stirling, the Carnegie manager seemed to think so. He has us sign a contract for a concert in the second week of February for the next five years. He even talked us into a three-night venue.

Once they turn the seatbelt sign off, I'm going to tell each member of our company how proud I am of them. I tell Evan what I'm going to do. He says he'll sleep right where he is. I'm on my own.

I start working my way front to back of the plane. The first couple I come to is Dr. Rich and his wife. "Terry, I must congratulate you on your vision for excellence. These two concerts have been as professional as any I have ever seen, and they all came from Augustine. You are more than ready for your Augustine concert in two weeks. I do have a concern I want to talk to you about." I don't say anything, but I'm guessing both nights are already sold out. "Both nights of your concert have been sold out for six months and we have a waiting list that would fill a third night. Any possibility for another night?"

"Let me guess. You didn't reserve any seats for guests you want to invite from other schools." He ducks his head and mumbles a soft yes. "I think we can if all the nights are not exactly the same. Monday morning, reserve your seats before you open the ticket sale." We also talk about David's schedule, and I move to the next twosome.

"Terry, I think you're ready for another recording session with you and your entire company. I think I can get you set up for next Saturday if that works for you. It's the best advertising we can do for Augustine in addition to your concerts. It also will give me something to sell your students with." Flora watches with amusement. Then tells me she would love to take David on as a doctoral student when asked.

I'm surprised when I find Pam and Cindy sitting together in the next seat, "Where's your men?"

"They had to sit together to discuss an up-and-coming project. Tom was so excited; he could hardly wait to get A.J. alone." Pam says. "Thank you for finding David; he is such a great addition to our ensemble. He's also going to add a much-needed dimension to the OC."

"Pam, what would you think if we also put him in the men's choir? His voice would help, and you could also teach him a little conducting… I love your new oratorio composition. I think it's better than last year."

"Thanks, Terry, I hope so. The thing that is much better than last year is the sound of the choir. Having the two prep choirs has made all the difference in the world. David would be a real asset to the men's choir. I also hope Dr. Rich will have him give private voice lessons. It's time we had a male voice teacher." I talk with Cindy for a few minutes. She has no idea what the men are up to.

Celia and Jefferson are waiting when I get to them. "Terry, I'm as impressed with your sterling code of ethics as I am with your playing, and that saying something. You didn't have to switch hotels, but I'm so glad you did. Everyone in our company had a much better time, and you gave Emmerson the boost that will save his hotel business," Jefferson declares.

Celia says, "He was about to lose the hotel; he should be good until we come and stay with him next year… But we want to talk to you about something else. We've been looking around our city and can see it has its section of poverty. We were wondering if you think we're ready to start a children's choir in their needy elementary school. We would meet with any children in fourth grade and up who would like to sing for an hour after school. If we started with a few, I'm sure more would join. I just don't know if you think we're good enough."

"You've always been good enough. I think you now have the piano skills to make it possible. That area of town could use your help. If you have so many children that they and the audience won't fit in your gym for your concert, let me know and we'll work something out in the Lilian Masters Auditorium. I'm proud of both of you; you did a wonderful job in the concert, but your new project will touch lives for years to come." I turn to leave then turn back, "I haven't forgotten your temple wedding in two weeks. Pam and I are so thrilled for both of you. She has everything ready for your reception. I'm also looking forward to meeting your parents."

This night must be musical chairs night. I find Dawn and Cheryl in the next row. "Where are your men?"

Laughingly Cheryl says, "Someone set them up with a concert of their own, and they said they needed to put their heads together… Terry, thank you for making us part of their world. It's so fun to be in the middle of their successes and not just hearing about them after it happens."

"Music will be their lives. You need to be involved in it every way you can."

Dawn changes the subject, "Will you be able to watch us play any of our tennis matches this spring, Terry?"

"Evan and I plan to be at your collegiate nationals in April and at the Open in the fall if all goes well. It will depend on this little fellow," I say as I pat my growing child.

"Stephanie and Russell, how was your first trip to Carnegie? I was very impressed with your duet. I think both of you are almost through bridging. You have been good for each other."

"Dr. Timpson, Dr. Lowrey was at the concert and came to the reception. She said she couldn't believe the change in my playing, the change in my confidence, or the change in my name. She's ready to take me back, but I told her I still have another year to get my doctorate, and I'm not leaving without it."

"How about you Russell, ready to work on your doctorate next fall? We should have a spot for you."

"Dr. T, that would be so cool. I'm so impressed with what Allen Prince is doing. I love his compositions. Do you think I could learn to do something like that?"

"What you compose will be different than Allen's, but just as rich and as entertaining. I'll hold a doctoral spot for you, probably with Dr. Prince. All you need to do is say yes."

"Yes, yes, yes!" I give him a thumbs up and move on.

I find Tom and AJ in the next seat, "What new project are you two cooking up?"

Tom looks at me strangely then almost whispers, "It's a secret. You can't tell anyone. Dr. Osgood from the Eye Institute called and said he has corneas that will give AJ back most of his vision. I'm going to take him there in ten days. It will be such a surprise for everyone when we come back."

I do not like where this is going, "AJ, how do you feel about leaving Cindy out of the biggest miracle that will ever happen to you?"

"Something doesn't feel quite right. She's been by my side through it all. She was there when I splashed chemicals in my eyes, supported me through the healing, and has been my eyes ever since. Tom thought it would be great to surprise her, and he is paying for everything."

Staring at Tom, he ducks his head to avoid my eye contact, "Tom Masters, has your money gone from your heart to your head and your pride? I can understand you wanting to be there, but Cindy has been with him every day through the pain and trials, would you rob her of the joy at AJ's first moments of sight? The moments of joy, when Evan took his first steps with his prosthetic foot will be forever etched in my heart. Don't rob Cindy. Don't become your father-in-law." I know I've put Tom down, but I can't let him become a control freak with his money. I love him too much…

I move on to Allen and Solomon, "Got your concert all planned? You both did a fabulous work at Carnegie."

"It was an amazingly rich experience, Dr. T, but you'll have to work hard to turn our heads away from Augustine… Tell me what you think of this idea. Solomon's jazz is amazing. I was thinking of taking one of his jazz numbers with all his embellishments and writing a duet in classical music. Kind of like a war between the two finally merging into one to end. Possible?"

"Allen, anything's possible. I think it sounds exciting. Go for it!" I tell them about the recording next Saturday and move on.

The next two rows are empty. I'm at the end of the first-class seats, and I've lost three people. I'm sure they got on; I think. I decide to explore the second class. Pulling aside the curtain, I am surprised to see it's almost empty for this red-eye flight. I hear laughter coming from the last seats on the plane. I'd recognize their voices anywhere.

They quiet down when they see me approaching, "I thought you three fell out of our jet. What are you doing back here?"

"We wanted to sit together, and the flight attendant said it would be okay if we came back here. I don't think we're disturbing anyone," Arundel says.

"You're fine. I just wanted to tell you what a fabulous job you did in the concert, and that we will be recording next Saturday. Keep having fun."

As I start to leave, David holds up his hand, "Dr. Timpson, will you be my preceptor?"

"Good grief no. You are a vocalist, not a pianist. Dr. Flora Martin will be your doctoral advisor."

He punches the air and yells, "Yes! What else will I be taking?"

"First of all, if you're serious about teaching, you need to learn how to play the piano. You need to be able to accompany yourself and your students plus play parts for a choir. Arundel, would you be willing to take him on as a student?" She nods her head revealing a broad grin. "Push him to get acquainted with the piano and become very familiar with on-hand theory."

She gives me a thumbs up. "In addition to the Oratorio Choir and my ensemble, we would like you to be part of the Men's Choir. You will strengthen the sound, and at the same time, Mrs. Masters will begin your conducting career. You will also give private vocal lessons. That should be enough to keep you busy."

David closes his eyes to stop his tears, "I think I've finally come home. Thank you more than I can ever express."

I put my hand on his shoulder, "Welcome to Music at Augustine."

I look at my third musician, "Maria, are you ready to start work on your doctorate next fall? I have a spot for you if you would like it."

"Dr. Timpson thank you. I am so, so ready. Will you be my preceptor?"

"I will, Maria. I am excited to keep you moving forward. You have a great future ahead of you."

# CHAPTER 8

I'm at my desk working on the final order of the musical numbers for my Augustine concert. Since it's supposed to showcase my work in the College of Music, I'm including numbers from everything I work with. It's good I have three nights. The Master's Touch and the Knights of Ebony will be on stage every night. I will also be able to showcase some other advanced students. I'm taken by surprise when my door opens and Tom walks in. I'm forgetting to lock it more often. "Good morning, Terry, got a few minutes?"

I'm amazed he's talking to me after the hard time I gave him on the flight home from Carnegie, "Tom, I always have time to talk to you. What's up?"

Avoiding my eyes, he takes a chair and slowly moves his head to look at me, "I wanted to apologize and thank you for keeping me from getting my head so big it would get stuck in the door. I told Pam about our conversation, wanting her to side with me, but she not so gently opened my eyes. You were right, it was okay for me to be there, but not for it to be my proud moment with me wanting everyone to know what a great thing I had done. Both you and Pam need to help me keep focused on what's important. I need to concentrate on all the good things that could be done with the money the Lord has put in my hands to build His Kingdom not mine."

I move from behind my desk to put my arms around him, "Tom, I love you. We all need to work together to help each other stay on the straight and narrow. Did you go with them?"

"No, Cindy went with him, and they're not back yet. She was so excited to go, and AJ was more than glad to have her escort him. Cindy called telling me the doctor said it looks like a success, but we won't know for sure until they take the bandages off in two days. It will take another month for things to heal to the point he will be able to see with glasses, and then another two months for everything to be clear with contacts. I didn't have a vision of how long it would take and what kind of support he should have… Be patient with me little sister."

I hug him again and change the subject, "I'm finalizing the program for the concert this weekend. I have you and Pam singing and dancing together each night. Is that okay with you?"

"It's perfect, I need to put my head and heart into something more positive." He stands up, hugs me again, and with a kiss on the cheek heads out the door. I love that he's my brother.

Tom hasn't been gone ten minutes when the door opens again, "Morning Stephanie, what's the excitement I see dancing in your face?"

"Do you think there's any way Allen would let Russell and me play four hands on my part in the piano choir?"

"I don't know. Do you think it will blend with the other parts?" I hesitate for only a moment not wanting to crush her enthusiasm, "Let's take it to the lab and see. I assume Russell is close by."

Russell is standing around the corner and Stephanie grabs his hand pulling him along. Once we're seated at the pianos, I ask to see their music. I read it through and am amazed at how well it will fit. "Okay, let's hear what it sounds like." I begin with my part, and they come in two measures later. It sounds even better in the air than in my head.

"Doctor Timpson, what do you think?" Stephanie excitedly asks.

"I think we had better get Allen in here." A quick call has him hurrying to join us.

"Where's the fire?" Allen asks, flying in the door.

"Take a seat at one of the pianos and I want you to play the progeny part you gave me of your concerto. I'll play your part. Stephanie and Russell have a part they would like you to consider."

We're in the middle when the music lab doors fly open. Arundel is leading Solomon into the room, "Are you all having a practice without us? We don't want to be left out," Solomon bellows.

"It was all impromptu. Turn on a piano and join us."

Allen stands excitedly when we finish, "That was out of this world. I loved it. Russell, will you play with us when we perform?" He nods his head, and we are all clapping.

My mind starts spinning, "By any chance have the two of you worked on the 'Allujah' and 'The Prayer'?" They both nod their heads to confirm my suspicions. We play part of both songs, "Russell, will you please join us on all three of those numbers." The hug he gives Stephanie confirms his answer. "The last four numbers of each concert will be in the following order, 'Moonlight', Allen's piano choir, 'Allujah', and 'The Prayer.' Allen, you need a name for your concerto." I am so proud of these pianists. Watching them develop their talents is the most rewarding part of teaching. I'm so hooked.

After three nights of concerts, Scott and I are ready for a break. I couldn't be prouder of the people standing beside me on stage tonight making up the reception line. They all performed magnificently. As we wait for the audience to make their way to the stage, I notice that security is holding back the line waiting for something. A tall very distinguished-looking gentleman is making his way to the head of the line with his elegant wife. When they reach the bottom of the stage stairs, I recognize President Drake, President of Augustine University.

He moves quickly across the stage waving to everyone until he gets to me. He extends his hand, "Terry, you were right. It takes a concert pianist to teach and develop concert pianists. You have completely changed our piano and vocal departments. I was at Carnegie for your concert. I realized then you could be the new shining star in the concert world, but instead, you have chosen to be a Music Mother. Your new developing child is most fortunate indeed. He will become the star."

"Thank you, President, I certainly pray that I can be a good mother. My mother gave me so very much… President, I would like you to meet my husband, Evan Timpson."

"Ah, Evan. Your name has come across my desk many times for the work you are doing with troubled young people. Your son is indeed fortunate to have you both as parents.

"Terry it's already evident what kind of parents you'll both be. You are a Music Mother to every person on this stage." Everyone on stage starts clapping and cheering while I give him a questioning look. "They all know you are the reason they have developed the skills they have." He turns to shake Pam's hand. "Mrs. Masters, you are also a Music Mother, two steps behind your sister. We desperately need to get you credentialed."

Pam smiles, "I'll have my BA next month."

"Great. Then you'll have your doctorate in August. Your oratorio compositions and placement at Carnegie have earned you that. Are you taking us back there again this May?"

"I sincerely hope so. I think our new oratorio is better than last year's, and the choir certainly has a more professional sound. We are about ready to record. You do know that I only write the vocal harmonies, and Terry fills in all the accompaniment. If we do win, we will not be going back to Carnegie until August. Carnegie has scheduled the competition for then because Terry is due in May."

"You two make such a formidable team. You've also taught me that the accompanist is as important as the choir. I know she writes the accompaniments, but your vocal presentation is what earns you the doctorate all on its own. Now I must let the rest of your fan club on stage." He takes each of our hands in one of his and squeezes it as he whispers, "I hope you will mother our music department for years to come. Now I just need to figure out how to enlarge this performing facility. We turned away more guests than those who had seats or standing room."

I finally need to give up standing and greet people while sitting on my piano bench with Evan standing behind me. It takes about a half-hour to clear the auditorium and another fifteen minutes for most of the performers to leave. We probably should be having a company party to celebrate, but I just don't have it in me. Stephanie and Russell are the last on the stage to thank me for making this night possible for them. They are both finally sounding like concert pianists and are so thrilled.

I don't notice the man who slithers up behind us, "Well Stephanie, you've become quite the pianist and a very beautiful woman." I lift my hand into the air and twirl my fingers, hoping the sound guys will notice I want the recording tapes to keep rolling.

She whirls around in shock, "If it isn't Uncle Mike. What a horribly unpleasant surprise." I slip my phone out of my pocket and speed dial Detective Douglas 'on stage AU'.

"Is that any way to welcome family? I haven't seen you for years. I've come to spend a couple of days with you. Give me a hug." He spreads his arms to receive her.

Stephanie backs away into Russell's arms, "Don't touch me, you pervert. You're never going to hurt me again."

"I don't know what you're talking about. I have only ever loved you. You have been mine since you were ten years old, and you will always be mine. You're coming with me now."

I stand up from the bench, "She's not going anywhere with you ever again."

"I see you've talked about our relationship. I told you what would happen if you ever told anyone. I will kill you and your teacher." He reaches inside his jacket and pulls out a small stiletto knife. "Remember this little friend of mine. It has made its mark all over you. You are mine."

At that moment there is a resounding crack as Evan's foot contacts Mike's knife arm. The blade goes flying, and he screams in agony as his forearm hangs with a new joint. "I'll kill you all," he yells as he reaches inside his belt.

Before he can pull his hand out, I bring a swift hand chop down on his fist, and a gun firing fills the stage with ear-shattering noise. Mike screams louder and doubles over, falling to the floor in pain. Blood begins to pool on the floor below him. I realize that Detective Douglas and five uniformed officers are surrounding us with drawn firearms.

Douglas yells, "Everyone move back, way back!"

I yell as I move, "He still has a gun in his belt."

I hear the detective, "Drop the gun." Then we hear another shot, and all is quiet.

"Douglas yells, "Everyone leave the stage to the right and don't look back." We all hurriedly exit through the curtains beside the piano.

Russell is holding and trying to comfort Stephanie. Evan has found a chair and makes me sit in it. We wait to see what will happen next. Shortly an ambulance arrives, and the gurney rushes onto the stage. When it leaves, the body of Uncle Mike is completely covered.

Detective Douglas follows the gurney and stops to talk to us, "He put the gun under his chin and pulled the trigger. I didn't want any of you to see what was left of him. Go home. I'll get with each of you Monday for a statement." He leaves with the other officers.

Stephanie turns and throws her arms around my neck sobbing, "Dr. Timpson, you stood up for me. No one has ever done that before. I owe you, my life. He would have slowly killed me and Russell."

"Stephanie, that's what mothers are for. You are now beyond his reach. Don't go back to his memory ever. Russell, take her out to a beautiful place for dinner and then take her home and love her. Neither of you is to entertain thoughts of what might have or could have happened. Give prayers of thanks for what actually happened. Only ever think of the blessing. Stephanie, your courage opened the doors for healing generations."

When they're gone, Evan lifts me to my feet, "My dear beloved, are you ready to go home? I think you've done all the mothering you can do for this day."

# CHAPTER 9

Pam and I are on our way to the OC, "Terry, I'm so anxious to be finally recording again for the competition at Carnegie. We're recording in the Lilian Masters Concert Hall at 9:00 am. Dr. Grandpa Martin has set us up with the new recording equipment the music college purchased."

"We'll just pray we don't have an unknown catastrophe. How did you like Celia and Jefferson's wedding? You went all out for their reception."

"That was one of my life's treasures to be with them and their families in the temple. Celia had no idea that her mother would be there. Jefferson's family started befriending her when it looked like he and Celia would get married. She had already looked at the church once. It didn't take much for her to decide it would be a blessing for her whole family. She and all the younger kids joined, but the college-age brothers are still getting their heads on straight… Terry, see that man leaning against the wall pretending to be reading a textbook, I have seen him in that spot for two weeks. At first, he was there every day when I walked past. Now he is only there when I walk past with you going and coming from the choir."

"I've noticed him too. I don't have a good feeling about him. After we walk past, I'm going to drop something. Please pick it up for this fat woman, and at the same time look back at him." We hurry past the guy who doesn't quite fit in with the college crowd.

I drop my keys and make a motion to bend over, but Pam beats me to it, "His eyes are on us like glue. He has such a malicious look." We hurry on down the hall to class.

We spot him again, only at the far end of the long hall. "Pam, our shadow has changed ends of the hall. If he is one of that doctor's dupes, he is sent to hit my baby, it will probably be a frontal attack. I wasn't ready for him last time, but I am now. If I yell, move as far away from me as you can get. Don't try to help me, you'll only get in the way." The closer we get the more his eyes are focused on me. I push Pam sidewise yelling, "Move."

He is running full-out with something in his left hand. He moves his left arm back to get a forward swing. As the swing comes forward, I step quickly to the side with my right foot in a side lung, while my left foot and leg stay planted. He misses with his knife, but trips over my foot. I swiftly turn around and place a kick at the base of his neck. All movement but breathing ceases, and blood begins to slowly seep from under his body.

Pam rushes to my side, "Terry are you okay? I'm surprised you can move as fast as you did as big as you are. Detective Douglas is on his way."

"I have to get centered every day." Pam looks strangely at me, "I'll tell you later." Then I yell, "Someone call security. This man tried to attack my baby."

Someone calls from the crowd, "Dr. Timpson, I saw it all. That man tried to stab you with his knife. I think he fell on the blade when he tripped on your foot. That was a great side-lunge."

Detective Douglas rushes to my side with uniformed officers again. When he looks at the scene, he yells at one of them to call an ambulance. He turns to me and asks at the same time he is putting something in my hand, "Terry, what's going on?"

Before I have time to answer one of my advanced students yells, "I saw the whole thing." He goes on to repeat what he has said to me. I look at what Douglas has put in my hand and smile while shaking my head.

My attacker is moaning and coming too. The detective leans over him, "You are under arrest for assaulting an officer of the law. You have the right to remain silent…" The ambulance crew arrive with their gurney and turn over my attacker. One of the paramedics winces at what he sees. The knife meant for me is sticking into his chest and has penetrated his lung. They quickly apply covering to seal the hole when the knife is drawn out. When he is ready, they put him on the gurney and cuff one wrist to the bar on the side.

As they roll him out, he looks threateningly at me, "The doc will get you in the end. He always does. He hates handicaps; they are such a burden on society."

Detective Douglas stares at him, "You're the only burden on society that I see here."

When all the commotion is cleaned up in the hall, Pam and I start walking back toward our offices. Pam asks, "Terry, why did Detective Douglas say that mugger was charged with assaulting an officer?"

I pull from my pocket the wallet-like folder the detective handed me. Pam opens it. "Terry, this says that you are a deputy detective for the police department. It has a badge and your picture ID. I didn't know you were the law."

"It goes with my FBI Agent badge. They think it's easier to protect me if I'm law enforcement since I seem to be a lethal weapon, and my list of deadly enemies seems to be ever increasing… I'm glad we're still going to record tomorrow instead of me being in the hospital or the morgue."

I'm back to my early morning practice session in my office. I would think my body would want to sleep longer since I get so tired by the end of the day. But my need to practice is stronger than my need for sleep when the sun is waking up. My concentration is not as deep as it usually is. My mind keeps wandering back to the hoodlum's last words. I ponder when and where that insane doctor will strike again. Yesterday's recording keeps trying to chase away the ugly thoughts of the attack.

Pam certainly has a beautiful gift for composing and conducting. The production of the recording went flawlessly. We're just planning on being back at Carnegie in August for the competition. With that behind us, I think my next big event will be delivering baby Scott in May. I will be so happy to have him on the outside. We must keep him safe before and after he's born.

My office alarm pulls me out of my dream world. I'm surprised to see Dr. Grampa Martin and Agent Fowler at my front office door. Once they're seated in front of my desk, I look at them waiting for a bomb to drop. Granddad opens the bay, "Terry, do you remember Cliff Pilgrim?" I search my mind. The name sounds vaguely familiar. "He was one of my doctoral students, but your mother spent a lot of time teaching him. He's the one who loved to talk to the audience when he performed."

"Oh yes, I remember. He was the funny one. He was always teasing me and challenging me to race on Hannon. What about him? He got married and has a family, doesn't he? Is he still performing?"

"Your memory is still as sharp as ever. He's supposed to be playing, but his left arm is in a cast with both bones broken…"

"Is he an insurance victim?"

"After receiving a panicked call from him, Agent Flower and I went to visit him. He lives in a small town on the East Coast that has a phenomenal domed concert hall. The sound is the richest I have ever heard. It is a very quaint rustic old building right on the coast. Cliff has been giving concerts there for years to capacity crowds. The insurance company moved in on him and has taken everything he has. They take all his concert earnings plus he's had to mortgage everything to meet their demands. When he couldn't make the last payment, they broke his arm. They told him he had to find another pianist to take his place for the next concert. They broke one of his kid's arms to let him know they are serious. It sounds like he's moved down to the bottom of the Derksin List. We've come to ask you if you could possibly do one more concert this spring the first week in April.?"

"Is this another Derksin?"

"We think this is Grampa Derksin, the instigator of the whole insurance scheme," says Agent Fowler. "We would be with you every minute just like before to keep you and anyone else you bring with you safe. We could really use your help, Agent Timpson. We think that if your name was up in lights, they wouldn't be watching Cliff and his family quite so close. We could get them all out of there before the concert and then take care of the elder Derksin after the concert. We are hoping this will put the insurance company permanently out of business."

I turn to Granddad, "Have you already signed a contract?"

"No, I had to check with you first to see if you could do it."

"Okay, I'll do it. But remember the contract must state that all the performing fees will be paid by direct deposit into Augustine's account within ten hours following the concert, and I am not authorized to take money. That way they can't shake me down or kill me for the money."

"We'll fly back out there tomorrow with the contract, and Agent Fowler will start working on putting Cliff's family into a safe house. They will be coming back to my old home. Eventually, we'll be getting him into college teaching."

Evan and I are eating dinner when he sets his fork down and stares at me. "Okay, tell me what happened today. You're way too quiet. I thought you'd be buzzing with excitement after the recording yesterday."

"Granddad and Agent Fowler visited me this morning."

"Do they want you to do another sting concert?"

I tell him all about their visit and the plans for the concert. "What is the exact date?" I tell him the first Saturday in April. He shakes his head, "I'm so sorry Honey. When you told me no more concerts until after Scott's birth, I signed up for the survival trip with the high school's troubled teens. I can't back out now, I've already contacted my boys. I can't go with you, but you can't go alone. Something doesn't feel right about this concert."

I don't answer quickly while I ponder a solution, "Do you have anything this weekend on Friday and Saturday."

"No, what are you thinking?"

"Allen and Solomon would be a good pair to take with me, but I want to see them in their own concert before I extend an invitation to take them with me. How about a little getaway back to Matilda's concert hall? We won't even tell anyone we're there."

"Just you and me alone for two days. Terry, I would never say no to that. Make the reservations."

"Terry, you've got rocks in your head if you think someone here won't recognize you tonight," Evan says as we make our way to our seats in the back of the concert hall. "I'll even bet you a second survival honeymoon this summer that you'll end up on that stage." I'm about to defend my position when the lights dim, and the concert begins.

They are better than I thought they would be. They have developed an easy banter between themselves that pulls the audience in. They are both playing with the confidence of a master, and their skills are suburb. I could take them to perform anywhere with me or send them on their own. The "War," as the battle between jazz and classical has come to be known, is brilliant. What's even better, the audience loves it. They even take sides with their clapping and shouting.

After the song, Allen turns to Sol, "Hay Sol, you do pretty good for a man that has to play in the dark."

"Bet you don't know anyone that can play as well as I can in the dark," Sol counters.

"I'll bet you and your wife a home-cooked dinner that I absolutely know someone who can play better than you in the dark."

"You're on. Prove it right here and now or the bet's off." I have a very bad feeling that I'm about to lose my bet with Evan.

Allen turns to the audience standing in front of the mic, "We would like to introduce all of you to our teacher, mentor, and doctoral preceptor Dr. Terry Masters Timpson. Since she's in the audience, we would be most negligent if we didn't let you hear one of the premier concert pianists of our day in person. Mr. Timpson, would you please escort your wife to the stage." The audience begins standing, facing me, and clapping.

I stand and hold up my hand. There is instant silence, "OK, play something while I waddle my way to the stage." The audience turns to the stage, and someone calls out "War". They soon take up the chant for "War". Evan and I are behind the wing curtain when their song ends. We give them time to acknowledge their applause and for the audience to be seated. Evan walks me onto the stage. I am taken aback when once again the audience is on their feet and applauding. I nod my head to recognize their appreciation, and Allen holds up his hand. Again, there is instant silence, "This is the setup for the bet. Sol, tell the Doc what you are going to play and let her ask questions. When you are ready, all the lights on the stage will go off, and Sol you will begin. The Master will come in when she's ready."

I hold up my hand, "Give me a few minutes to check out this piano." He nods his head, and I play the most complicated warm-up I can create to check out all the keys quickly. I signal I'm ready. Sol tells me the jazz number he's going to do. It's the first piece I ever played four hands with him; this is going to be fun. The lights go out, I close my eyes, and we're on our way. When I get up in the middle of the night to play the piano, I never turn on the lights.

When we finish, the stage lights come back up and I move to stand by Sol. I take his hand, and we bow together. The audience is ecstatic. Allen is at the mic again, "Dr. Timpson, would you be so inclined to play one solo for our friends in the audience?"

"And just what would you like me to play, Mr. Prince?"

"'Flash Fire!'"

I look at the sound booth, "Do you remember the number with the thunder and the lightning?" They flash the lights to signal their readiness as the scrim lowers. "Remember, left for thunder and right for lightning." I sit at the piano I played with Sol. "Let's have a little practice." I play a little and lift my index finger on my left hand. Thunder rolls across the stage. I lift my right finger a little and a small flash of lightning strikes behind the scrim. I announce my song and begin.

I can tell my piano guys have given an outstanding performance; they have created an exuberant audience. When they calm down, Allen goes to the mic and invites me to join them for their last number, "Wild Winds", his piano choir composition.

Solomon is guided to one piano and Allen and I go to the other. As we are sitting, I whisper, "You play the prodigy part, and I'll accompany you."

He takes in a sharp breath and whispers back, "Don't bury me, please."

"Allen, I will never do that again. I will only make you look good. Calm down and play your best. There is no competition here," I whisper back. Allen begins timidly, but relaxes quickly, to play with confidence. The number is a thrilling end to their performance. We finally need to leave the stage for the audience to stop clapping and begin leaving.

The concert hall manager is the first to greet us behind the curtains, "Fantastic show gentlemen. You are welcome here anytime. Dr. Timpson, you know I'll book you in a heartbeat, even if it's two years out. Tell that manager of yours that I'll contract anyone from your university if they are the caliber of these pianists." He looks at the guys, "The money for your performance tonight has already been sent to Augustine

University. We even included a bonus for such an exceptional show." He shakes our hands and walks away.

"Way to go men. I'm so proud of you. Get your clothes changed. Evan and I are taking you and your wives to dinner to celebrate. We should have time before our journey home; I think we're on the same flight."

I track down the manager and ask him to recommend a good eatery. He pulls out his phone and makes a reservation for us, "Our van will take you to my five-star restaurant, and the tab is on me tonight. Thank you again for the brilliant show. If you call when you're finished, the van will take you to the airport."

I stop the couples before they can change, "Maybe we'll switch clothes at the airport after we eat at the restaurant."

After we're seated at our semi-private table and our orders are taken, Evan exclaims, "It's a good thing we're still dressed formally. I have never been in a place as elegant as this." He looks at me, "It's a good thing I married above my station."

"Evan, I don't think there's any more grandeur here than sitting around a campfire eating sandhill crane on a survival trip. It probably lifts my spirits more than all this extravagance. But I will enjoy every moment we're here with good company."

I can tell he would like to say more, but Allen has a burning question, "Doc, are you here tonight to check out how we would do?"

I laughingly answer, "Yes and no. I have no doubts about your abilities to function on your own, but I needed to see if your program would blend with mine in a concert that I'm doing in one week. I'm thrilled to know it would blend perfectly. I am inviting you to perform with me in the Sea-Side Concert Hall." I spend the rest of the dinner explaining the insurance fraud thugs, FBI involvement, and sting concerts. "I'm committed to this concert to help a fellow pianist and finish off this gang. But Evan can't go with me, and in my current shape, I can't go alone. We wouldn't be taking your wives; family is too easy to snag for hostages. You don't have to decide right now. I want you and your wife to decide together. This adventure comes with an above-average amount of risk." We are all very silent as we travel to the airport.

We've only been in the air for about thirty minutes when Allen makes his way up the aisle to where Evan and I are sitting. He stops and smiles, "I'm with you all the way Doc, and so is Cheryl. You have pretty much given us everything. It's the least we can do. I'm looking forward to a real adventure."

Solomon and Dawn are ten minutes behind Allen, "Doc T, I don't know how much I will be able to help you, but I would defend you with my life."

Evan gives him the same instructions he did Allen, "From the instant you get off the plane, you are to be on one side of my wife and Allen on the other side. Never let her away from your touch unless you are performing on stage, or she is in the restroom, which happens quite often. Stay attached no matter who tries to get her alone. Please take care of my most precious possessions, my wife, and my son."

# CHAPTER 10

I am sitting next to Agent Fowler in first class and my two piano guys are sitting in the seats in front of us. I was finally able to convince Fowler that I no longer had the stamina to fly, do a concert, and fly out on the same day. The concert manager doesn't know we're coming a day early and spending the night locally. It makes security more difficult for the FBI, but it makes doing a good concert possible for me. I can't believe how much energy this baby is stealing from me.

Once we've taken off, Agent Fowler turns to me, "Terry, you do have your agent's badge with you, don't you?" I pull it out to show him. He takes it from me, opens it up to show the badge and ID, then lifts the badge up. "There's a small tracking device embedded in the leather under the badge. We will be monitoring your exact location every second. The only place it doesn't work is underground." He takes a box from his pocket, "Trade me your diamond for your necklace mic." We make the switch. "This should go as smoothly as any of our past operations, but we aren't taking any chances. Almost everyone you see tonight at the hotel and backstage at the concert tomorrow is an agent. We even have you in adjoining rooms at the hotel with your boys. You will enter and leave through their door, then lock yourself into your room. Their side will be left unlocked. There will also be agents in the hall all night guarding your rooms."

"Sounds like I'll be safe. It's just that something about this sting doesn't feel the same." He looks at me strangely and then tells me how tired I look and that I should get as much sleep on the plane as I can.

My men and I sleep until about 10:00 am. Crossing three time zones while flying doesn't make for waking early. We eat a substantial breakfast/lunch, dress in our concert clothes, and arrive at the Sea-Side at 2:00 pm. While pulling up to the front doors in the hotel shuttle, several people rush out to meet us. Before they get to us, we are out of our vehicle and Allen is on one side of me and Sol on the other.

"Dr. Timpson, we are so glad to see you here. We were beginning to think you had changed your mind." The man I assume is the manager hurriedly speaks. "We thought maybe you would be a no-show when you didn't let us know when you would be arriving at the airport. I see you came from a hotel."

"I needed a good night's sleep. I explicitly informed you that we would be arriving at 2:00 pm for staging, sound prep, and piano inspection. I trust you have the two electronic grand pianos, and that they have been placed and tuned." My insides tell me I need to be as businesslike as I can be. Something is definitely not right.

"Yes, Dr. Timpson. We are ready for you. Please follow me." He leads us directly through the main doors of the concert hall. I stop and look around in amazement. This is a domed-shaped building with seating on the main floor and a wrap-around balcony. I figure that there are over two thousand seats ready for use tonight. We continue walking through the auditorium and onto the stage. Before I begin the setup, I get him to show us where the restrooms are.

While we were walking through the auditorium, I began to feel the amplification of sound surrounding us. Seating myself at the grand piano, I play one note. No matter what follows the program, this will be a magnificent concert tonight. This building has acoustics like I have only ever dreamed of. I begin my piano check-out and music swirls around us.

"Dr. Timpson, what's happening in here? It sounds like music is coming from every direction, and I don't think the mics are even on." I can't resist, I begin playing part of Beethoven's "Hammerklavier"; I'm in heaven.

When I finally stop, I'm laughing., "Gentlemen, you could play in concert halls all over the country and never experience these acoustics. This is going to be a celestial concert." The guys are as excited as I am.

We spend the next four hours making sure everything is exactly how we want it. But mostly we bathe in the phenomenal sound as we play. At 6:00 PM we are ushered into the performer's lounge where we are served light refreshments. We relax until it's time to go on stage. I've almost forgotten this is a sting and start wondering if all the FBI agents are in place.

I watch as the patrons begin filling the seats. I have never seen guests dressed so lavishly. These seats must cost hundreds of dollars each, maybe into the thousands for the dress circle. No wonder they were antsy about a no-show. I can't wait to fill this place with the masters' music using my touch.

When I am introduced, I step onto the stage. The audience all stands, but there is no clapping or noise of any kind. I begin to rehearse my mantra, 'Credibility, you have to establish credibility' in my head. I announce that I will begin with "Beethoven's 9$^{th}$ Symphony." I begin playing straight Beethoven then gradually introduce my improvisations. When I'm playing half and half, I begin hearing a slight buzz in the audience. When I finish, the original is still there but my improve has taken over. The audience finally comes alive leaping to their feet, clapping and cheering.

I play one more number, then introduce my men. I can tell that the audience isn't used to any interchange on stage as the guys begin their dialogue getting to play "War". It doesn't take long until the audience has taken sides and are clapping for their favorite style. When the guys blend the two music forms together instead of playing back and forth, the listeners are ecstatic. Their enthusiasm lifts the pianists to play at their best. The audience is now ours.

Everything goes as we planned; the night seems perfect. We even include our bet for playing in the dark. When I sit down to play the second to last number, "Moonlight", I whisper, "Mom, if you're here, you're welcome to play with me. This is such an impressive place to perform." I feel her presence by my side. As I begin, she takes over the melody. I can hear the buzz in the audience again, not understanding how I can be playing all the notes coming out. I don't care; I'm just excited to be playing with Mom in this heavenly setting.

The audience is wild as I stand to acknowledge their appreciation. I finally lift my hand for calm so I can announce the last number. The three of us will be playing Allen's "Wild Winds." Allen guides Sol to his piano and then escorts me to mine. As we sit, he whispers, "Doc, this is your concert tonight, and we are your guests. I will play the prodigy part and Sol will play his part, but you give them everything you've got, completely bury us."

"Thanks, Allen," I play out of my mind with all the energy I have left.

The standing crowd claps, cheers, and shouts wanting an encore as we three stand at center stage to take a bow with me in the middle, but I have nothing left. I think the guys are almost holding me up. We finally leave the stage as a threesome while waving to the audience. I fall into the first chair we come to totally exhausted. Sol puts his hand on my shoulder, "Doc T, that was the most incredible thing I have ever done. Thank you for letting us perform with you."

I lift my hand to squeeze his, "I hope you are still thanking me when this night is over." I close my eyes, take deep breaths, and try to gain back my strength. I'm probably praying more than anything… It takes a long time for the concert hall to empty. They seem to know each other well and are discussing every unusual, different, or exciting part of the program. I am so thankful they finally warmed to us… I could play in this concert hall at least once a week, empty or full. Someway, I'm going to bring my whole company back here to experience this place.

It takes a while, but finally, my bladder wins over my fatigue. On the way to the restroom, I realize that I'm still in my thin piano slippers, and my feet are getting cold. I ask Allen to retrieve my black velvet bag from under the piano that holds my tennis shoes. I'm back in my chair making the shoe switch when a young man with slicked-back greasy hair appears in front of me. "Dr. Timpson, the manager would like to see you in his office. Please follow me." As soon as I stand, Allen and Sol are standing beside me each holding one of my arms. The messenger looks perplexed, "Dr. Timpson, he needs to see you alone. He doesn't bite."

Sol turns his head in the direction of the voice, "Her husband made us promise to be by her side from the time we got off the plane to the time we get back on. You either get three of us or none."

He shrugs his shoulders, "Whatever, come on he doesn't like to be kept waiting."

We follow him through curtains at the back of the stage and down a dimly lit hall. He opens the door at the end and walks through. We follow him. I sure hope Agent Fowler is keeping track of us. It is rather a large comfortable office with modern furnishings and four burley men in addition to the messenger. None of them are dressed in concert attire.

The man behind the desk stands, smiles, and offers his hand, "Dr. Timpson, that was a remarkable concert. Tell your agent I will do business with you any time. I'm being flooded with emails praising your program. Our patrons were especially impressed with the caliber of your performance. They think you are world-class, and so do we." He hesitates for an instant and picks up a large puffy envelope. "Here is all the money from tonight's performance. You can count it if you like. There should be two hundred thousand dollars there. If you just sign this receipt that you are taking the money, you can be on your way. We'll be contacting your agent to set up a future concert."

How dumb does this man think I am? I speak my words slowly and distinctly, "You know I can't touch that money. It explicitly states in the Augustine contract that I cannot receive money for this performance, and that all the money must be in the university's account within ten hours of the program or legal action will be taken."

A man in the far corner rushes to the desk and slams his fist down on the shiny oak surface, "Did you sign a contract that says that, and you didn't tell me?" I recognize this man without any introduction. He is an older version of the Derksin boys, Grandpa himself. Our odds are not very good in this office behind a closed door. I probably shouldn't have come in here.

The manager tries to defend himself, "I didn't think it would make any difference. You'd just get her to sign the paper, and we'd be on our way."

"The wording on that contract makes all the difference in the world. It changes everything. I've got to have a minute to think. Take them down to the big room in the catacombs, lock the door, and turn out the lights" Two of the men take out guns and begin herding us to the opposite door from the one we came in. Once I reach the threshold, I can see it is a long flight of rickety stairs extending down into the dark. One of the gunmen flips on a light switch, and my stomach drops further. I'm sure we're going underground. The only positive is that there's a handrail.

I move back and let Sol go first with his stick. I start after him, and Allen follows me. The two gunmen bring up the rear. When we arrive at the bottom, one of the gunmen pushes past us to open a door and turn on a light in the room. The switch is outside the door. They force us into the room waving their guns. The wall straight across from the door is paneling. The other three walls have two doors each. We are standing in one of the doorways of our wall. The thugs snicker, "None of the doors in here are locked, but this one. Each leads to a winding catacomb maze. You're welcome to try any of the passageways. It will save me trouble if you go through one. You'll be lost in the mazes for days or more. You might even trip over the other bodies that never found a way out. Your blind guy ought to feel right at home when we turn the lights out." He slams the door, and all goes dark.

Allen turns on the flashlight on his cell phone. He rushes to open each door to find a dark passageway in front of him. With the dim light coming from Allen's phone, I walk with Sol beside me to the wall with paneling. I've got to have something to lean against. Allen is beginning to panic as he joins us, "What are we going to do? I don't want to die here. Maybe we can kick the door down. No one even knows we're down here! We're all going to die."

"Allen, calm down. No one is even hurt yet. Panic is the last thing we need to do. Pull yourself together. There is one who knows where we are, and we need to talk to him. Will you two join me in a prayer?"

"Sorry, I don't do well in dark or closed-in places. You're right, prayer is what we need." Solomon just squeezes my hand. I take Allen's hand, and we have our prayer.

"I don't think I can stand much longer. My baby is getting awfully heavy. I think I'll slide down this wall and sit on the floor."

Solomon finally speaks, "I think that's the best idea you've had so far. Allen, get on the Doc's other side and we'll push our backs against the wall and slide down together. If your flashlight is still on, you need to turn it off to save the battery." We link elbows and slowly push against the wall to slide down as a unit. We are about halfway down when all of a sudden, we're falling backward. It's a short fall, but we land flat on our backs on what feels like wet sand.

There seems to be a light that's growing brighter. I can see that the wall was two large swinging doors that opened when we leaned against it. We seem to be in a cave of some sort.

Allen is the first to speak, "There's light in here and what's that smell?"

"Bro, that's the smell of the ocean, and that light is a ghost. I saw her at Carnegie at the piano when Doc T and Arundel were playing 'Moonlight'. Maybe she's come to scare us to death."

"I almost laugh out loud, "Solomon, she's not a ghost, she's a ministering angel and has come to help us. She's my deceased mother, Dr. Lilian Masters."

Mom moves to stand in front of Solomon, "I'm impressed Sol, you may not have mortal eyes, but your spiritual eyes are sharp and clear. I'm not here to hurt you or scare you. I have been sent to help you. You seem to be in the middle of a soggy mess... Allen will you push those doors shut? When they come to the room to kill you, they won't know which way you've gone for a while. We need to get moving. Follow my light."

While we're walking, Mom starts giving us a running commentary of where we are, "This is a tide tunnel. It leads all the way into the ocean. When the tide's out the tunnel is empty, but when the tide is in, the tunnel fills up depending on how high the tide is."

"So can we just walk out of this tunnel into the ocean?" Allen asks.

"If the timing was right, we could, but at this time the tide is turning and coming back in."

Sol asks, "What determines how high it gets? Are we going to get caught in a tidal river?"

"The moon usually decides the height and depths of the tides with its gravitational pull. When there's a full moon and the sun adds pull, the tides are higher and lower. When the moon is closest to the Earth it adds extra pull. When those things happen at the same time there are extreme tides. The low tides will go out for a couple of miles because of how flat the ocean floor is right here. When it comes in, it will completely fill this cave. It's called a Spring Perigee Tide. We are in the middle of that right now."

My memory of this event is starting to raise the hairs on my arms, "How fast will this cave fill up, Mom?

"That is where the danger lies. It takes a little less than six hours for a tide to go out and the same to come in no matter how far it is traveling. When it's way out it's a rushing turbulent river on its way in."

"I'm really lost," Allen says. "If all this is happening, why are we walking toward the ocean to meet our doom?"

"Because it's the only way out." At that instant, all of Mom's light vanishes, and it's pitch black. The three of us scream together.

Mom's instantly back in front of us, "Sorry to leave you in the dark. I had to make sure the passageway is clear all the way. Sometimes there are cave-ins below the tide level. Follow me into this crack. I think the men will fit if they turn sidewise and squeeze hard."

Finally, we all squeeze through the crack, although Sol lost the buttons on the front of his tux, and Scott barely fit. I can touch both sides of the tunnel we are in now, and we are definitely climbing uphill. The sand slowly turns to rocks, and the walking is harder. We are brought to an instant halt when we hear three consecutive explosions echoing in the tide cavern. I almost think they're gunshots.

The timid voice of the manager follows, "Derksin, why did you shoot your two sons and your grandson?"

"The fewer people, the more money each of us gets. If you hadn't signed that contract, we might have been able to take full advantage of that Timpson woman. She was a real top-notch pianist. The way I figured it, the only choice left was to kill the three pianists and for us to move on to greener pastures with all the take." Their voices are coming closer with every step they take. Sound is so amplified that we can't tell how close they are. I'm praying they won't discover our tracks leading into the crack. "There's standing water on the sand here; I don't see their footprints anymore. Do you think the tide's turned?"

"We still have plenty of time. It's out at least two miles. We've got to catch those pianists and do away with them before they get out of this tunnel. Then we'll slip out of the cave's opening and be gone. You can swim, can't you?"

"I doggie paddle a little; you may need to help me."

"You live on the ocean and can't swim, how ridiculous. I've reconsidered; there's only enough money in this waterproof pouch strapped around my waist for one." We hear another echoing gunshot. Our Angel motions for us to start moving upward again.

Solomon stops, "Angel Lady, what are all these shiny rocks?"

We stop and Mom turns to face Sol, "Pick up as many of those shiny rocks as you can put in your pockets, both in your pants and in your tux coat. You'll be needing them."

"I don't see any shiny rocks," Allen says disgruntled.

"Turn off your flashlight and look where my light shines on the ground. Put a couple of pieces in your pocket, Allen. Terry, pick up as many as you can carry in your shoe bag, you're already carrying enough extra weight." I feel like I'm carrying fifty extra pounds. I'm getting so tired.

"Mom, can we stop for a little break? I don't know how much further I can make it without a rest. I need to sit down."

"Hold on Terry, just around the next bend this tunnel opens into a large cave-like room with plenty of places to lie or sit. We will also be above the high tide line, I think."

When the tunnel finally opens into a large cavity, it feels like we've reached heaven. The place is filled with rocks sitting height and some flat enough to lay on. We all find a place that's close to one another. I find a spot where I can get my feet up and recline against another rock half sitting up. Mom just seems to be standing watching over us.

Again, we are assaulted by a thunderous sound. The only noise that comes to my mind is standing in the middle of Nigra Falls. We each automatically cover our ears. After a few minutes, there is no sound at all. Mom finally says, "The tide tunnel is full, and you are safe now. There will be no noise when the tide turns to go out."

I notice Sol is intently watching her, "Angel Lady, I've never seen what a woman looks like, but the only words that come to my mind are you are beautiful. Are you real? I don't think you look like a ghost although I've never seen one of those either."

"Of course, I'm real Sol. My physical body died, but what you see is the body of my spirit. Spirit bodies never die. When I'm resurrected, my physical body and my spirit body will become one again. Then, I will never die. Do you believe Jesus opened the grave for all to be resurrected?"

"Oh yes mam, I just never thought about the spirit not dying. That makes sense. So are there spirits floating around everywhere that lost their bodies?"

"Most of the time we spirits stay in another realm where there is work to keep us busy. When we're needed here, we come as ministering angles. Now I have a question for you Sol. How certain are you that you would like to spend your life teaching the blind."

"Since Doc T helped me to learn that I can teach blind people to play the piano, my head won't leave it alone. I just don't know how to go about making it happen. You might say my vision is limited." Mom has my attention as well as Sol's. I have no idea where she's headed.

She switches subjects again, "Sol, would like to see what Doc T looks like?"

"Now that I've seen you, there are two women that I would give anything to see, so I can keep their images in my mind eternally. My life will be changed forever because of these two women. I love both, but not in the same way. The first is my wife, Dawn, she has taught me what pure love is and how heavenly it is to be married, and the other is Doc T who has given me faith in myself."

"The last one is easy, take a good look at me. Terry, or Doc T as you call her is my beautiful daughter. If you could see us together, you would not be able to tell us apart except for her large abdomen that's growing a baby… Dawn is a little more difficult, but I think I can come close. Hold on for a minute." Everything is pitch black again.

When the light comes back on again, I can see two angels, "Sol, this is Dawn's grandmother. They look alike enough that you can keep her image in your mind when you think of Dawn. Personalities are also similar."

"Solomon Tune, thank you from the bottom of my heart for taking such good care of my Dawn. She is the sunshine of my life and such a brilliant woman. I can tell that you love her very much. If you want that love to last forever, you need to take her to the temple."

Before Sol can reply, another angel appears, "Soly, you need to get baptized so all the rest of us can."

"I don't recognize your face, but I could never forget your voice. You're Polly, my older sister. You were killed in a gang shooting when I was ten years old. You will never know how much I missed you. You were the only person who ever believed that I could be something other than a street beggar."

"Oh Solomon, I know how you hurt, I cried with you and tried to comfort you as best I knew how. Your spiritual eyes were just starting to develop back then, so you couldn't see me. I've been whispering to you for years. Now I'll speak loud and clear. You need to go to the temple." All three lights begin to fade. Polly's last words are almost too soft to hear, "Ask Jefferson about the temple." After her last whisper, the cavern is plunged into the darkest night.

I awake sometime later to find Mom standing by my side, "Terry, I'm sorry to disturb your sleep, but I must tell you one more thing. When you have the opportunity, buy the Sea-Side Concert Hall with one of your gold rocks and the concert money you earned. Get it affiliated with Augustine University as a performing arena for music students.

"Then sell land to Solomon and Dawn. He has enough money to restore the concert hall to last for another two hundred years. There is enough acreage that comes with the structure that they can build a nice home with a work office for Dawn and a music school for the blind. They could even develop a tennis academy if Dawn wanted to coach underprivileged kids in her spare time away from engineering, managing the hall, and mothering. Don't let anyone know he has the gold; get it converted to currency quickly. Have Allen do the same. He'll have more than enough money to buy the family van he needs for his new twins."

This time when I wake it's because my body is rebelling against the rock I'm curled up on. It's still pitch black. I look at my phone and am startled to see it's 8:15 am. My eyes are drawn to a pool of water on the floor and a few small animal tracks in the wet sand. I guess the extreme high tide spread across the floor of our cavern, but it's gone now. I flip off my phone to save the battery and stand to get centered. My mind starts calculating if there are animal tracks, there's a way out of this tunnel.

I begin growing an urgency that we need to get moving, "Guys, it's time to be up and hiking."

I hear moans and groans, then Allen is instantly awake, "We're trapped. We're going to die. We'll suffocate; I can't even breathe." He's in a panic mode and hyperventilating. This is the last thing we need.

He's sitting next to me, and I can feel his thrashing movements. I'm finally able to grab one of his arms, and I yell, "Allen! Allen, we're not dying. You're not suffocating; you're panicking. Calm down!" He calms a little, "Slow you're breathing. Solomon and I are right here."

"But it's black in here. I can't even see my hand in front of my face. We'll fall into a deep dark hole and be lost forever. The batteries in my phone are dead." His breathing begins to quicken.

"Hey man, that's how it is every morning I open my eyes. Yesterday with the Angel Lady is the only time I have ever seen with my eyes. If I lead us, we won't fall into any hole."

I grip his arm tighter, "Allen, do you trust me?" He mumbles yes, I think, "Will you trust me enough to do exactly as I tell you?" Now I can hear his 'yes', "You are growing scenarios in your mind that are not real. Your mind is telling your body to prepare for the worst. None of those things have happened to us and none are going to happen. After we have a group prayer, I want you to start praying to your Father in Heaven a prayer of thanks. The only things you can think of are things to thank him for. Start with your wife. Thank Him for all the big and the most minute things you appreciate and love about her. Then go to your son. Until we are off this mountain and down to the concert hall, you cannot stop that prayer. Will you do it?"

"I'll try Doc, but what if I start slipping?"

"Tell us what's happening, and we'll get you back on track... We've got two flashlights left. Solomon will lead. With his long tapping stick, he can see better than any of us in the dark. Allen, you go last and use Sol's phone to light the way for both of us. If we need my phone, we'll use it, but I'm trying to save the battery to make a call to the FBI once we're in the open. Let's start... Allen, why don't you pray out loud, I think it will engage your mind more." Sol leads out and Allen is muttering softly behind me. I'm praying that the light in his hand will not grow dim. I'm struggling to see where to place my feet among the rocks.

It seems like we have walked for hours; I have no concept of time in this lightless cave. Solomon slows and stops, "Doc T, I feel the movement of air on my face, and it's colder. If we're coming to an opening, I want you to be in the lead."

I'm amazed when I lift my head. My eyes have been so glued to the ground that I haven't noticed that the tunnel is filled with dim gray light up ahead. I still need my light to see the ground as we move forward again, but it quickly becomes lighter as we move forward. When the tunnel turns sharply to the left a window filled with light appears in the distance. "Solomon, you nailed that one. There's an opening at the end of this tunnel with sunlight streaming in." Our pace picks up as our visibility increases. We stop about ten yards from the cave opening. I direct both Allen and Sol to find a boulder to sit on. I don't want either of them close to the opening until I can examine the rocks and the flooring at the edge.

I slowly make my way to the opening testing every step before I transfer my weight. Everything seems to be solid. The opening is large enough for each of us to get through one person at a time even with a large bush-like tree choking one side. I lay down to inch close enough to look down. The sight almost takes my breath away. It's a thousand-foot drop straight down sheer rock walls to the ocean. I try to look up, but there's an overhang and I can't tell how far we are from the top.

It's time to call the Calvary. I'm praying the whole time I'm punching the speed dial to call Agent Fowler. He answers on the first ring, "Terry, where on earth are you? Are you alright? I've been going out of my mind with worry since we lost your tracking signal. Hang on a second… We finally have your signal. It shows that you are somewhere near the top of the cliffs behind the concert hall. Can you flash me?"

"We're in a cave on one of those cliffs. I don't have anything to flash you with."

"Can you see the concert hall?" I tell him yes. "Use your badge. It's shined to function as a mirror. You also need to know the edge of the badge away from the fold is razor sharp. Sorry, I didn't get to finish all your orientation."

I remove my badge from my knee-high socks and start sending an SOS signal. "Terry, we've got you located. You're about a hundred feet from the top. We can get a chopper with a drop line, but we have no way to get the harness into your opening."

"Get that helicopter on its way. You've given me everything I need to make a hook. Make sure that the harness is strong and big enough. I have two large men with me, but neither can help themselves. I will send them down one at a time." We end the call, so I can save what little battery I have left.

I thought I kept my knife sharp, but I could shave the hairs on my arm with this piece of steel. While still sitting on the ground, I scoot over to the other side of the opening. I cut the thickest and longest branch I can reach. I think this is some kind of a maple. It's not going to reach as far as I need, so I cut another long one. They are about an inch thick. I also cut one that has a fork three-fourths of an inch thick.

Now for lashing material. My concert attire looks like a dress, but it is actually a blouse and pants. The legs are full of material, so it looks like I'm wearing a full-length gown. I have stretch pants on under the skirt in case I need to become a martial artist. I cut the material in the skirt into strips to use for lashing. I tie the two long poles together then I invert the fork leaving one limb long and lash it to the end of the long pole. I cut the other limb of the fork to about 18 inches long. Now I have the hooked pole to capture the harness and bring it into the cave. While we wait, I explain to the guys what Mom said we should do with the gold.

When we hear the chopper, the guys start moving toward the noise, "Not so fast, they can only take you one at a time. I don't want either of you to move until I have the harness ready. Allen is going down first." They both sit back down. "Allen, can I also assume that you don't do well with heights." He nods his head looking somewhat embarrassed. "I want you to keep your prayer of thanksgiving going." I take one of the material strips and put a blindfold on him. I reason if it works for horses in scary spots, it might help get Allen to the ground. I caution him, "No matter what you're feeling, don't take this blindfold off until your feet touch the ground."

The harness is easy to snag, and very quickly Allen is strapped in ready to go. I walk him to the edge of the cave holding his arm tight. I'm back on my phone again this time talking to the pilot of the chopper, "Slowly, move out toward the ocean to take-up the slack. When I tell you to go, keep moving in the same direction. Don't go up or down, or your passenger will swing into the cliffs. When you're clear, put him down on the lawn behind the concert hall. Hurry back for your next commuter."

While I'm buckling Sol into the harness, he takes hold of my arm, "Doc T, I know you didn't describe where we are because you didn't want Allen to panic again, but would you give me a verbal tour?"

"I'd be happy to Sol. The tunnel we walked up opened into a big cavern with an opening that looks like a large window." I explain what the view looks like and try to give him a feel for the size of the cliffs. "You will be hanging by a cable from a helicopter. It will carry you out over the ocean for a bit, then bring you back and set you down on the lawn behind the concert hall. When you feel the wind on your face, you will know what it's like to be a bird soaring through the sky. Enjoy your ride."

"Doc T, thank you for keeping me safe and helping me to understand ministering angles. It was a beautiful experience to be able to see."

"You're welcome, Solomon Tune; thank you for a great concert. Let's do it again… the concert part I mean."

My ride down is magnificent. The ocean, the cliffs, and the green expanse of the grounds around the concert hall. I love this bird's eye view. The only thing missing is Evan. As my feet touch the ground, I feel arms slide around me from the back and a kiss on the neck. I'd know this kiss anywhere. As soon as I'm unbuckled, I whirl around and throw myself into Evan's arms. Our hug and kiss are long enough that Scottie rebels with violent kicking. Finally, I get my tears under control enough to speak, "I thought you couldn't come."

"I will always come when thugs kidnap my precious family."

# CHAPTER 11

Our embrace ends when I feel a hand on my shoulder and the voice of Agent Fowler, "Terry, are you and your baby okay? I have never felt so helpless as when we lost your signal along with all the Derksins. What happened to you?" I don't let go of Evan, and he keeps his arm around my waist as we face the agent. I spend the next ten minutes reliving our experience with help from Solomon and Allen who are attached to their wives. When I finish, I ask the obvious question, "What's been happening out here?"

Agent Fowler looks like he doesn't know where to start, "This morning when the tide came back in again it washed up four dead bodies. They were finally identified as the Derksin's Grandpa, his two sons, his grandson, and his brother-in-law. They had all been shot except for the old man. Your explanation sheds light on that curiosity. All the bodies were almost unrecognizable. They looked like they had been thrashed in a large washing machine. I guess the tidal river knocked them against the cave walls repeatedly. The Elder Derksin still had the waterproof pouch strapped to his waist with all the concert money. This is not how I expected to wrap up this case, but I think this insurance scam is now permanently out of business. Good work Agent Timpson."

I sigh and look up at Evan. He is looking at me with concerned eyes, "Terry, that is a most interesting outfit you have on. You are usually a little more conservative in your dress."

I look down at myself and am embarrassed. I try to act natural as I explain, "My concert skirt went into lashing material and a blindfold for Allen. Agent Fowler, do you have our travel bags with you? I desperately need to change clothes." I eye the closest building, "Do you think the Concert Hall would be open so I could change in there?"

"It's not, but I'll open it for you," comes from an elderly man I don't recognize. "Follow me, and I'll let you in." We move toward the building, and Agent Fowler sends his men to retrieve our bags from his van. As we walk through the hall the acoustics begin to reveal themselves again.

We are about halfway to the restrooms when Dawn grabs my arm, "Terry, do you know what this is? It's almost a perfect acoustical dome. The engineering in here is phenomenal."

"Let me change my clothes, and I'll show you just how incredible it is." The three of us performers change and quickly move everyone to the stage.

I'm about to sit down at the grand piano on center stage when Agent Fowler interrupts me, "Evan and Dawn have arranged for you to stay here for another night, but Allen and his wife want to return as soon as possible. I need to leave now to get them to the airport on time."

I turn to give Allen and his wife a hug, "Allen, I'm proud of you. You played a masterful concert. I would take you with me anytime."

"I didn't do so well off the stage Doctor T, but I think you've given me clues to help me conquer my fears. I want to talk to you more when you get home. Thank you for everything." I hug him again. I don't think most doctoral candidates have experienced what we did in the last twenty-four hours. He starts to turn away then turns back. "Doc, will you keep this for me? I don't want to risk losing it or having to answer questions I don't know how to answer." He slides his one piece of gold casually into my hand as he shakes it. He yells as he walks toward the concert hall doors, "Don't have too much fun without me."

My fingers fly all over the keyboard sending out notes to swirl together in acoustic perfection. I'm in heaven. I play for about five minutes when I feel a hand on my shoulder. I turn to look into the sad eyes of the elderly man who let us in, "Dr. Timpson, you are the most accomplished concert pianist I have ever heard play in this hall. It's fitting that you should play the last notes to be heard in this building."

I gape at him in profound shock, "What do you mean? What's happening to the building?" I feel like I've just been stabbed in the heart.

The man hangs his head with tears rolling down his cheeks, "The Derksins have robbed this place of every penny possible. They faked receipts for needed repairs which were never made. They've pocketed all the profits from concerts in the last three years, and this year they have even failed to pay any of the employees, which is most of the town, who make a concert possible. All that's left is the money recovered from your concert which old man Derksin had on him when the tide washed him up. You deserve the last of it. You took us out in style," he says as he hands me the waterproof bag full of money.

"We are so far in debt that selling is our only choice. We are just a small struggling community that loves music performed in our hall. Before the Derksins started stealing, the Concert Hall was our jewel. It made enough money to support itself and take care of everyone in the community. There's a real estate company that's offered us millions for the hall and the 500 acres. They want to turn it into luxury estates. It would destroy our town, but even more, it would end the most exciting performing venue in the States." He looks at me with pleading eyes, "You know the worth of this place. Can you buy it?"

Evan squeezes my shoulders he's holding. I know he's going to think I'm crazy, but now I totally understand Mom's intervention. With an excited voice, I ask, "How much do you want for it?" I hear Evan's quick intake of breath, but he doesn't say anything.

"If you will promise in writing to repair the hall and keep it a place for the very best performers to give concerts, I'll sell it to you for the cost of our debts, six million dollars."

"Will you take this $200,000 as earnest money?"

Evan whispers in my ear, "Terry are you crazy?" Before he can protest more, I reach into my shoe bag pulling out a large hunk of gold, "I have gold. Will this work?" Evan is speechless.

"I can see that you've found some of the Chinaman's load. It always seems to appear when it's needed most in this community. I can't take the gold, but I can take you to the company that exchanges gold for cash. They will even deposit it directly into your bank account. It cuts out all the middle people who have their hands out."

"Let's do it now. You get your lawyer to draw up the papers and we'll finish this deal this morning. Evan, I assume you have a rental, is there room for five of us in your car?"

Evan is still standing with his mouth open. I turn and kiss him on the cheek. "Ah. Oh yes, there's plenty of room. Follow me."

Our experience at the gold exchange worked seamlessly. We are just finishing up at the lawyer's office when my cell phone rings, "Terry, this is Agent Fowler, where are you? I need to get your full statement."

"Agent Fowler, I needed to take care of a little business. I'm finished and was heading back. Where do you want me to come to?"

"I'm at Sea-Side now. I'll meet with you as soon as you get here. Thanks."

I thank Bruce Underwood, the Chairman of the board for Sea-Side. I can't believe I own a concert hall, let alone one as magnificent as this one. Now my brain begins to think logically. I can't do this on my own. I need all the people that have been running the hall for the past three years. "Bruce, do you think it would be possible to have a board of directors meeting on stage at Sea-Side tomorrow evening at 7:00 pm?" He smiles and nods his head.

"Sure Doc. If you still want us around, we'll be there. We'll help in any way we can. We just want to keep our beautiful building and still have concerts here. We'll all be there."

I'm sitting on a bench under a beautiful chestnut tree finishing up my recording session with Agent Fowler. I still can't believe the grandeur of this place. My attention is drawn to a man hurrying across the lawn toward us. When he's close enough to read his face, I sense furry. I feel Evan put a hand on my shoulder from behind. The other men who have been wandering around gravitate toward us. I think most if not all of them are FBI agents.

The man stops in front of me and snarls out the words, "Are you Dr. Timpson?" I decide to level the playing field a little and stand up to answer him. I am at least eight inches taller than he is, and he needs to look up to see my face. He takes two steps backward before he feels comfortable again.

"I am. What can I do for you?" I don't think Fowler turned off his recording device.

He spits out his disgust, "No empty-headed female broad who isn't even smart enough to not get pregnant is going to cut my grass."

I answer him with no sign of intimidation, "Who are you, and what grass have I cut?" I'm confident this is about the property.

"I'm Mickey Barlow, and I was told that you bought the properties. They really should be mine. By the end of this day, you are going to sell them to me, or you'll wish you'd never been born."

I'm still as calm as I can be, and I never lose eye contact with him, "I'm sorry Mr. Barlow, but it's not for sale. I plan on making it the premier concert venue in the United States."

"I will trash that building; I'll burn it to the ground tonight. There will never be another concert in that horrid building."

"You are wrong Mr. Barlow. There will be a concert there tomorrow evening. Help me understand something. If I am the legal and lawful owner, why should it belong to you?"

He is beginning to lose his gusto, "I'll tell you why. I paid Derksin two million dollars to run this place into the ground and force bankruptcy. He told me last week that it would be going into receivership any day, and I could step in and buy it for peanuts. Somehow you got word of that and beat me to it."

"It never made it to receivership. The board of directors offered to sell it to me if I restore the building and continue offering concerts. That's exactly what I'm going to do… If I'm understanding you right, you and Derksin deliberately tried to trash a beautiful, magnificent concert hall and steal the livelihood of the townspeople who keep this place running, so you could scoop it up and make a fortune selling real estate."

"Hey, that's how this world works. The smart people get rich any way they can, and the rest of the people get by the best they can. Where is Derksin anyway?"

Agent Fowler finally stands, "Terry, would you like to do the honors?"

"Mr. Barlow, I would like to introduce you to FBI Agent Fowler."

"And Mr. Barlow or Mr. Tungsten, this is FBI Agent Timpson, and you are under arrest on multiple charges. Your days of destroying people to get rich are at an end."

"I'm not taking the wrap for all this. It was Derksin's idea. He was raking in money from everywhere. He was the head money maker."

I'm still glaring into Barlow's eyes but calmly reply, "All of the Derksin men are now facing a judge that passes out eternal sentences. They all died trying to get rich at someone else's expense."

Barlow is finally realizing that he has hung himself. His eyes tell me he is going to try to run. He surges forward to push me out of the way, but I sidestep his hands, and his momentum carries him into the bench I had been sitting on. FBI hands quickly cuff his hands and feet and carry him away. It doesn't help his image that blood is smearing over his face from the broken nose he received when he smashed into the bench.

Agent Fowler extends his arm to shake my hand, "Terry, do you know what I love the best about you? The crooks always spill enough information to put themselves away for a long time. You seem to know how to bring out the worst in them. While you were talking to him, I did a background check. He's played this game before under the name of Andy Tungsten. We could never get enough solid evidence to send him to prison...That should wrap up everything here. You and Evan enjoy your little vacation here. This is such a beautiful place.

Evan puts his arm around my shoulder and backs up to sit us on the bench. I snuggle into his side, "This has turned out to be almost more adventure than I can cope with. Just hold me for a while."

There's a peaceable silence between us long enough that I almost fall asleep. Evan finally whispers, "I can't believe you own all this. Tell me again how all this fell into place."

"We own all this. Your name's on everything with mine." I tell him all the details including how Mom set the whole thing up. Now the future hinges on what Dawn will want to do. I guess we'll soon find out because I realize they are walking across the lawn toward us.

"Terry, this is the most beautiful place I've ever been in. When I was young, I used to tell my mom that I was going to live in a big house with a green lawn and be able to see the ocean. She would laugh and say 'Dawn, that dream is only for rich white people not for poor Black People. But Terry, this is my dream. If I had a house here, I would never leave this place."

"Dawn, sit down here with Solomon, and let's talk. I could deed you and Solomon five acres of land over there starting on the lawn behind the concert hall. That would be enough room to build a nice home with a well-equipped engineering office and a school for Solomon to teach blind piano students. You could even build tennis courts if you wanted to teach disadvantaged students how to get a college education. In return, I would like you to be the on-site manager of the concert hall. With your engineering skills, you would be the perfect person to oversee the renovation that's desperately needed. I know you could do it, but what I need to know is if you would like to take on the manager position."

"Terry, I'd become your manager in a heartbeat." She turns to Solomon, "Sol, is this where you'd like to build your school?"

"That's a no-brainer. I don't know of a pianist alive who wouldn't give everything he or she had to have daily access to practice in a hall with those acoustics. Certainly, I'd build my school here. Could you leave Fletcher and Masters Electronics and the tennis world with Celia?"

She throws her arms around Solomon's neck and kisses him soundly on the lips. "Sol, with all my heart I want to be here. AJ doesn't need my eyes any longer only my ideas, and I can accomplish all I need to do online. Celia and I only want to play the open tournament this fall one last time. She's ready to start a family and so am I. Every time I look at Terry and Pam, I'm jealous."

"It's settled then. As of right now, you are the manager of the Dr. Lilian Masters School and Sea-Side Concert Hall. We are having a meeting tomorrow night on stage with the board of managers which will become the board of advisors and introduce you."

Evan squeezes into our conversation, "Will you be drawing up the plans for your home?" Dawn nods her head, "Will you draw up another set for our retirement home back near the edge of the woods close to the ocean? It might be good to have five cottages back there also for visiting guests and performers."

With a grin from ear to ear, Dawn says, "I'll have some rough sketches for you tonight."

Everything seems to be catching up with me all at once. I feel a heavy fatigue settling over me like a thick dark fog. I turn to Evan, "I think I'll lie down on this bench for a while; I am so tired."

Evan puts his arm around my waist and pulls me up off the bench, "A couple of steps to the car and a short ride will have you in a real bed. I'm sorry, I've been so caught up in your excitement that I haven't noticed your fatigue."

As we're walking to our rooms, Dawn says, "We found this charming little restaurant. We'll pick you up at six." Evan nods and carries me through the door and gently lays me on the bed.

I think I hear Evan calling my name, but he is so far away. I just want to stay asleep. Finally, his voice pierces my fog enough that I understand what he's saying, "Terry, Dawn and Sol will be here in ten minutes. I know you're tired and need to rest, but I'm also pretty sure you haven't had anything to eat for two-plus days. As soon as you've eaten, I'll put you back to bed." As if to add credence to his statement, I'm kicked repeatedly from the inside. Scott must be starving. I get up, clean up a little, and am ready when they knock on the door.

I almost laugh when I see they've come to pick us up with a four-seater golf cart sitting ten feet from our door. They take us to an outdoor barbeque. Evan was right, as soon as I take my first bite, I know I'm famished. I eat double what everyone else does. After all, I'm eating for two, I tell myself. Once we're seated back in our transportation, Dawn turns to us with mischief in her eyes, "How would you like to see the property you just bought from inside." Both Evan and I just stare at her with no understanding. "You can't drive a car around your property, but we can drive this golf cart across the lawns. That's what they're made for." I can see the excitement growing in Evan's eyes. Dawn can see it too, so we head for Sea-Side. Once we're on the property, she becomes the tour guide. I have the feeling that she and Solomon have already made this excursion.

She drives to a grassy area a hundred yards behind the concert hall and stops, "This is where we would like to build our home. It's far enough away to give us some privacy yet an easy walk to the hall. About 25 yards away to the east, we'll build the school," she says as she points. "It will be a two-story building with all the classrooms and practice rooms on the main floor and a dormitory with a modern kitchen on the second floor. There will also be a large family room for relaxing and visiting on the second floor. We will try to match the architecture of the concert hall, so it looks like it belongs here."

We are off again, this time heading toward the ocean. We make a turn to follow the shoreline north. It is breathtaking, with areas of sandy beaches mixed in with craggy rocks extending into the surf. Our next turn heads us away from the water toward the forest backed by the towering cliffs. When we reach the edge of the woods we stop again. "This is where I think we should build your home-away-from-home. If we put it twenty feet back in from the tree line and make it rugged woodsy, no one would realize that it's there. You could put five cottages in there with about twenty feet in between, and they'd still be concealed."

"Dawn, when did you learn so much about architecture? I thought your schooling was in engineering."

"When that cheating Coach Armstrong lured me to Draper, he convinced me that their engineering college was top in the nation. He didn't know the difference between architecture and engineering. I took the required classes at Draper to keep my scholarship, but I studied engineering on my own. I have rough sketches for you. Look them over and tell me what you think tomorrow."

On the way back to our rooms, we set up our schedule for tomorrow. It includes a trip to the bank to set up new accounts, shopping for clothes, and organizing a concert for Saturday.

When we arrive at 6:30 pm to get ready for the meeting, the front door is unlocked, and chairs are set up on the stage. I don't know if I'm excited about this, or if I should be concerned. Bruce Underwood greets us as we climb the stairs to the stage, "Thought I'd get everything set up. Is this placement ok or do you want it arranged differently? Everyone will be here tonight and maybe a few extras. Everyone is curious about the future."

I have frantically been trying to figure out the best way to build credibility with these people. It always comes down to playing the piano. I just don't want to come across as a show-off. We move the circle of chairs closer to the grand piano and open one end to include it. People must be anxious because the chairs on the stage begin filling, and the front of the auditorium seating is filling as well.

Well before 7:00, everyone seems to be seated. I stand beside the piano, so I am facing the board of directors in the circle of chairs as well as those sitting in the auditorium. All the town must be here. Half the seats on the floor are filled. There's no noise, just anxious silence, and all eyes are riveted on me. "Ladies and gentlemen, thank you for meeting with us tonight. I am Dr. Terry Masters Timpson, and this is my husband, Evan Timpson. We are the new owners of this magnificent building and the beautiful grounds that surround it. It is truly a heavenly place…I would like to ask how many of you attended the concert I gave in this building last Saturday?" Not one hand goes up.

One man in the circle stands up, he is the only person I know by name except for Bruce in this entire building of over a thousand people, "Dr. Timpson, may I speak?"

"Please do Kenny." This is the sound engineer who ran the boards during my concert.

"No one was there because it was not allowed unless we bought tickets at double the price." He turns so he is talking to everyone, "This woman is the most accomplished pianist we have ever had perform here in our Hall. She is totally awesome. On top of that, she's genuine and not full of herself. She even talks to the audience. I looked her up on the net. She has performed at Carnegie Hall several times. She is the accompanist for the Oratorio Choir which won first place in the national contest. They were invited to give all the Christmas Day concerts. In February, she gave her own concert including the preshow with her own performing company. It was a two-nightstand with sell-outs both nights." He turns to me, "Doc why don't you play something for them."

I could run and give him a hug and a kiss, but instead, I sit down at the piano. He saved me just like Lenard did on my first day of teaching. I play for about ten minutes my Medley of the Masters. When I finish, there's a reserved standing ovation. Kenny comes to my rescue again, "Why don't you do that duet with the blind player? We won't turn out the lights, we'll just blindfold you." Dawn guides Sol to the piano to sit beside me. He takes out a large red handkerchief from his back pocket, and Dawn ties it around my head. I can't see a thing.

"Alright Doc T, I'm going to play something you have never heard me play. I'm not even telling you what key it's in. I'll lose you in the dust."

"I'll take that challenge. You begin." I can tell the audience is coming alive. This is just what we need. It only takes me a few measures to find his key, and then I fly with an accompaniment. He changes keys several times, and I stay with him. He finishes, and I continue with my own ending. The audience goes wild.

When the audience calms down, Sol stands to face them, "Doc, I don't know how you do that. But someday I'm going to figure out how you compose on the spot."

It's my turn to speak again, and I am so thankful that the audience has relaxed, "I am a concert pianist, and I can sit at this piano and make wonderful music, but me and my piano cannot put on a concert. It takes a whole team of people working together to make a successful evening." I turn to the board of directors. "I know each of you has an area of expertise you take care of. I would like you to stay in that position as a board of advisors. For being in that position, I will see that each of you receives a stipend four times a year. Each of you will also receive a reserved seat that is permanently yours to use or give away at any event that takes place in this building. Who is in charge of paying the employees?"

One man raises his hand, "Bill Thorn here. For the last four concerts, I made out the checks, but none of them cleared the bank. Derksin's took all the money."

"Give me two days to get everything set up with the bank and you should be able to print checks for all four concerts." There's a gasp from the entire audience. "The money from my concert was recovered and it should be adequate to make everything right. We didn't buy Sea-Side to become rich in money, but to enrich the lives of those on our team and those who listen to our music. I am currently a full-time professor at Augustine University and director of the piano department. Augustine needs a place to showcase its talented graduating students who have reached professional performance levels. We will use this hall to do that. I make you a promise that no students will perform here that I wouldn't take with me to Carnegie. We will also invite professional musicians from around the world. Once a person has performed here, they will want to return again and again. I envision this becoming the premier concert venue in the States."

"The name of this venue will be changing. It will be The Dr. Lilian Masters School and Sea-Side Concert Hall. Behind the Concert Hall, we will be building a music school to teach piano to the blind. Dr. Solomon Tune will be the teacher at the school. Since I will not be here most of the time, the on-site manager will be Dawn Tune, Solomon's wife."

I am surprised at an outburst from a board member, "A Black woman?"

I turn and look at Dawn then turn back to the man, "You're right. She is black, and she is a woman. I hadn't noticed... What I did notice is that she is a highly sought-after engineer and totally capable of directing the renovation of the Concert Hall, making sure it retains its beautiful acoustic qualities. I also noticed that she is the number two-ranked amateur women's tennis player in the nation. She may even put in tennis courts by their home which will be built next to the school. If she does, she will teach disadvantaged kids how to use athletics to get a college education. She is the on-site manager."

"Dr. Timpson, I'm very sorry. That was a very rude remark for me to make. Mrs. Tune, please forgive me. I will support you in every way I can. I am not prejudiced; I have just never seen a woman in that role. But then I look at what the Derksins did, maybe we need an honest woman." Laughter and clapping come from everyone in the room. Dawn looks pleased.

"I have just one more announcement." I have instant attention, "Before we start the remodeling of Sea-Side, I want to have one more concert. Next Saturday, I will bring as many of my company as can come on such short notice, and we will fill this magnificent building with music. This concert is for all the employees and their families and friends. There will be no admission charge. I will need all your help to put it on and all of you inside to listen when we begin." That rates a noisy standing ovation.

As everyone starts towards the exits, I head to Kenny, "Thank you for the credibility boost." He smiles and shakes my hand. Then I have another thought, "Kenny, will you check the third organ pipe from the left side? I think something like a squirrel has built a nest in it. Everything else seems to work fine."

"The Derksins said it was broken and not repairable. I'll see what I can do." I'm going to enjoy working with that young man.

# CHAPTER 12

Oh, what a wonderful evening we had. I don't know where they came from, but the whole hall was crowded with excited guests. The performers were even more ecstatic with the acoustics of the building. Dr. Martin couldn't stop raving about the sound and what an absolute boon it would be to have it affiliated with Augustine University. Everyone left on a high. Mom did know what she was doing by leading us to the gold.

"Terry, this was such a magical night. I have never heard a better concert or felt a more thrilled audience," Evan says as we are lying in bed talking. I think you have the community behind you. That was such a great idea to give them their own concert.

"They are the ones who will make the concerts possible. I want them to feel a degree of ownership. I think we will give them a concert once a quarter, and make sure they get paid what they've contracted for and on time." We continue to talk late into the night about the future and at some point, we both fade away to sleep.

On one of my routine nightly trips to the bathroom, I hear Evan's phone ringing. It stops leaving an ominous feel in the air. No one ever calls with good news at 3:00 am. On my way back to bed, I pick up his phone to see who had been calling. It starts ringing again, and I almost drop it. I lean over to shake my zoned-out husband, "Evan, wake up. It's your mother, and this is the second time she has tried to get through to you."

He slowly comes too. I flip it to the speaker as I hand it to him. "Hi Mom, what's up?"

"Evan, I wish with my whole heart that I didn't have to do this over the phone... Your father had a heart attack this evening and passed away."

Anything she might have wanted to say is cut short with Evan screaming, "No! no! no! It can't be allowed! He can't be dead. I need him to be alive. He can't leave me." He throws the phone and face plants onto his pillow, and sobs with repeated no's.

I retrieve his phone from the chair, "Sorry Mom, can you tell me what happened?"

"Terry, I'm the one that's sorry. I didn't think Evan would take this very well. I wish I could be there with you.... Scott has been having heart issues for twenty years. The Lord has repeatedly been putting him back together so he can continue his service. Tonight, He finally took him home. Kenneth, our oldest son, was here with his family having dinner with us. We had moved into the living room and were reminiscing about

Kenneth's struggles growing up when Scott closed his eyes and seemed to go to sleep. When I touched him, I knew he was gone. We had agreed that when this moment came, I would just kiss him and tell him goodbye. No frantic call for an ambulance, nor any attempts at resuscitation. He would quietly move on to his next mission."

"Mom, do you have any idea yet about the funeral arrangements?"

"Yes, Terry. We are going to hold the funeral here in Seattle, Washington where we have been serving. We will intern him in the cemetery in your city. We have reserved rooms for the family at the Addison Hotel not far from where the services will be held. I would like everyone to be here the day after tomorrow for a family dinner at the hotel. The viewing will begin the next morning, and the funeral will follow at noon. Scott and I put the program together a month ago, and everyone knows their part except you. He wanted you to play the pre and postlude music and a piano solo lasting about five minutes somewhere in the middle. Would you be willing to do that?"

"I would love to do that. Does Evan have a part in the program?"

"I'm sorry to say, no. He refused to even consider the possibility of his dad dying even with all the signs magnifying themselves. Terry, he's going to go through a rough time. Be patient with him and show him your love in any way you can. Call me if you get to your wit's end." After we hang up, I ponder her words. I sure hope his rough time doesn't last as long as mine did.

Walking back into the bedroom from the bathroom, I sit down on the bed and put my hand on his sobbing body. I don't say anything. Finally, he calms down enough to get out a few words, "Why, why did the Lord need to take him now? I need him! He has been healed so many times before, so why not this time? It isn't fair. I don't think the Lord loves me very much if at all." I lean forward wrapping my arms around him and just hold him. I finally crawl into bed and hold him the best I can with Scott between us. As the sun begins to lighten the sky, we both fall asleep.

It's late morning when I'm finally forced awake to make another bathroom run. When I return, I kneel beside Evan's side of the bed for our morning prayer. He looks at me with anger in his eyes, climbs out the other side of the bed, and slams the door going into the bathroom. I pray without him. This is going to be harder than I thought.

Buckling into our seats for this red-eye flight to Seattle, I wonder what our communication will be like. Any time today that I've asked him about his dad or the funeral, he only stares at me with angry clenched teeth and says nothing. If I bring up another subject, I only get short, clipped answers. He starts no conversation. I'm going to try one more time, "Evan, can we talk about what's happening inside of you? I think it will help if you can talk about it."

I get his angry stare again, but this time his mouth comes open, "Terry, I do not want to talk about my father or the funeral. We have a big day tomorrow, and I think we should get all the sleep we can." He turns away from me to put his head on a small pillow resting against the hull of the jet. I wonder if I was this bad when Mom and Dad were killed.

Evan's mom and brother meet us at the airport, and we are swept into a whirlwind of activity. By mid-afternoon, I must not be looking too good. Evan's mom rescues me by taking my arm and leading me to my room, "Terry, we don't want you to have this baby in the middle of the funeral. I'm going to put a do not disturb sign on your door, and you are going to spend between now and dinner resting, preferably sleeping." I give her a smile and a giant hug, then walk straight to the bed. The next thing I know, Evan is shaking me and telling me it's time to get ready for dinner. At least he's talking to me.

Evan and I are the first to arrive for the viewing. The family gets to spend an hour alone with their dad before the doors are open to the public. I move to the casket to stand beside my acquired mom, and Evan follows behind me. Elder Timpson is resting so peacefully. I reach into the casket and gently squeeze his hand. I have come to love him as I did my father, such a great Man of God.

I turn to Mom and engulf her in a tight hug. She whispers in my ear, "How's Evan?" I shake my head and whisper back that he is not good. I turn to see him with both hands on the side of the casket just staring at his father. No tears, just anger.

I turn back to Mom, "Would it be okay if I go to the chapel and get the piano ready for the services." She gives me a knowing smile and nods her head. She moves to put her arm around Evan's shoulders.

There's no one in the chapel when I beeline for the piano. I give it my get-to-know-you drill and find it's not in too bad of shape. There's only one key I must avoid. I spend the next three hours putting together the music for the meeting. They have chosen "Nearer My God to Thee" for the opening song and "Each Life That Touches Ours for Good" as the closing. The prelude, postlude, and solo are mine. "Be Still, My Soul" with embellishments will be my contribution to the program. When I'm satisfied with the direction it will take, I settle into playing the prelude with music that's right for a funeral. I love this kind of playing because I can add my improvisations to my heart's content. I play to the point that the casket is placed up front, and the audience is seated. I have never seen so many people crowded into a building. The chapel is full, the cultural hall is full, and there are even chairs on the stage.

A General Authority is conducting the services. As he begins, a peaceful calm settles over everyone. Everyone that is except Evan. He looks angrier than I have ever seen him, scowling with clenched teeth. I don't remember getting angry until months after my parents died.

Each of Evan's four brothers has a part in the program. I seem to be taking Evan's place since he wanted no part in a funeral that shouldn't be taking place. His brothers paint a picture of their father's life, giving everyone a sense of what a great man he was. It feels like a celebration for a truly wonderful servant of the Lord. He seems to have been loved by everyone here.

When my number is announced, I detour to the microphone, "I am going to play all three verses of 'Be Still, My Soul'. It would have a much deeper meaning for you if you were able to follow the words as I'm playing." I hear a rustle from the audience as they search to find the words in hymn books and on cell phones. When silence prevails, I begin. The melody is there, but there are added notes from all over the keyboard. It is in grand concert style. As I progress through the three verses, my music becomes more and more mellow. On the last line of the third verse, I begin playing only four notes at a time, then two notes of the harmony, and finally on the last two measures, only one note melody, "...we shall meet at last." I look out over the silent audience, and their tear-streaked faces let me know they have been deeply touched.

The casket is the first to leave after the services. Row by row people leave in an orderly manner to follow behind the casket. I play postlude music until the last man walks through the doors leaving a silent memorial. I am engrossed in feeling and thoughts as I feel a gentle large hand being placed on my shoulder. A whisper follows, penetrating my solus, "Terry, that was magnificent. Thank you. I am so thankful that I can claim you as my daughter." The Spirit sends fire through every fiber of my being. I almost feel consumed.

I can't believe that Elder Timpson has taken time on this day of all days to thank me. My mind races to my most demanding concern, "Evan?"

"I know, Terry. I am also concerned. Please be patient, and I think we can get him there."

"I don't know what to do."

"Love him. No confrontations, just love him. But you must also stay firm in your faith."

I want to ask more, but at that moment a lone figure runs through the cultural hall doors, "Terry, everyone is waiting for you in the multi-purpose room. Come on. We're going to miss our flight." When Evan finishes yelling, he turns and disappears again.

I finally find him waiting outside a door. He doesn't look so happy with me, "Where have you been? The funeral's been over for almost a half hour."

"Funeral etiquette dictates that the postlude music is played until all the guests have left."

He shrugs his shoulders as if he doesn't care and turns to open the door. When we walk in, we are met with clapping and bravos from all of Evan's brothers and their wives. They are all standing at their places at a long table piled high with food. As the noise is dying out one of Even's brothers loudly says, "I thought you were a teacher at some college, but you are a world-class concert pianist, Terry."

There is no noise now as Brad, another brother, interjects, "Evan, if I had a wife that could play like that, I'd be her manager, and we'd travel the world over making millions." Everyone laughs, and I'm lost for words. These are my new brothers and sisters, but I don't know them at all. I can't tell if they are teasing, being sarcastic, or genuinely impressed.

His last brother must get his comments in, "I can see that you married Miss. America, and you've changed her into Mrs. America." More laughter follows.

Evan puts his arm around my waist and pulls me tightly to him, "I'd like all of you to meet Dr. Terry Masters Timpson, my wife. She does teach at Augustine University where she is the piano chairperson and concert pianist in residence. She is also the youngest person to ever receive a doctorate at Augustine. She is very much a world-class concert pianist. I even got to be introduced with her on stage at Carnegie Hall last February where she performed in a two-night sell-out. She does make big bucks, but most of the money goes to the Lilian Masters Scholarship Fund for gifted musical students who cannot afford higher education. We had just finished her last concert on the coast when we got the call to detour here. Terry liked the Concert Hall and its acoustics so well she bought it. It will be affiliated with Augustine University to give graduating music students a place to appear professionally... I did marry Miss America, and she's all mine."

Now I don't know what to do. I want to be friends with these people, but I get the feeling there's deep sibling rivalry, and I'm being swept into it like a pawn on a chessboard.

Mom Timpson intervenes, "Enough of this sparing. Terry, you were phenomenal. Thank you for bringing the Spirit so richly to our funeral service today. I know you need to be on your way to the airport, I've had a lunch prepared for you to take with you."

She hugs Evan and then turns to me. As she hugs me tightly, she whispers in my ear.

Evan complains, "Hey, her hug is longer than mine, and I'm your son."

"Since you two were sealed for eternity, Terry is also my daughter. I was asking her if after I spend a week or so with each of my boys' families, it would be okay if I come and live with you. I would like to give Terry a mother's help with her first baby."

I don't even wait for Evan to comment, "I would love that more than anything." I give her another hug.

At first, I can't figure out what's awakened me. That was the worst plane ride I have ever had. Scott couldn't settle down for five minutes. He felt like he was doing gymnastics all the way home. When I finally got to my bed, I passed out from sheer exhaustion. Now my hunger is screaming that it can smell eggs, hash browns, and bacon. I finally wake enough to throw on a robe and head downstairs to the kitchen.

"Thought you might be hungry," Evan says as he hands me a plate of food. Something in his tone of voice alerts me to be on my guard. I bow my head and say a blessing on my breakfast or maybe it's lunch. I look up at him and tell him thank you. When I start eating, he starts talking, "Terry, if you just did concert tours, could you really bring in millions?"

I answer emphatically, "No!"

"Why, I think you're good enough."

"My heart would not be in it…Do you remember last summer when you changed your major from engineering to recreational rehab?" He nods his head. "Why did you do that if it meant a significant drop in the salary, you would be making?"

"I get your point. It was an interesting thought that we could be rolling in millions." He pauses looking straight into my eyes. I can tell that he has much more on his mind, "Terry, I'm finally ready to talk about my father." I don't say anything but give him my full attention. "I have decided that there will be no more prayers or scripture study in this house anymore."

I'm so ready to fly into protests but the words quickly come to my mind, 'No confrontation, just love.' I answer, "Why?" as calmly as I can.

"Why, because God stole my father from me. That's why. He could have healed him like he has so many times before, but He snuffed out his life when I need him the most. If He were a loving God, He would have spared his life for me."

I wait for words to enter my mind, "Evan, your dad's not dead. His mortal body is gone, but his spirit is very much alive. He's just moved on to another realm."

"I stood by that casket for a long time. I even touched his cold lifeless body. He is gone, and I will never see him again."

"Evan, will you listen to me for a few minutes?" He looks at me and finally nods his head.

"Last summer before you came home, I was poisoned. I ate doctored chocolates that were meant to kill someone else. They destroyed my liver very quickly. The only thing that saved my life was Tom giving me part of his liver for a transplant. During that operation, my spirit left my body while I was on total life support. In essence, I was dead, but my spirit was not. I found myself in the most peaceful beautiful place. My mom was there to welcome me. She told me that she had been sent to offer me a choice. I could end my mortality and remain there with her, or I could go back and finish my earthly experience. I was ready to stay until she reminded me of you. If I wanted to be your eternal companion, I needed to go back and be sealed to you in the temple. I had also promised that I would wait for you. I decided that I would return to my mortal body and the horrid pain I knew was coming, so we could spend eternity together. Evan, spirits don't die."

"It sounds like you had a pretty wild dream or nightmare while under the anesthetic. It's all your imagination."

"If that's what you want to believe, so be it. But this house is a dedicated house of prayer to the Lord. You have your agency to do as you like, but my prayers and spiritual time will continue. I will not join you in a war against God. I did that once and almost died. I never want to go through what it does to your mind and spirit again. Hate destroys you."

I can't read the look Evan has on his face. Finally, he opens his mouth, "They called to say that the new Jeep I ordered is in. I'm going to pick it up and get ready for the survival camp." Oh, he is such a Jekyll and Hyde. But, I'm not sure I was any better when my parents died, but I hold it all inside.

I'm still sitting at the table when I hear the front door open, and I'm assaulted with a kick from inside. I relax a little when I hear Pam's voice, "Terry, are you here?" I yell back that I'm in the kitchen. Pam walks in bringing golden sunshine. I hope it will dissipate my thunderhead gloom. She stands looking at me in the kitchen doorway, "Terry, never at any time have I seen you with a full plate of food that's gone cold. What's happened?" I explain my morning with Evan to her.

"Pam, I don't know what to do for him. It's almost like I'm living my parents' accident all over again, only this time I'm watching from the outside. I'm sure thankful my brothers were patient with me, especially Tom. I don't want to wait seven years for my real Evan to come back."

"Trust the Lord and let the Spirit guide you…Now tell me about you. What's happening with you and baby Scott?

"On the airplane coming home yesterday, he felt like he was trying to do flips. I think he somersaulted right inside. That was the most horrid ride I have ever been on. I couldn't get comfortable no matter what I did. Now I can't get centered no matter what I do, and I feel like I'm waddling like a duck. I wish I didn't have to wait another two weeks to have him on the outside."

"Oh Terry, you get a set due date which has nothing to do with reality. When your baby is ready, he'll do his own thing. We just need to be prepared for whenever. It sounds like he is getting ready to leave the womb behind. Do you have all the things packed I gave you the list for? I think we need to leave for Red Rock before it's light in the morning."

"I'm ready. I am so ready!"

"Do you think you have one more small concert in you?"

That almost makes me feel sick, "What small concert?"

"Arundel fell and broke her arm this morning."

The thought hits me like lightning, "This is Celia and Jefferson's concert with their elementary school choir tonight, isn't it? Of course, I'll play for them." The thought that I can help them make their dream come true gives me the rush of energy to know I can do it.

"Good, I'll pick you up and bring you home after the program. I want to be there for them. I think I'll stay with you tonight just in case. My car will be all packed.

# CHAPTER 13

"Did you see how excited those kids were as they sang with all their hearts? The simple harmonies Celia and Jefferson taught them made the whole group sound incredible. But Terry, if you've taught me nothing else it's that the choir should only get half the credit. A good accompanist should get half or more of the accolades. You made them shine."

"That's why I would never just be a concert pianist. It lifts my soul when I can help others reach for the stars. But now that it's over, I'm more than ready for bed. Evan texted that he has already left for his survival camp, so you can park in the garage and feed your car electricity for our trip."

I'm in bed and asleep before Pam even changes her clothes. My motherhood must be closer than I think because she isn't letting me out of her sight. On one of my bathroom runs, she asks how I'm doing, so I know she's awake when I am. It has become such a routine that I never turn on a light. For some reason, when I'm finished, I move the window shade to look down on the street in front of our house. The same car is parked there like the last five nights. Only this time I think I see light. I call softly to Pam, "Come in here, but don't turn on any lights."

She is quickly by my side, "Are you okay Terry?"

"I'm fine, but that car has been parked there every night for five nights straight. I think someone is in that car watching our house."

Pam watches intently for several minutes then we both see it. "Terry, someone is in that car, and they just lit up. Do you suppose that's Dr. Twig and company?"

"If nothing else he's persistent. He knows my due date and we've been expecting another attack. What time is it anyway?"

"It's 4:00 am. There's no way I could go back to sleep. Let's get dressed and leave. Maybe we can shake him going out of town." We kneel and both offer a fervent prayer for protection. I grab our lunches from the frig, and we're on our way. About a block down the street, we see the car following in our mirrors. He doesn't even have his lights on.

"When we get to the freeway, I'll go North instead of South to the next on-ramp. I'll try to get far enough ahead that he won't see me take the next exit. We'll wait under the overpass for him to continue north, and then we'll head south." Pam makes her bright red dart fly. We take the exit and wait under the bridge. Right on schedule, the perp is speeding north over our heads still without lights. When Pam knows for sure that he can't see our taillights, we take the southbound on-ramp. That ought to be good to give us a couple of hours' head start.

"Terry, I don't think you can sit straight up for this trip. Move that lever on the side of your seat and recline until you're cozy. Try and sleep if you can." This is the most comfortable I've been in days.

"Good morning sunshine. I can't believe you've been asleep for four hours. We're coming up on a rest stop, and I can't imagine you don't have to use it. Thought I'd get you awake before we stopped." By the time we take the off-ramp and stop, I'm more than ready to rush with my waddling stride to the restroom.

Pam is standing by her red dart watching the freeway when I finally make it back, "See anything suspicious?"

"Nope. I figure we should be a good hour ahead of them. You watch while I use the facilities. Want anything to drink? I see vending machines in there.?"

I shake my head and reach for my water bottle. I'm intent on watching the interstate traffic when two biker-looking guys stop to talk, "The mountains behind you are much more interesting than the freeway."

I smile and turn to look at the mountains, but that doesn't divert their gaze from my motherly shape. The other can't resist, "I'm sorry lady, but you look like you're about to burst open. I hope you're not traveling far." I lie to him that we're headed for Los Angeles. He shakes his head as Pam joins us, "I doubt that you'll make it that far. It's still twelve hours away."

Pam picks up on what I'm doing, "Her husband is waiting in LA, but if we need to, we'll stop in Vegas. We better get moving." We tell the guys goodbye, and they wish us luck.

"Terry, as soon as I joined you, I think they recognized us from Red Rock. That won't help if anyone stops asking questions. I hope we're far enough ahead that they won't catch us when we need to stop to charge the batteries. That takes about an hour. The town just before we start over the mountain has a charging station."

We fill our time with talking and singing until we see a sign telling us we're ten miles away from our charging station. I'm about to comment when I cry out instead with a pain that almost doubles me over. It's like I have a giant muscle cramp in my stomach.

"Terry, what's happening?"

I try to catch my breath and can finally get out words when it passes, "I've never had a pain like that before. I didn't know you could get cramps in your stomach. That was a doozer."

Pam just looks at me in unbelief as we pull into the charging station, "Is that the first one of those pains you've had?" I nod my head; I'm still kind of out of breath.

The charging part of this gas station is on the back side of the building. They have a lounge for waiting customers. We go in to use the restroom again and relax in the comfortable air-conditioned environment. I'm not very hungry, but we get a light snack and a bottle of ice-cold water. I can see through the windows to the front part of the gas station. I randomly watch the cars fill up with gas while we talk. Forty-five minutes and another trip to the restroom later, I notice an ambulance pull in for gas. The driver and the passenger both exit the cab. I gasp when I recognize the driver. It's the punk that tried to sock me in the stomach at school. The passenger must be Dr. Forest.

"Pam, it's the baby butcher himself in that ambulance. I know he's after me."

Pam grabs my arm, "We have more than enough charge to get us to Red Rock. Let's go. They can't move until they're full. We still have a little head start." I move as fast as I can toward the car. By the time I'm buckled up, Pam has us disconnected, and she's pulling onto the highway. But not before Dr. Twig spots us. I watch him point and hear him yell as we drive away.

As soon as we're away from the town, Pam floors it. We don't even stop at the intersection but take the road over the mountain. That ambulance could never hold the road like Pam's dart does, and she pushes for every second of speed. She handles her car like Tom's been giving her driving lessons. As I begin to worry about meeting a car head-on coming down the mountain, I get another cramp. This one is harder and lasts longer than the last one. Just as it finishes, I have the uncomfortable feeling I'm wetting my pants. I can't believe this.

Embarrassed, I turn to Pam. "I am so sorry, I'm urinating, but I can't stop it. I'm getting your seat all wet." Pam does the last thing I expect her to do. She almost slows to a stop and turns off the highway onto a rough dirt road.

"Hold on Terry. This road gets quite bumpy if I remember right." She is right about the bumpy part. Even though the car is barely crawling up a small hill, I am bouncing all over. Then I scream with another of those cramps; they seem to be getting stronger. We stop at the base of the small hill we just came down. I finally recognize the spot.

"Pam, this is where we hid when the mob was after you and your baby. What a smart idea. Do you think all the bumping could put me into labor?"

Pam is laughing, "Terry, you are in labor, and those cramps are contractions. You didn't urinate, your water broke. It's the amniotic fluid that your baby's been swimming in for nine months. Welcome to your survival birthing parlor. Can I put my hand on your stomach?" I nod my head in disbelief. Pam feels all over my stomach like she is developing a picture of where my baby is. Looking at me she says, "Good, head is down and facing your back. I think he's even engaged or very close to entering the birth canal. We've got to get busy."

She flies around the car and starts pulling things out of the back seat. I haven't moved. She looks at me, "Terry, stand up and strip from the waist down!"

"Out here?"

"Yes, out here. This is where your baby has chosen to be born. Think about it. It's the ultimate survival experience. I'll bet this tops anything your mom did." She looks at me and then at the blanket she's spread on the ground. Changing her mind, she spreads the blanket on the seat while I remove my wet clothes. She pushes me back into the seat, so I am sitting with my legs on the ground and leaning back in a reclining position. She then lifts my feet up, so they are resting on the bottom of the door frame. Another contraction hits, and with it, she gives me directions, "Push." I push as hard as I can.

Pam laughs, "He has dark red hair, much darker than Tommy's. You're crowning. Next time the contraction comes, I want you to pant and try not to push. I'm going to see if I can stretch your opening, so you won't tear when he comes out. I'm also using baby shampoo to lubricate the opening to make it slippery." Stretching is not comfortable, but I think tearing would be much worse. When the next contraction comes, his head pops out.

"The hardest part is over. I'll clean his face a little while we get ready for the shoulders." The next contraction brings the baby shooting out. "I'll suction his nose and mouth, and we'll see what kind of lungs he has." I watch Pam hold him head down cradled in her arm and palm of her hand. With her other gloved hand, she uses a small suction bulb to take the mucus from his mouth and nose. His cord is still attached to something inside of me. She rubs his back with a small towel, and he screams like an Indian on the warpath. I can't believe the consuming joy I feel. I hold out my arms; I want to hold him like I've never wanted anything.

"Hold him on your abdomen while I take care of his cord." I can't believe the love I feel; I never want to let him go. I watch as Pam clamps the cord close to where it's coming out of Scott's tummy. Then she clamps it about two inches away. Opening a small package and taking a sterile razor out, she looks at me, smiles, and cuts the cord. I now hold a new human being in my arms that will someday be a world-famous concert pianist.

Pam looks deep into my eyes, "Terry, I'm now going to give you an experience that few women in our society get to have." She quickly puts a very small diaper on Scott and says, "Lift your shirt. I'm going to unhook your bra so you can snuggle him right onto your chest." I work to get both him and me comfortable. Pam pulls my shirt down over the top of us, "Now sing to him with all your heart. He has heard your voice or vibrations from deep inside, but now let him know his mother's voice that will guide his future."

I feel a little self-conscious at first, but then it feels so right. I know just the perfect song, "I pray you'll be our eyes, And watch us where we go, And help us to be wise, In times we don't know…Let this be our prayer, Just like every child,

Needs to find a place, Guide us with your grace, Give us faith so we'll be safe." The Spirit has filled me to the point that tears are spilling down my face, and I can hardly finish the last verse. Pam finally joins with harmony to help me end. I reach out with one arm to hug Pam and whisper, "Thank you, thank you."

We are holding each other in silent joy when we begin to hear a siren coming up the canyon. We each hold our breath as it passes by, "Terry, that was two sirens. That creep must have asked for a police escort so he could continue his charade at maximum speed. Where's the satellite phone? I'm going to call the Red Rock Sheriff."

I'm still wrapped in ecstasy, but I follow most of their conversation. He knows about the murdering baby doctor. He will let the sheriff's office in the other town know what's happening so they can call back their officers. In the meantime, he will alert Agent Fowler. The Sheriff is going to escort us from the air again to his ranch and his waiting mid-wife mother.

"So, I guess we just wait for our escort. I probably should get dressed.

"Not quite so fast; you still have a tail. You have only completed two of the three parts of birthing. You need to deliver the after birth and it's taking a little too long. I'm going to massage your uterus to see if we can speed up the contractions."

"Can't you just pull on the cord and bring everything out?"

"I wish it were that easy, but if I pull on the cord it will tear the placenta, and you will bleed to death. When the uterus contracts like it's supposed to, all comes shooting out at once." She massages hard on my abdomen, but I don't feel any contractions. "Okay, let's let Scotty do his work. Put him on one of your nipples."

"Oh, I've dreaded this moment more than you'll ever know. When I tried to feed Tommy on our little survival expedition, I thought I was going to pass out from the pain."

"This will be very different, I promise. Tommy was a three-month-old hardy eater. Scott doesn't have the muscles or the suction to do that yet. Direct your nipple into his mouth. I doubt you'll even notice his sucking."

As he latches on, I brace for the pain. I am completely unprepared for the pain that comes from the contractions in my stomach. I scream and jerk forward. Pam makes sure I don't drop Scott. My yelling and contortions don't phase Scotty a bit. He just continues sucking. Pam breaks his suction and moves him to the other nipple. He sucks, and the contractions continue but are lessening in intensity. When I can finally breathe again, I scowl at Pam, "You're right. I didn't feel him sucking at all. You could have warned me a little...Did I expel the afterbirth?"

Pam holds up a large clear plastic bag that looks like it's full of blood, "Got it all…I hope. I'll let Grandma Daisy check it. Now I can get you cleaned up."

When she finishes, she hands me clean clothes and reaches for Scott, "Come on Scotty it's time you get to know your Aunt Pam." She wraps him in a receiving blanket and cuddles him. I am so thankful for her. Now that I'm dressed in regular pants again, it feels so good to not be pregnant. I begin my centering exercises. "Terry, what are you doing? You just had a baby. I don't think you should be exercising."

"It's not exactly exercising; I'm trying to get centered with my new weight loss. I'm certain there will still be a confrontation with Dr. Twig, and I must be ready for anything and everything he throws at me."

The satellite phone rings at the same time we hear the chopper. I answer it, "Hi Sheriff, thank you for coming to our aid again. Should we continue over the mountain or go the long way?"

"Might as well go over the mountain. The ambulance and its occupants are in Red Rock trying to find you. You'll come to the ranch several miles before you reach the town. Terry, do you and your little one need a quick transport to the ranch?"

"Thanks, Sheriff, but we're doing fine. Pam has taken extra good care of us. We have no emergencies. I'll just continue with Pam. We'll be back on the road in a few minutes."

Pam hands Scotty back to me. I do a double take when I look at his head, "What happened to his face? The empty eye sockets are gone, and he looks like a normal baby."

Pam is laughing at me, "Oh Terry, he is a normal baby. He just can't see. I talked to the eye specialists at the hospital, and he told me that they make artificial eyeballs in all sizes. I had a pair made for a newborn, and they just fit into his sockets. What will be a little disconcerting is that his eyelids work. When he is awake, they will open, and you will see emerald green slits peering at you. You can change the color of his eyes any time you want."

# CHAPTER 14

"Evan, why in the world are you here?"

"Dad, you are alive. Terry was right. I am so, so happy to see you."

"Of course, I'm alive. Spirit bodies never die. You know that, but it seems like you have forgotten more than you learned." I'm not sure I understand what he's saying. It also dawns on me that he thinks I should be somewhere else.

"Now everything will be okay. I can talk to you again. You have no idea how much I miss you. I can't function very well without you."

"Evan, things are far from okay. I've come to see if I can help you sort things out and tell you goodbye."

"Are you leaving me again? If you do, nothing will be right."

"Listen very carefully to what I'm going to tell you. In the preexistence, Elohim was the Father of your spirit. Your mom and I agreed to be your mortal parents here on earth. When we were married, we committed to being your mental, emotional, physical, and spiritual support while your mortal body grew to be a fit home for your spirit body. We had two goals to achieve before you were considered an adult. First, we were to teach you how to communicate and receive directions from your Heavenly Father. Second, we were to help you be prepared to enter an eternal commitment with a woman who would be your partner and other half for eternity. It seems we have failed in both areas."

"Dad, I think I was following that path until I went on my mission. I received inspiration all the time, and I knew I wanted to marry Terry. I even helped her learn how to receive inspiration for herself."

"Son, I think the blame rests with me. I thought it would be so neat to have you serve your mission where I was serving mine. It backfired. Instead of helping you to become more dependent on the Lord as missions do for most young men, you turned more to me."

"You were right there and only a phone call away. It became easier and easier to just turn to you for advice and help with my struggles."

"You're almost back to your twelve-year-old turned-in self. If something didn't go the way you wanted it to, you would create a scenario in your head to justify your actions. God didn't kill me or murder me to take me away from you. It was my time to go, and He lovingly helped me cross to the other side. I had such a joyous reunion there with all my deceased ancestors. And this business of having a war with your Eternal Father is ridiculous. I don't know if He's crying or laughing. If you continue, you're going to find yourself in outer darkness as one of Lucifer's minions."

I'm stunned. I wanted my way so badly that the consequences of my behavior never entered my mind. I'm beginning to feel the guilt of my actions. I feel like I'm caught in a void.

"You want help getting past my death, well Terry is way more qualified than anyone I know to help you. She lost both of her parents at a young age. She hadn't had enough time to know how to turn to her Heavenly Father. She's done it the hard way almost dying in the process. Let her help you."

"Something else you need to understand son is that I was only your mortal father, and mortal fathers die. I will never be your eternal partner. Your mother is my companion for eternity. We have worked and will continue to work to become one. The man is not without the woman nor the woman without the man. Together we are a single unit, and we build our eternity together. We do this with Heavenly Father as our guide. So…why are you here and not at Terry's side when she gave birth to your first child? You have made eternal promises to take care of her and that baby and you left them on their own. Now, you are leaving them to face a maniac murderer."

"I need to go find them."

"No! You need to spend the night in prayer pleading for forgiveness, so the Lord can be on your side and not hedging up your way. He needs to be your guide and support for the rest of your life. It's time you stepped up to become the head of your family, and you had better take care of my wife. I love you, Evan… Goodbye."

I mumble a goodbye as Dad's light fades away, and all I feel is lost. Have I blown eternity? Tears roll down my cheeks as I slowly kneel. My first thought is I hope the repentance process is real.

# CHAPTER 15

Pulling up to the ranch house Grandpa Sandy and Grandma Daisy are anxiously waiting on the porch. She rushes out to meet us as we come to a stop. I step out of the car holding one arm across my chest. Grandma gasps, "Where's your baby?"

Pam leans over the roof of the car, "She's holding him Grandma, skin on skin. I couldn't talk her into the car seat."

Grandma walks up to me and opens the top of my blouse. "He does look awfully comfortable. Bring him into the house, and let's get you two checked out. Pam, did you bring the afterbirth?"

We follow her into the house and spend the next hour checking out Tommy. He doesn't particularly like the process and registers his complaints with deafening screams. In the end, he is pronounced a healthy normal baby except for having no eyes. "Pam that was a good idea to have the prosthetic eyes ready to put in at birth. It is a little disconcerting to have emerald green slits peering at you when he opens his eyes."

"The man who makes them said his eye sockets will change size so quickly it's too expensive to make real-looking eyes yet. We'll do that when his growth slows down." Pam signs the birth certificate as the attending physician and Grandma Sandy as the witness. We fax it in, and Scott is a living, legal citizen. I don't think that will stop Dr. Twig.

Grandma Daisy turns to me, "Terry, how about you? You aren't looking like the usual mother that delivered four hours ago."

I'm sitting holding Scotty and feeling like I'm going to fall asleep any second, "I'm okay. I'm just a little tired."

"You should be very tired. You've let Scott sleep, now it's your turn. Pam, how did the delivery go? Any tearing?"

"I did lots of stretching and used baby shampoo to make it slippery. No tearing at all. The placenta was a little slow coming out, but Scott took care of that. I want to watch you check it. I'm not quite sure what to look for. I think it's all there."

"Let's get Terry in bed, and we'll check it." Scott and I are led to a bedroom in the middle of the house. There is even a bassinet right next to the bed. I gently lay him down and fall onto the bed. I think I hear Grandma Daisy tell me to keep the door locked when I'm here alone with Scott. That's all I know for the next three hours until I hear someone screaming. I wake up enough to see Pam pick up Scotty and walk out the door with him.

When I wake up again, the skylight tells me it's dark outside, and Pam is in bed with me. The moonlight through the window in the ceiling shows me Scott is asleep in his bed. My movements wake Pam, "Feeling any more rested? Having a baby drains every ounce of energy you have. I was surprised you lasted as long as you did. When Scotty screams again, you feed him from both sides. Make sure you burp him as you go along. When he wakes up again, since I'm still nursing, I'll feed him. We've got to get your energy back as fast as possible for whatever's ahead. Sleep till he cries." I turn over, and I'm gone.

When I wake to Scott's crying in the late afternoon, I almost feel normal. After feeding him, I take a quick shower to get ready for our planning session. Grandma Daisy brings me a huge plate of food which I down like I haven't eaten for months. My appetite's back to normal. I clean and bundle Scott up, and we head to the meeting. I almost don't recognize Agent Fowler; he's dressed in a full Western outfit from head to toe including dark sunglasses. I can't resist a comment, "Are you supposed to be undercover?"

He laughs, "At least from a distance I don't think you'd recognize me. You're looking good for someone who just gave birth yesterday. Glad your little guy made it here safe and sound... If this man is who I think he is, he knows who I am on sight. I would prefer that he didn't know I'm in town...Alright everyone, let's get the meeting started."

The Sheriff takes charge, "Terry, the two guys you talked to at the rest stop recognized you and Pam. When the ambulance pulled in and a man who looked like a doctor started asking concerned questions about a pregnant lady, they were quick to help. After the ambulance left burning rubber, the guys got to thinking that maybe you and Pam didn't want anyone to know where you were going, so they contacted me. The ambulance came roaring into Red Rock with the police escort and sirens blaring. They must know you've had your baby, but they are still hanging around town. They've traded their ambulance for a rental jeep to not be quite so conspicuous."

Agent Fowler raises his hand, "This murdering jerk prides himself on never leaving a witness to his atrocities. He eliminates babies and mothers, and it doesn't matter if it's before birth or after. Terry, I think you have wounded his pride. Now Sheriff, what's the plan to stop this perp?"

"There's a bedroom at the back of our house that has a window that you can step through to get in or out of the room. We never let any of our kids use it before they graduated from high school; it is too easy to sneak in or out. We set up three surveillance cameras in the room and several more outside, and we set up the command station next door. We already know they suspect Terry is here. They've been lying on the top of a low hill all afternoon with binoculars scouting out the ranch. What they don't know is that from the butte behind them, every move they make is being observed.

"When evening comes, we'll leave a lamp on and the curtains open. Terry will go into that room and put her sleeping baby in the crib. She'll open the window for fresh air and sing to her newborn infant. She'll then turn down the lamp, close and lock the window, and lie down on the bed. If they sneak up to the window in the night, we know we've baited the trap. The next night she will forget to close the window.

"When he sneaks into the room, we hope Terry can do her usual and get the monster to spill his guts. We will be ready to enter through both the door and the window in an instant…What do you think?"

I'm the first to respond, "Sounds okay except for the part about having Scott there."

"I need to clarify," the Sheriff says. "That bundle will be a carefully swaddled baby doll. Scotty will stay safely in Pam's arms in the family room." Pam looks like she is going to object. "I only want one of you in that room. It's too hard to protect both of you at the same time. Besides, I think Terry has some skills that you don't, and she is an FBI agent as well as a Deputy Sheriff. Pam closes her mouth. Terry, we'll give you an earpiece for tomorrow tonight, so you'll know what's happening. I don't think you'll be in there any longer than thirty minutes. Any questions? If not, dinner is served in the family room."

I don't know if I want to do this or not, but I don't think I have a choice. This maniac is going to be after me until he gets me, or I get him. I begin silently praying.

It's almost ten when I begin making my way to put this baby doll to bed. I can't believe how quickly they put together the surveillance room next to the bedroom. They gave me a quick tour after dinner. Three cameras were focused on everything in the bedroom and maybe five outside covering the whole side of the house and hill. They even had a night infrared camera focused on the window.

A lamp is on high when I walk into the room. It's on a small table next to the bed on the wall opposite the window and silhouettes me to anyone watching through from outside. I walk to the crib and lay my bundle down. I turn and walk to the bed and sit down. That was what the Sheriff scripted me to do, but that's not me as a new mother. Putting me into my part, I walk to the window and open it while speaking as if my baby can hear, "Scotty, it's a bit stuffy in here, I'll let in a little fresh air." I walk back to the crib and pick up my child. I cuddle him close talking nonsense even though he is supposed to be asleep. I lay down on my bed with him in my arms and sing to him. I am about to fall asleep when I hear three taps on the wall. That's my signal if there's a problem. I quickly stand and take the doll to the crib, "I better let you sleep before you're hungry again." I turn to leave and remember the window. I take three quick steps and slide the glass shut. I replace the wooden board that was cut to fit the window. Such a simple lock, but pretty much a failsafe. I lay back down on the bed and turn off the lamp. I wait for a count of fifty, slide to the floor, and crawl out of the room.

The Sheriff is waiting for me in the hall with his flashlight. "Did I make good bait?" I ask quietly.

He pulls me to a stand and guides me into the surveillance room, "Almost too good. Show her the infrared tape."

I gape in horror as I watch me in the room and another person outside the window. They are just standing to step through the window when I slam it shut. I had no idea they were even there. Now I have the real stuff for nightmares tonight.

Pam is feeding Scott when we get back to the family room, "Well, did you bait the trap well without me?"

Agent Fowler answers her, "She was such a convincing mother with her baby that she almost had company coming in the window. I don't think it was Forest, but I will bet it will be tomorrow night. We have security in place for the night. Everyone better get some sleep." I explain the whole thing to Pam as we make our way to our real bedroom. After tucking Scotty in, we have a long prayer before we crawl into bed.

Pam doesn't seem to be sleepy when she turns to face me, "Terry, how are you doing?"

I can feel Pam's concern for me, "Ok, I guess. That was a little scary tonight when I found out how close I came to having company."

"My question probably has more to do with Evan than this crazy doctor."

"Pam, you know me much too well. I'm really worried about him. I can't believe he hasn't even called to ask about the baby. I don't want to be a single parent. I love him so deeply, and I want him to be with me through eternity. I want to help him, but I can't if he won't let me. He didn't even say goodbye when he left…" Uncontrolled tears begin to spill.

Pam hugs me until we both fall asleep.

I feed Scotty both times when he wakes up in the night. Even with that, I'm up with the sun and working on my centering exercises. I'm feeling pretty good, but nowhere as strong as I have been. If I do have a confrontation, I must make leverage work to my advantage. The rest I'll leave in the Lord's hands.

This must be the longest day of my life. By mid-afternoon, everyone is climbing walls. We can't go outside or even look out a window. I'm amazed at the number of law enforcement individuals who are roaming around the house, inside and out. Taking care of Scotty is the only thing we do to pass the time. Scott's feedings take a little more time now. My milk has finally come in, and he can't drink it fast enough. He looks like he's been swimming every time. He needs to have a sponge bath and a change of clothes with each feeding. I become more and more withdrawn. I'm sure people think I'm worried about the confrontation this evening, but in reality, I'm praying harder and harder for Evan.

A commotion at the front door brings me back into the present. The Sheriff comes into the family room making a beeline for me, "Terry, why don't you let Daisy hold Scotty for a while? There's someone here that would like to talk to you." I look at him with concern. "I promise you it's safe." He takes Scotty and places him in Daisy's waiting arms. He then takes my hand and pulls me up out of my chair, "Come with me." We walk down the halls in silence until we come to a closed door.

He turns the knob to open the door, and I stare into the room. I scream and rush forward, "Evan." Before he can say anything, I throw my arms around his neck and cover his lips with the most passionate kiss I have ever given him. My heart sings with ecstasy as he instantly returns my passion.

Finally, he takes hold of my shoulders and pushes us apart. He peers deeply into my eyes, "Terry, can you ever forgive me for being such a fool?"

"Forgiven now and forever! Even I love you so much." I want to kiss him again, but he puts a finger on my lips.

"Are you angry with me?

"No, just extremely concerned. Most of my waking moments are in prayer that it will not take you seven years to come back to me and God."

"Seven years! I couldn't be without you for seven days. Why would you think it would take me seven years?"

"That's how long it took me to find God after my parents died."

He throws his arms around me again and holds me tight while I sob.

We spend the next hour catching each other up on the details of the last two days. Finally, he says, "If I ever start acting like I've slipped into another dimension, will you hit me over the head with your tennis racket? I am so sorry for the way I behaved. When I was younger, I would build scenarios in my head and then act on them like they were real life. It was kind of a get-my-way behavior. I want to be done with all that, but I think I'll need your help to do that."

"The Lord and I will help you in any way we can. One thing's for sure, I'll never let you leave so easy again. I think it's time for you to meet your son."

We stand, and he gives me another hug and kiss. He backs up with a shocked look on his face, "Terry, is your blouse wet?"

I look down horror-stricken. "I completely spaced out Scotty's feeding. I'll bet he's screaming his head off. Come on, let's go," I say grabbing him by the hand and rushing down the hall to the family room.

Everyone looks up when we rush in. All is tranquil and quiet except for a jabbering Tommy who is precariously balanced on Pam's lap while she is feeding Scotty under a blanket draped over her shoulder. Tommy is not happy to have someone eating his dinner.

The irony hits me, "Tommy is Scotty stealing your dinner?" He looks at me for an instant and then holds out his arms for me to pick him up. I pick him up. If I'm holding him at least my leaking milk won't be so obvious. I have underestimated this little bundle of energy. He begins trying to unbutton my blouse. I do quick reasoning, If Pam is nursing my baby, then I might as well feed hers. I'm so full of milk that I'd drown Scotty. I grab a blanket from the back of a chair and sit down with Tommy. The room is exploding in gales of laughter. I even join them; this is so utterly ridiculous.

Pam finishes long before I do. She gently places Scott in Evan's arms. I watch him gaze down at his son for the first time. With tears in his eyes, he brings Scotty up close to his face and touches him cheek to cheek. Scotty is going to change both of us. Still cradling Scott in his arms, he walks up to the Sheriff, "I'm going into the set-up tonight with Terry. This is something I must do!"

The Sheriff looks into his eyes for a long time, then whispers, "I know."

At 10:00 pm, we walk into the family room with a sleeping Scotty. There are now only five individuals in the room instead of twenty-five. Grandma Daisy stands and holds out her arms to take Scotty from me. Pam and Tom are on a couch with Tommy curled up and asleep on his father's lap, and Grandpa Sandy is sitting at the table reading. When Grandma Daisy has Scotty snug in her arms, she speaks to all of us, "When this is all over, I wish all of you would stay with us for another two weeks. I would love to spoil every one of you; especially these two little young ones."

"Oh Grandma, you have no idea how inviting that sounds."

"Terry, I still need to be on my way to the survival camp, but you could stay here, and I'll come back to pick you and Scotty up after the camp."

"Pam, I need to get back to the company, but you and Tommy could use Grandma's spoiling. I'll come back with Evan and drive you home."

Pam and I look at each other, "Let's do it." We both chorus in unison. But my thoughts go on. That is if we make it out alive from the trap we've set.

Evan is holding the swaddle-wrapped doll when we enter our supposed bedroom. I make comments about stale air in the room and move directly to open the window. We then go to the crib to lay the baby doll down. This time I hear the stalker coming in through the window. His voice turns us around, "Well, aren't you two the perfect caring parents of that freak of a baby."

I know I need to get this conversation going, but I would rather smash him into the floor. "Well, Dr. Twig you are not quite what I was expecting. You don't look much like a doctor." Evan slowly lets his arm drop from my shoulders and pushes me away from himself.

"Don't call me Twig. I am Dr. Forest, and I can say you are not what I was expecting. You look more like a model than a mother. I would think you would be happy to be rid of this child."

"I am happy to have my child and would be even happier to be rid of you. You seem to thrive on this baby killing. Tell me, just how many infants have you put in a grave, or is it too many to count?"

"I'm just clearing the world of misfits and freaks, but I remember every one of them. They are all thoroughly documented with every detail. I need to have all that information for reimbursement. It is my business, you understand. It saves the government millions."

"Do you keep records of the innocent mothers you've killed who have objected to your slaughter?"

"Of course, I keep track of everything, and I keep all of my records with me at all times." I thought he brought a medical bag with him through the window, but now I see it's a briefcase. He has set it down right behind him. "You know, you almost got away. If those guys at the rest stop hadn't recognized you, I never would have found you. No one gets away from me!"

"You're not really a doctor, are you?"

"Since you'll never be able to tell anyone, I admit that I'm not a doctor. I am a certified midwife, so I can deliver a baby.

A diploma from a highly credited university is so easy to get. Now it's time to tell you all goodbye." He carefully pulls a syringe out of his pocket and uncaps it. "One tiny drip of this under your skin and you enter eternal sleep. I usually do the baby first so the mother can watch, but in your case, I think I'll have to take care of you two first."

He smiles taunting us with his needle. Evan draws his attention, "Are you one of those freaky babies that didn't get annihilated? At 5'6" you didn't grow to be much of a man." Twig is now focused with rage on Evan. I sure hope he knows what he's doing. "What's the matter Twiggy, got cold feet. Not the same facing a man as a hysterical mother trying to protect her newborn."

Twig screams and rushes with his needle toward my husband. Evan seems unphased. He waits until the last second and jumps for an aerial kick which he solidly plants in the middle of Twig's chest. At the same time, the fake doctor pushes the needle into Evan's ankle. Twig is knocked backward getting tangled in his briefcase which causes him to fall straight back with his neck landing on the edge of the bedside table. The table shatters, but I also think I hear bones crack. Twig is screaming above all the commotion as the room fills with law enforcement men. I rush to Evan who is sitting on the floor. Agent Flower gets there at the same time.

Evan reaches for the syringe, "I've got to get that thing out of my ankle. I think the needle is wedged into the joints and my foot won't move."

Fowler grabs his hand, "Don't touch it. It's got fingerprints on it." He yells for a team member to bring an evidence bag. I'm waiting for Evan to die any moment. Instead, he reaches down and pulls up his pant leg. The syringe has gone through his sock and is stuck in his prosthetic foot. I throw my arms around his neck and kiss him while I'm crying and laughing at the same time.

Once the needle is taken out, Evan can move his foot again. The three of us stand and turn our attention towards our attacker. He is surrounded by law officers. At Agent Fowler's command, a passageway opens, and we move towards a sprawled-out Twig. He is on his back with his head supported by the shattered nightstand. We finally move into his field of vision. "Fowler, arrest those two. He just tried to kill me!"

"Cool it! Bruce. You've just won the Academy Award for Killer of the Year. We have it all recorded."

Twig is beginning to realize he has been set up, "You can't prove a thing. I have never seen these people before. I was just trying to help this woman with her baby, and I am here at her request."

"You picked the wrong woman to force an abortion upon. You have been stalking an FBI agent for the last six months."

His eyes shift to me, "You're a Fed? I don't believe it."

I lift my pant leg and remove my ID from my sock. I open it to show my picture and badge, holding it ten inches from his face. He spits at it. He is then very agitated, "I'll kill you if it's the last thing I do. No woman has ever outsmarted me." His agitation increases, and he stares at his hand. "Why won't my hand reach into my pocket for my other syringe?" Then he notices Evan, "And why aren't you dead? I know that venom works. I just used it on Mike thirty minutes ago." Evan lifts his pant leg to reveal his prosthesis. "I can't believe this. I'm taken out by a one-legged man. What did you do to me? I don't seem to be able to move at all."

"I only kicked you in the chest. You got all tangled up by all those babies and mothers you've murdered when you tripped over your briefcase. Your neck collided with the nightstand, and I think you severed your spinal cord. I believe you've done the last thing you will ever do…Agent Fowler, do you need us anymore? We would like to get back to our son. I think it's time for Terry to feed him."

He waves us out of the room, "Go, I'll get statements from you tomorrow." We head back to the family room and spend the next hour reliving our experience with Tom and Pam and with Grandpa Sanda and Grandma Daisy.

This has probably been the most relaxing time I have ever spent. Evan and Tom left the day after the capture of my stalker. They said they would be back in two weeks to bring us home. Evan also told me that he had scheduled the baby blessing in church for three Sundays from now. I am so thankful to have my old Evan back.

The more time I spend with Scott the more I cherish every moment. Grandma Daisy taught me how to use a baby wrap carrier, so I could have both hands free. We spend time together at the piano and hours of walking through the Red Rock Canyons. Pam and Tommy did some walking with us. Sometimes he walked, but most of the time he rode in his carrier. Pam spent time with Grandma Daisy learning about midwifery. She went with Grandma on three deliveries. Grandma thinks that with her paramedic training, Pam would make an excellent midwife. I can tell she is thinking about it. She certainly has my vote. While she learned about delivering babies, I learned how to be a mother.

Scotty looks so grown up in the blessing outfit Grandma Daisy made for him. Our chapel is overflowing with people mainly because of how many we invited to attend Scott's blessing. The Sheriff and his wife from Red Rock even flew up in the helicopter along with his parents. I've adopted them as my grandparents. Evan's blessing is on the long side but is everything Scotty needs to succeed in this life. I am glad that he included us as parents to have the inspiration to teach him and keep him safe.

The majority of the congregation follow us to Tom and Pam's ranch for a luncheon. I'm not ready to let Scotty be passed from person to person, so I keep him close to me in his baby wrap carrier. As I sit watching the guests, I finally feel life is where it should be. Everyone that I care about is here except Dawn and Solomon, and Evan's mother moved in with us yesterday. I'm brought out of my musing when I realize my cell phone is ringing. I'm not surprised to see it's Dawn on the caller ID, "Hi Dawn. How's everything?"

"Terry, I'm so, so sorry… The last Derksin brother torched the Concert Hall, and it burned to the ground last night."

# CHAPTER 16

"**N**o, no, no! This can't be happening. I have too many plans!" I yell and then I crumble on the sofa and sob.

I don't even realize when Pam takes the phone out of my hand, "Dawn, I've put you on speaker. Will you tell us what you said to Terry?"

"I guess the direct approach was not the best idea. The last Derksin brother torched the concert hall last night. Can you get Terry calmed down enough that so I can tell her all is not lost?"

Pam moves to stand in front of me, "Terry, Terry" she yells. I finally lift my head to stare at her. "Terry, Dawn has more to tell you. Bring some of those exploding emotions under control. Dawn is on speaker so all of us can hear."

She hands me back the phone and I speak with a trembling voice, "Dawn, I'm sorry. I've been on a wild roller coaster ride the last few weeks, and I'm not very settled. Tell us what happened."

"Sol and I have gone to the Hall every day to work on the renovation. We moved everything out of the office to our apartment. While going through all the paperwork, I found the original company that built Sea-Side. It is now owned by the great-grandson of the original architect. I have been working with Terance Udall, the owner and architect, on our restoration. I called him after the fire, and he said that it may be more of a blessing than a curse. It will cost you less to start from scratch on solid land than to do the renovation. He also said that he has studied the phenomenal acoustics in the building for years and has finally been able to replicate the beautiful sound. I just need your okay to move the site a hundred yards closer to the mountain and a thumbs up to begin construction. Oh, one more thing. Can they quarry the stone from the mountain for the walls of all the buildings?"

"Dawn are you sure we have enough money?"

"Terry, I think we have more than enough money. We have the money from Sol's gold, the insurance money, and the hidden money."

"What are you talking about? What insurance money and what hidden money?"

"You can't believe everything that's happened in the last twenty-four hours. When I was going through the files, I found a new insurance policy for the Sea-Side. It made it pretty obvious that arson had been planned for some time. The policy was for one million dollars, and if something was to destroy the hall, the current owner was to receive the money. I think

Grandpa Dirksen was scheming to move into the ownership position. I believe you are now the current owner and beneficiary."

"The afternoon before the fire, Sol wanted to go back into the catacombs and to do some more exploring. Sol is amazing down there. He remembers every twist and turn and found three more exits or entrances. He felt like there was one more area he hadn't gone into, so I with my flashlight, and Sol with his cane made our way back into the tunnels. He was right. We found a room with a locked door which he easily pushed in. It was kind of a storage room for a very old safe.

"When Sol explored it with his hands he laughed and said he could open it. It was the same safe his father had. His father would bring home his cashed paycheck and put the money in his safe. He would give very little money to Sol's mother. Said she needed to earn her own money to feed her kids. After he left to go get drunk, she would take Sol to the safe, and he would put his ear on it and could hear the tumblers fall. His mom would take enough cash to run the family and leave his dad enough to get drunk once a month. Sol opened our safe in less than a minute. It was full of gold bars. We spent the rest of the night moving the gold to our apartment. We went out a different exit on our last trip and Sol said that he could smell fireworks. I shined my light around and found some sticks of dynamite attached to the wood over our heads. We were going to alert the Police when we got to our apartment, but by then it was too late."

"Dawn, you and Sol could have been killed. If anything would have happened to you, I could never forgive myself. This is turning into a hideous nightmare." My mind begins to swirl with all the possible things that could devastate my family and friends. Evan slips down to sit beside me putting his arm around my shoulders.

Pam kneels in front of me, "Terry, you are letting your mind build scenarios that have never happened. What you should be doing is thanking the Lord for His protective care of Dawn and Sol. You should also be thanking Him for making the Sea-Side campus a real possibility. The sound might not be as magical, but it will be concert quality, and there will be a school to teach the blind. Smothers your fears with thankfulness and faith."

I look at Pam with tears running down my cheeks, "Oh Pam, you are so right. I don't know what's happening to me. I feel like an emotional basket case."

Pam laughs out loud, "Terry, you just had a baby. That by itself stretches any mother's emotional web. You had a very intense abnormal delivery and unusual emotionally impacting postpartum activities. I'm surprised you are functioning as well as you are."

Evan directs his next comments toward Dawn and the phone, "What about that Derksen jerk? Is he behind bars?"

"That's the saddest part of it all. When the fireworks went off, we turned around and headed back to Sea-Side. It was a roaring blaze when we got there. There was a young boy about eight years of age crying hysterically in the parking lot. He just kept screaming that he had killed his dad and was going to be locked in the basement and never get out.

"The police and the fire department arrived at the same time. All they could do was watch as the flames soared fifty feet into the sky. Sol was holding the sobbing child, and I was trying to calm him down to make sense of what he was saying. From out of nowhere appeared a small shabbily dressed unkempt woman. She held out her arms to the boy and he lunged for her. Sol held on to him enough that the boy didn't knock the woman over. The Police Chief had worked his way over to our trauma corner. He was listening intently to what the boy was trying to say. After more rambling and crying from the boy, the woman turned to look at the Chief.

"She told the Chief that her husband was an arsonist. Thinking he was protecting himself, he would always make their son push the button to set off the explosions. That way he could never be convicted of arson. He would set the explosives and then return to Ronny and make him push the button. When they were leaving early that morning, she heard him tell Ronny that when the alarm went off, he was to push the button even if he was not there. No matter what, he was to push the button when the alarm rang, or Ron would die in the closet in the basement.

"The alarm went off and he pushed the button to strike the explosion. Ronny thinks he has killed his father, but at the same time thinks he is going to be beaten and thrown in the cellar closet like so many times before. This was the wife and son of the last Derksen.

"When the fire was finally put out, they found Derksen's body on the floor at one of the exits of the catacombs just inside the door. The explosion jarred loose a piece of timber which fell blocking the door. It might take a while, but with the right kind of help the mother and child are finally free to live normal lives." There is a long silence as no one knows what to say.

Finally, Dawn speaks again, "Terry, I have something else for you to consider… Terance knows that most of your love for Sea-Side comes from the phenomenal acoustics it had. He wants to convince you that he can duplicate that in your new building. He has just finished a concert hall on the West Coast in Southern California. They are getting ready for a grand opening. He has talked to the owner, and he is more than willing to offer you and your ensemble a pre-opening venue so you can immerse yourself in the incredible sound. Terance is even willing to fly you and your group out there at his expense. Making you a satisfied customer is the best advertising he could ever get. Your concert would need to be during the last week of June. Think about it and let me know in the next couple of days."

"I've probably tied up your baby blessing party long enough. Wish we were there. Love you all."

The line goes dead, and all eyes are drilling straight through me. I don't know what to say. As my head clears a little, I blurt out, "Give me a day to digest everything that's happened."

Pam isn't about to let it drop, "Terry, I want to do the concert."

I look around and see everyone in my group giving me a thumbs up. Grandma Timpson, who is holding Scott, even throws up her thumb. Looking at Scottie, I open my mouth, "What about the babies? Isn't it dangerous for them?"

Tom laughingly answers, "Terry, you were on your first survival trip when you were three weeks old. You never left Mom's side until you could crawl. You went to every lesson, every class, and every concert. If you want your child to learn what you know, they need to be with you doing your thing until they can do their own thing. Why do you think I'm an electrical engineer?"

"That's why I came to live with you and Evan, Terry. I would love to go to your concert and take care of Scottie behind the stage while you dazzle your audience," Grandma Timpson says. Grandpa and Grandma Martin voice the same assurance for Tommy.

I look around at all the hopeful faces, "OK, that gives me three weeks to put life back together. I think we can make this work." The clapping and yelling startle both Scottie and Tommy into shrieking screams. I think—this will give us a warm-up for going back to Carnegie in August for the Oratorio Competition. I move quickly to the piano and begin playing, both boys instantly calm.

Not long after we started our redeye flight to the West Coast, everyone, including the babies, appeared to be sleeping. I'm so full of anxiety that I could never sleep. Instead, I close my eyes and begin pleading with my Heavenly Father for peace. About midway through the trip, a calm for the infants settles over me, but I still have a nagging apprehension. I decide it must be for the new concert hall. I want so badly for it to have the acoustics of the burned Sea-Side Hall, but fear that would never be possible. I continue my prayer until I finally doze off. I wake in time to feed and change Scott before we land.

A minibus takes my entourage to our hotel and a private car takes me and my luggage directly to the concert hall. I need to make friends with the stage crew, the sound crew, and the piano, and I only have about six hours to do that. When we arrive, I am amazed at the massive domed structure. It does have similarities to Sea-Side and is a beautiful building. The manager opens my car door to greet me then escorts me up the stairs to the front doors. We walk through the foyer and onto the main floor of the hall. I stand staring in awe. It is a magnificent arena.

I am jolted out of my stupor by a familiar voice, "Good morning, Terry!" I look all around and finally find Dawn standing by Sol and another man at the back of the stage. That greeting ultimately makes its full impact on me. She isn't using a mic, and I can hear her loud and clear. The acoustics are everything she said they would be. I want to run to the piano they are standing by, but I guess I need to have some decorum. The manager escorts me through the empty hall to the stage.

I give Dawn and Sol hugs. Dawn turns to the man standing beside her, "Terry, I'd like you to meet Terrance Udall, the architect and builder of this magnificent building."

He reached for my hand, "It is such an honor to finally meet you. I can't wait to hear you play in this hall."

I throw my burning question at him, "Can you make the new Sea-Side have the same acoustics that this building has?"

"The sound will be better than this building. We are using stone instead of wood and interior building materials for the walls. With the bare stone on the inside, it will not absorb as much sound, so the acoustics will be tighter. Are you ready to test out your piano? I'm ready to hear you play."

When I move to the piano, the stage crew moves to surround me. They lift the lid, turn on the switch, and motion for me to sit. I play a few get-acquainted notes and scowl. It is horribly out of tune. I stand and reach for the red tuning button. Another hand beats me to it. "The installers said it would take several playing attempts to get it tuned properly. It was just delivered this morning, and your hands are the first to touch the keys," the head of the stage crew says.

I try again and again to work my way up the keyboard. Each time I get a little further before it needs to be retuned. When we reach that point, I decide to play music that makes jarring percussion. Beethoven's "Hammerklavier" seems like the perfect piece. I get five minutes before we retune again. This time I almost get to the end before we push the tuning key. I decide to give it and me a break.

Terance moves to the piano, "Dr. Timpson you are even better than Solomon said you were. Your concert tonight will be the best to ever play in this building. The only one that will be better is the one you play opening night in your concert hall at Sea-Side. I think we should be ready to do that in June." I look at him with tears in my eyes; I can't even speak. I just nod my head.

I take a deep breath and address the sound booth. We spend the rest of the time outlining the program and the sound needs. I don't know how much mixing the numbers will need, but the sound crew assures me they will stay on top of things every minute. They will only augment the natural sound when necessary.

Four hours later, Scotty arrives with Evan and Grandma Timpson. He is more than ready to eat. After his feeding, I decide to change into my concert clothes. I'm not sure why, but I feel impressed to dress in my long black stretch pants and shirt under my concert attire. I even stuff a few packets of braided paracord into my pants pockets.

Coming out through the lounge door, I almost run into Arundel. Before she can speak, I ask, "How are you coming on your accompaniment for the oratorio music?"

"It's ready to go. Do we have time that you can listen to it?"

I hand Scotty off to Grandma T, and head toward the piano, "No. Come and play it with me right now. Are you playing high or low?"

She answers as she sits in front of the bottom of the keyboard. I begin to play, and she comes in five measures later. The singers recognize their music and quickly begin moving into place while singing. Pam is the last to move into place with a blanket draped over her shoulder and Tommy in her arms. The singing falters slightly as the group struggles to contain their laughter. Finally, we're all working smoothly together.

When we finish, I ask the group, "What do you think about adding Arundel's accompaniment to the song?" They respond with clapping, shouts, and cheers.

Pam holds her hand up for silence, "I think it's a masterful addition. No pun intended. Arundel, it's fantastic. You must come to Carnegie with us in August. I had no idea you two were scheming together." Everyone seconds the invitation with more clapping and praising.

I hold up my hand for attention. We talk through the order of the night and then walk everyone on and off stage in their order. We finish as the doors are opened and guests begin finding seats. I'm blown away that the seats quickly fill. I didn't expect any audience at all. There hasn't been time for much publicity. We all move off stage, and my Knights of Ebony move on. When Sol finishes his first number, there are no empty seats, and no one is sitting in their seat when they give him a thunderous ovation as he ends. I am so proud of all my Knights; they could appear on any concert stage.

Following the preshow I move onto the stage to the mic to officially begin our concert. I welcome the audience and give a little introduction of our group and our affiliation with Augustine University. I also publicly applaud Tarence Udall for this magnificent structure. I even have him come onto the stage to take a bow. I move to the piano, push the button one last time, and begin playing my medley of the great composers to officially begin our concert.

I play for about thirty minutes and turn the stage over to Sol and Allen for their piano competition. I'm standing offstage watching as Arundel moves to stand beside me. She whispers, "Doctor Timpson, I want you to know how much I appreciate working with you. I love having you as my mentor in so many ways. You are so beautiful, and you don't have to wear revealing clothes to enhance your beauty. No strapless gown concert pianist could ever hold a candle to you. I so want to emulate your values. Thank you for being my preceptor and my friend." I turn to face her with tears in my eyes and give her a giant hug. I can't get out any words.

She changes the subject, "Do you think your mother will join us for 'Moonlight' tonight? I love it when she does that."

I swallow hard to be able to speak, "It would be so exciting if she would, but I never know. I hope you're okay with doing it before the final number. It just felt like the Oratorio number should be last."

"I totally agree with you. That is such a powerful piece of music that Mrs. Masters has written. It deserves to be last. I'm more than excited to be part of it." Following the guys, the Master's Touch moves onto the stage for two numbers. I then play two of my own compositions and Arundel, Mom and I play 'Moonlight'. The audience is ecstatic and mystified. Arundel and I stay at the piano while my singers move back into place. I've had this uneasy feeling all evening that something in this concert feels missing. I look at everything once again. They look so professional in their long white evening gowns and black tuxes as they move into place. Dawn stands with her arm holding on to Sol on the edge of the group as does Cindy linked up with AJ. Everything looks fine, but it doesn't feel fine.

I look at Pam for her nod and then at Arundel for hers. I say a quick silent prayer and begin. The four hands begin exactly on cue, and we are off. This is by far Pam's best piece, and in this hall, it sounds celestial. Everything is building toward the grand finally. I can hardly wait to hear it ring in this building when we end. It will be heavenly! We only have eight measures to go when I feel something hard in my back, a hand on my arm, and a voice yelling, "Stop!" Everyone is stunned into silence.

"This is a gun in your back. You are coming with us, Dr. Timpson. If anyone moves or says a word my partner will shoot them. On your feet lady. If you want to see her again, it will cost you three million dollars."

They start to lift me, and I yell, "Pam, feed Fowler, my watchdog." The next thing I feel is something crashing down on my head, and I'm out cold.

I'm being carried when my consciousness returns. I decide I'll live longer if I pretend to still be out. I can feel that I'm being hauled down the stairs, I hear a car door open, and I'm thrown into the back seat. I feel something thrown over me and hear a man say, "Cover her up with the blanket. We may have to stop at a few traffic lights, and we don't want any curious eyes in other cars to see her."

Once we start moving, I hear a different voice, "That was the easiest hijacking we've done so far. It was a piece of cake with no security. It was a mistake I'm sure they won't make again." That's it. That's what didn't feel right. There were no security guards. Wow, did I ever blow that one. I think I'll keep playing dead for a while. At least that's what the Spirit's prompting me to do. I begin with the one thing I can do; I pray. I plead with my Father in Heaven to help me not build unreal scenarios in my head that haven't happened yet. Made-up thoughts will send me into a panic attack, and that's the last thing I need right now. I must be able to listen to the inspiration from the Holy Ghost.

I think we've been traveling for about fifteen minutes and have stopped at several traffic lights when I begin to smell the ocean. I make sure the blanket is over my head and that I'm holding onto it. I'm picked up again and dumped not so gently onto plastic-covered seats. From the rocking motion, I'm guessing that I'm on a boat. That guess becomes fact when the engine roars to life and we begin to move. We go slowly at first then the boat jumps to full throttle. We are making a beeline for someplace. I'm sure glad I hung onto this blanket, it's quite chilly out here.

After about a half hour, we begin slowing and finally, the engine is cut. Now I can hear conversations. The man that hit me on the head laughs, "I wonder how the princess is going to like her castle."

The bigger deeper voice asks, "Are you going to ruff her up and get her scared before we leave her stranded?"

"Naw, they're no fun if they're not kicking and screaming. She'll be scared enough when she wakes up and finds herself on a platform in the middle of the ocean. Leave her with that sack of coconuts. If she's smart, she'll figure out how to crack them and get a little to drink and eat. Lift her onto the platform. The water is just at the right level."

A big voice booms out, "I don't see why you don't kill her now."

"Jake, use your head. We must have her alive to show a video to the family with her pleading to be ransomed. After we make the video, she's my toy, and then she's shark bait. We'll be back in twenty-four hours for the next high tide at night." I'm lifted and shoved onto a wooden floor. I make moaning sounds so they will know I'm still alive and coming too. I lift the blanket from my head and watch the boat quickly disappear into the night.

I quickly shift my position to get my cell phone out of my stretch pants. My 'castle' sways violently, and I hold my breath. This structure is anything but stable. Moving much slower, I retrieve my phone. I doubt there is any signal out here, but I do have a flashlight. Chills run up my spine as I take in the water six inches below my sheet of plywood. I am literally on a plywood island attached to four telephone-looking poles. There is another sheet of wood at the top of the poles. I'm guessing it might be for shade, either that or the tide gets extremely high. I turn my attention back to my phone. I punch in Evan's number but see the no service bar instead.

I'm debating what to do next when my cell rings. I look at it mystified. Cautiously I answer it, "Hello?"

"Terry, this is Agent Fowler. Are you okay?"

A surge of hope exploded in my body. The words fly out of my mouth, "I have never been so glad to hear your voice. I'm alive and unharmed except for the bump on my head from the kidnapper's gun." My brain slowly begins to engage, "If I have no service, how can you call me?"

"I have an FBI satellite phone. I can call anyone anywhere even if they have no service. We've been tracking you since you left the concert hall. Thanks for keeping your badge on you. Your message to Pam was brilliant, but sorry it gave you a bump on the head."

"Passing out probably saved my life and that of many others. I was only out for maybe two minutes, but I played dead until they dumped me on this board in the middle of the ocean. However, I did learn a great deal."

"For your information, you are on a tidal island about five miles from the Southern California shore. You are at high tide now and it's turning to go out. It will be low tide about gray dawn. The small island you're on will be above the water line. Using the satellite mapping and tracking system, we could tell you were being transported. We tracked your car ride and your boat ride. When the lights of the boat moved and you didn't, we guessed that they had stashed you on the island. I'm so thankful it was above the water. I prayed that you were alone when I made the call. We can get a helicopter with a drop line out there to pick you up in a couple of hours. I'm sure you're ready to leave."

"I'm not sure that's the best plan, Agent Fowler. I'm not their first victim. I know there's been at least two before me and maybe more. They move around checking weak security at performing venues. When they find a place with a good performer scheduled, they move on to the stage while the show is in progress and walk off with the star. They threaten to shoot anyone who makes a sound or moves to help. They are silent for 24 hours and then make a video of the hostage pleading to be helped. Once the video is aired to the financial target, the hostage suffers a hideous death and becomes shark bait right under my floor. If I leave, it may take many more deaths to catch them. They will be back tonight at high tide again."

"What are you suggesting, Terry? We can always bring in the Coast Guard, but that doesn't guarantee your safety."

"I need to be able to see this place in the light. Call me back about two hours after sunrise. The tide will be turning again. Will you tell my family that I'm, okay? When they get contacted for the ransom money, they need to play along but give them nothing. They have no plans to return me."

# CHAPTER 17

I decide that the best use of my time would be to get some sleep. I get about two hours' worth when I wake up soaking wet. I have milk dripping everywhere. Tears roll down my cheeks as I think about Scottie not getting his dinner or night feeding. No that's not right; he's getting dinner just not from me. Maybe we should never have come here. While I contemplate that, I try to express milk. I'm not very good at it, but it does relieve some pressure. Scott does such a good job of taking it all. I've never even needed to pump. He has never been away from me before. I take turns sleeping and trying to expel milk. I've also pondered my question about being here. I did have a positive confirmation that we should do this concert, and the Spirit has been guiding me. The Lord must want me here to thwart these evil thugs. I just pray He'll get me back to Evan and Scottie soon.

Even in the first gray light of morning, I can tell I'm on an island, and poles are sticking up out of the ground all over. They are all 4 to 6 inches in diameter and leaning in every direction. My perch is the only recent construction anywhere. When the water is down to a foot in depth, I use my pants/skirt like an electrician's sling and walk backward down one of the poles. I have what's left of the blanket wrapped around my neck and shoulders. I cut two big squares out of it for makeshift shoes. Piano slippers are hardly what you want to walk on coral with. It is now light to see through the shallow water. There are rocks, coral, and sand along with more of the long poles.

I look at my sea-house. A picture begins to paint itself in my mind. I push hard against one of the standing poles and it sways dangerously. I walk over to one of the solitary leaning poles and push on it. I can feel it give. I push hard and don't let up until it's on its way to the water. I hold my breath. It goes under the water, and then it bobs to the surface. Yes, yes, yes, I think this is going to work. I slosh back to my platform and begin pushing it back and forth. It doesn't take too many back and forths' to timber the whole thing. I couldn't be more excited with the way it fell. The eight-foot length of the plywood stayed attached to two poles at the corners and now lays flat on top of the timbers. I have the beginnings of my raft.

The roof piece of plywood broke completely free from the poles. I float it over and push it onto the poles with the first piece of flooring. I move the other poles one at a time to the raft and push them under far enough that they stick out a foot on the other side of the raft. I leave the rest of the length to stick out as far as it will go. I begin harvesting more poles. The tide is now out far enough that I can't float them anymore. I just leave them where they fall until the tide starts coming in again. When I'm finished, I should have a giant pinwheel with my eight-foot square raft in the middle.

Right on schedule, my phone rings, "Hi Agent Fowler. I think I have a plan."

"Terry, you are amazing. With it being light we have been zoomed in on you with our satellite camera all morning. You so think out of the box. They can't get close to you in their boat unless they ram in between two spokes."

"Got that covered. I'm going to run paracord at the end of each spoke to the next spoke. If they try to ram me, they will only succeed in pushing my raft out to sea. They might shoot me if they can see me. These poles are so loaded with creosote that I can turn every inch of my skin black. You know the route they used to go and come. Get Coast Guard vessels surrounding this area but leave the nappers a path to me. Once the kidnappers are inside the perimeter have the CG tighten their circle. I plan to disable their boat. Once disabled the authorities can move in and pick them up. Just so you're aware there's blood all over the wood on my raft. You might want samples. Once the crooks are secure, you can drop me a line and get me back to my baby and my husband."

"It sounds great. What can I do for you? Do you want me to send a team down there? Do you want weapons?"

"No more people! It's too easy for someone to get hurt. No weapons. What I desperately need is water and food. I'm getting dehydrated, and I can't drink this salt water."

"I'll be there with a drop in thirty minutes. I'll send a package down on a line. I'm going to include an FBI phone in that drop. I've decided that you of all people need to have one. It has all the features of an iPhone plus satellite capabilities, and it's waterproof. When they start talking to you, turn on the record feature. It even records underwater."

"It would make my plan a little easier if I had a mask, snorkel, and fins. They need to be all black with nothing on them that reflects light."

"Considerate it done, Terry. I'll see you within an hour. If you run into any kind of trouble and want a quick lift out, just let me know."

I say thanks, but I think the line is already dead. I'll just relax for a few more minutes, then float the rest of my logs into position. It doesn't take too long until my raft is floating two feet above the sand and rocks. It finally hits me that if I don't anchor it to the bottom, I'll float away. I tie a length of paracord to one of the waterlogged submerged poles and tie it to the raft. By the time we reach high tide, I have eight to ten feet of water below me, and I'm enjoying my hoagie and a gallon of water.

I use my new phone to call Evan. I assure him I'm ok, and He assures me that Scott is being well taken care of. I even say 'Hi' to Mom Timpson. Next. I call Pam and Tom. Pam and I share a laugh over the gift she put in my care package. It's funny but oh so needed. Now I can pump all the milk I need to. At the next low tide, I make bolas. If they can catch birds, they should be able to catch people and boats, I hope. Slowly the sun sinks below orange clouds and dark moves in. I have one more communication with Agent Fowler, and I think we're set. My showing skin is smeared in black creosote, and my swimming gear is adjusted. I wrap up in what's left of the blanket and try to rest. It's 2:00 am when I hear the boat heading in my direction. I don my gear and slip into the water.

I'm guessing they are quite puzzled by what they see. There are still a few standing poles, but their prison and prisoner are missing. They shine their spotlight around until they spot the raft. The boat inches slowly toward the strange-looking creation. When they are at the edge of the spokes, they kill the engine. I am on the other side of the raft from them and out at the end of a spoke. I stay low behind a pole.

I'm not surprised when they call out to me, "Dr. Timpson, we've come to take you home. Come to the boat." How dumb do they think I am? The only home they want to put me in is the one in Heaven.

I do, however, need to let them know I'm here. "The only home you want to put me in is a watery grave. No, thank you." I sink below the surface and swim hard toward the boat. I surface by the end of one of the poles halfway to my goal. I have tied the end of a paracord onto this pole. It goes all the way under the raft to the pole on the far side. I yank it back and forth to make the pants of my concert dress move in the water. I hear instant gunfire. I must be very careful how I move. From the next pole, I remove a bola and swim with my snorkel tip just out of the water toward the boat. I come up by the motor. I take my cords with rocks attached and wind them around the propeller. I then dive and swim deep in the opposite direction of the boat and raft. I'm so glad I have the flippers on because when I surface, I'm out of range of their spotlight.

But not so far that I can't hear what they're saying, "She's got to be out there somewhere. Let's just ram that raft and leave her to the sharks." They start the engine and then engage the prop. It makes a brutal sound of screeching metal, but nothing moves.

I punch the speed dial for Agent Fowler, "They're all yours. Send in the Coast Guard and come get me. I'm in the water about 50 yards west of the boat and raft. When you get close, I'll flash my light."

The Coast Guard gets there before my ride comes. The gang fires shots at them and then changes tactics. "Sorry officers, we thought you were pirates coming to rob us. We're stranded. Can you help us? Something happened to our engine."

I laugh at the Guard's reply, "You are under arrest for kidnapping and murder. You should have never taken an FBI agent, especially that one."

"She's a Fed?" I can't hear the reply because the helicopter is too close. I start flashing my light.

I'm whisked out of the water to a sandy beach. After depositing me on the shore the chopper sets down for me to board. Agent Fowler opens the door and stares at me, "Are you sure you're my agent? You look more like an alien."

"I feel more like an Eskimo after that breezy ride in wet clothes. Do you have a blanket?" He laughs and helps me into my ride. Thankfully there is a blanket, and it's warm inside. He puts a mirror in front of my face while I'm snuggling in. With my face smeared black and my wet hair in pigtails, I am unrecognizable.

Taking out his phone he snaps a picture, "Terry, you are going to be our undercover poster child."

We both laugh then I get serious, "That little island is a literal graveyard. There are bones and bone shards scattered everywhere. While I was swimming with my mask on, I saw a leg bone with a foot attached caught in the crack of a rock. I decided I didn't want to find anything else."

"Terry, I'm so sorry you had to go through all of this, but extremely thankful that you put an end to these insane criminals. We did a computer search for matching MOs. We found ten kidnappings of performers in Southern California where ransom was paid but were never found alive. The Coast Guard picked up the plywood you told us about. We'll send a whole team of divers out there to pick up everything they can find... What can we do for you?"

I say with urgency, "Get me back to my family as fast as you can!" I pause thinking, "Find out what's the best and fastest way to get this creosote off my skin."

He takes out his phone and, in a few minutes, says, "Alcohol. We'll have some waiting at your hotel. But we'd like to get you checked out at a hospital first."

"I look at him with fire in my eyes, "I need my baby now, and he needs me."

"That's what we thought you'd say. We'll land at the helipad on the top of your hotel." The copilot hands me a small bottle of alcohol and gauze pads from the first aid kit. I spend the rest of the ride talking and washing my face while Fowler records every detail of my experience.

I'm irritated when the elevator doesn't stop at my floor. Fowler smiles, "All the people who want to greet you and make sure you're alive won't fit into your room. We're going to one of the conference rooms. This is just your entourage. We'll hold the press until you're cleaned up looking like a concert pianist. We don't want to broadcast that you are also an FBI agent." I didn't even think about the press.

Agent Fowler opens the door, and I walk into cheers and clapping mingled with tears. I'm so full of gratitude to my Heavenly Father for bringing me back to my family, I am speechless and overflowing with tears of my own. Terance is the first one to get to me, "Dr. Timpson, I am so sorry. I never should have brought you here."

I cut him off, "Terance, I'll get back to you."

At that instant, the room is filled with the shrillest loudest scream I have ever heard. The whole room is stunned into silence as the scream continues. The crowd parts and Evan is running toward me with a protesting Scottie in his arms. I give Evan a quick kiss and reach for my baby. He starts to nuzzle, and Pam whispers in my ear, "There's a chair behind you." As I'm sitting, she throws a hotel blanket over me and Scott and ties the corners behind my neck. Bless her for knowing my every need. When he latches on, I breathe a huge sigh of relief. I never thought I would be grateful for this agonizing moment.

No one has said a word. I look around at the expectant faces and relax. With Evan's hand on my shoulder, I am at peace. I begin with first things first. "Thank you all for your constant prayers…Terance, where are you?" He moves to stand in front of me. "Terance, you did absolutely the right thing. This whole experience was heaven-directed. Before we left, I knew that I was supposed to come. I just didn't know why. I loved the acoustics and want the same sound in Sea-Side…What you and everyone else doesn't know is that the kidnapping was originally planned for the next week at the grand opening. If I had not come, that performer would have been kidnapped and killed just like the ten previous ones along with stage and security workers at each venue. The gang's boss opted to change their plans at the last minute thinking they were getting a bigger fish. The main boss even decided he would step in and take charge of this big one. They would be getting millions instead of thousands. My bump on the head was even part of the plan. It slowed me down so I could listen to directions from the Spirit who told me to play dead. I was only out for a couple of minutes, but by seeming to be unconscious I learned about the whole gang and their operation. They even took me to their special cage without harming me. They made the mistake of leaving me alone, and the rest is history. If I hadn't been knocked out for those two minutes, I probably would have fought. Many of you would have joined me and would have been shot or killed. As it is, the Lord watched over all of us." I look down, "Even you Scottie." I answer their questions until they have the whole picture, and Scottie is satisfied and has fallen asleep. I look back at my music family, "Let's go home."

Flights going home always feel so relaxing. The seatbelt sign has just turned off and Evan situates himself to look at me. "Terry, I was behind stage holding Scott when those thugs stopped the last number. When I saw that bozo carrying your lifeless body down the stairs to go out the door, I thought my heart would explode. I tried to move, but my feet were nailed to the floor. When my brain started working, I knew I couldn't move with Scott in my arms. I started praying and surprisingly was filled with assurance that you were okay. I have never experienced so many powerful, diverse feelings in a matter of seconds. The thing I did realize is that I would never make it through this life without you and Scott." He has tears rolling down his cheeks as he leans over and kisses me.

When he finishes, I kiss him back. I so love this man of mine. I then voice a thought I had while I was waiting on my ocean perch, "Evan, you know we have our first anniversary coming up and we both have the two weeks in the middle of

July open. I do owe you a second honeymoon survival trip. Where do you want to go?"

"Why do you owe me a second honeymoon survival trip...Oh, I remember, the bet." He stares at the plane's ceiling for a few seconds. Then a light of mischief fills his eyes, "I want to do a survival trek at Sea-Side and explore our new property, five hundred acres of woods and a mountain right on the ocean. I want to see if it might work for me to run my own survival school. Do you think that's possible?"

I look at him in total surprise, "Evan's that a perfect place to go."

"What about Scott?"

"If I could go when I was only three weeks, then he shouldn't have any problem at eight weeks. This might be the easiest time to take him while he still can't move on his own." We spend the rest of the flight home planning our second honeymoon. There is no one else to talk to, everyone else is sound to sleep.

## CHAPTER 18

We snatch our fully loaded backpacks and two suitcases from the luggage carrousel. We don our backpacks, Evan takes the two suitcases, I carry Scottie in his car seat, and we find an Uber ride to Dawn and Sol's rental house in the next town. They upgraded from their small apartment when they moved all the office materials from the old Sea-Side Hall before it burned. They assure us they have room for us to spend a night with them before we head out on our survival adventure.

Dawn and Sol rush out the front door and down the porch steps as we pull into the driveway. We share hugs all around then move our luggage from the back of the Uber van. I sit Scott's carrier on the ground to put on my pack. Dawn squats down beside Scottie. I think she's going to pick up the carrier but surprises me by unsnapping him and lifting him into her arms. "Scottie, you are such a precious little bundle of joy." He rewards her with a smile and a gooing sound. She lifts him to put his cheek next to hers and whispers in his ear. He squeals with delight. She is so natural with a baby; I hope they don't wait too long to start their family. We follow them into the house while Dawn continues talking to Scottie and nuzzling his neck. I may only get to hold my baby when he's hungry. We deposit our things in our room and return to their living room. Now Solomon is talking to and caressing Scott in his big strong arms. I've never seen either one of them happier.

"Terry, are you sure you want to leave on your survival expedition first thing in the morning?"

Evan answers for us, "We'll be out of here at gray dawn. I can't wait to get my son on his first survival trip. We'll be out there about five days, I hope. We'll spend a few days with you when we come in before we fly home. I know that Terry wants an update on everything."

"After dinner, we'll take you on a tour and give you a quick update," Solomon says with a proud smile. "Our house is about ready to move into and the school is well on its way. The tennis courts are even finished, and they have lights. Dawn already has her first student."

I look at Dawn for an explanation, "Terry, it was the neatest thing. We were driving our cart through the far side of town exploring and came across two old crumbling cement tennis courts. There was a fifteen-year-old girl there practicing against a splintered backboard. We stopped, and I watched her for a while. It must have made her nervous because she stopped hitting and angrily yelled at us. 'What'd you want?' I walked over to the fence and said 'Hi' to her. She just stared at me. I smiled and asked, 'Would you like to play on some courts that don't have cracks?' She laughed and told me that there was no such thing within a hundred miles. I told her that my courts didn't have cracks. She then sneered, 'Where are they?' I told her behind my new house at the Sea-Side School. 'There's no such thing there just a burned down concert hall.' I told her to get her tennis things and climb into the back seat of our cart, and we'd show her. She was skeptical but curious at the same time. Once we started, she asked if we were kidnapping her. I laughed and told her we were going slow enough that she could jump out anytime she felt afraid.

"When we reached the Sea-Side properties, I turned to drive across the grass lawn. She yelled, 'Hey, you can't drive in here, it's private property. Please stop! I don't want to get in trouble.' We drive right up to the Security Guard heading in our direction. She tries to hide by crouching down in the back seat.

"'Good morning, Mrs. Tune. What are you up to this morning?' He then spots our passenger. 'Dezzie, what are you doing hiding back here?' I let him know that she isn't hiding but coming to play tennis with me. He tells us to have a nice day and waves us on. When we drive up over a little rise the house, school, and tennis courts come into view. Dezzie's mouth drops open. I drive straight to the courts and stop. I tell her if she would like to practice on a backboard for a few minutes, I'll run Solomon home so he can practice on his piano and get my tennis gear."

"She seemed to have one last question, 'Why doesn't your husband look at me or talk?'"

'Solomon is blind, he can't see. He takes his ques from what he hears and touches. If you talk to him, he'll extend his hand to shake yours and hold it while he talks to you.'

"She walked to stand beside him, 'Hi Solomon.' He extended his hand, and she took it. "It's so nice to meet you, Dezzie. Thank you for playing tennis with my wife. I think she is tired of playing against the backboards… Dezzie, my friends call me Sol.'

"A light seemed to come on in her eyes, 'I know who you are. You're the manager lady, and he's the blind jazz pianist who's going to teach music in the school. You're an engineer and a nationally ranked tennis player.'

"I told her she will have to be the final judge for that. I also warned her that each backboard does something different. None of them send the ball straight back. After one session with her, I couldn't have been more excited. She has raw talent coming out of every pour, and she is an extremely hungry learner. Her high school won't know what to do with her next fall."

We head through the kitchen door into the garage to get our transportation. I am surprised to see two four-passenger golf carts. Dawn puts her hand on the bright yellow one, "Terry, this cart belongs to you and Evan. When you're gone, we'll keep it in our garage. Otherwise, it's your transportation when you're at Sea-Side. We'll all go in our cart this evening, so I can be your tour guide."

Five minutes after dinner we're going down a hill overlooking the Sea-Side properties. I had never really noticed that the concert hall was at the bottom of a large bowl with low hills on all sides. Now all I see is the catacomb maze with burned timbers sticking up in places. The fire must have been hot enough to burn up everything. My stomach turns over just looking at the destruction. I get more nauseated thinking that Dawn and Sol could have been caught in that blaze.

Dawn's voice breaks into my reflections, "Terry, do you know much of the history of this spot?" I tell her I don't know anything. "It's fascinating. When the town was first settled here, this low spot was an inland tide pool. It was fed by the underground tide cave you were in. The residents of the town decided to make it into a swimming pool. They built the door so they could control the level of the water. I'm not sure how it happened but someone drowned in the pool. Then they decided to drain the pool and turn it into a concrete maze. It became quite the carnival and pulled thousands of tourists. When the maze went out of vogue, the original architect and builder purchased the area for next to nothing and used the maze as a foundation to build the Sea-Side Concert Hall. Now you must decide what to do with it."

I look over the area with new eyes, "What are my choices?"

"You could bring in dirt and fill the whole thing in. You could restore the maze. You could even take it back to its swimming pool days. Your last option would be to clean everything out and restore it to an inland tide pool."

Evan's eyes are glowing with excitement, "Terry, this is such a serene place, we only want to add to that beauty. I think we should dig out all that cement junk, lower it a little more, and bring the tide pool back. It would so match the feeling of the entire grounds. It would also preserve your elegant concert image."

"I side with you, Evan. What do you think, Terry?"

"I think it's a beautiful idea. Go for it, Dawn."

We turn to walk back to the cart where Solomon is waiting. "Now let's go see your new concert hall," Dawn says as she drives the cart up out of the bowl.

As we crest the rise, my mouth falls open. There on a more level piece of ground is the most magnificent structure I have ever seen. It's an oval with rock walls. I was expecting gray limestone, but this is out of this world. There are foot-by-two-foot rectangle blocks of tan stones with dark streaks and blotches running through them. Even though they're ruff cut and not polished, they seem to glisten in the setting sun. The walls are high enough to almost be finished. There are holes in the walls for doors, but not for windows. This hall will hold several thousand people. Any harboring images of the old Sea-Side vanish from my mind.

Dawn is watching me closely, "Like what you see, Terry?" I can't even speak. She goes on, "The walls are at their height, the next row will hold the windows. They will only be as high as a row of stone to conserve the sound. They will begin the domed roof when the windows are in, probably in two weeks. The floor is already in."

I've finally find my voice, "I don't know what to say. It's breathtaking. I assumed that the walls would be gray limestone like the mountain. Didn't you quarry the stone from our mountain?"

"When they cracked the facade on the face of the mountain to open the quarry, they discovered a huge deposit of marble. That's what all the buildings on the property will be made of. There will be no other concert venue like this anywhere in the world." I'm back to not speaking, just bathing my face with tears. What an auxiliary campus this will be for Augustine. Mom did know what she was doing.

Dawn grabs my and Evan's hands, "This is as close as we can get with all the hardhat construction going on. Let me show you the rest of the campus." She pulls us away back to the cart. I love these rolling green lawns as we ride further East. Cresting another rise, our new campus comes fully into view. The piano school is twice the size of our music space on Augustine's main campus. Ice chills rush through my body as I contemplate the possibilities. Dawn touches my arm, and I shift my gaze. Their new home is stunning.

"Oh, Dawn, the marble makes everything so elegant. I love your new home. When do you get to move in?"

"It's finished. We should be moved in by the time you get back from your survival trip. Terry, I have never been happier. Sol and I plan to grow old right here in this spot. We will never be able to thank you for what you've done."

"Doc T, Can I give you a hug?" Sol holds out his arms. Evan takes Scott and nudges me forward. He does know how to give an unbreathable hug.

I step back to catch my breath, "You're welcome for my small part. Your thanks mostly need to be sent heavenward. I had very little to do with most of it. We'll just keep moving forward where the Spirit leads." Scott begins to scream while Evan rushes toward me. "Scott's finished with sightseeing and ready for his second or third dinner," I laugh.

While the sky lightens this morning, we are packing up to head out. We plan to silently move through the house to the kitchen and out the door to our new golf cart. Scott's been fed so he shouldn't make any noise. When we walk into the kitchen, I hear noises and smell food. I find a light switch and flip it on. We laugh when we see Sol at the stove cooking food. "Sol, what are you doing?"

He turns toward my voice, "I'm just fixing you folks breakfast before we send you out to live off the land. You can come back anytime you get hungry." Dawn joins us, and we fill our stomachs before we take off.

We drive due East toward the ocean. We arrive there just as the sun is peeking its head over the horizon. What a breathtaking place. We park our cart far enough into the trees that it's not visible. As an added precaution, we put a camouflage covering over the entire vehicle. We walk along the coast heading toward the towering cliffs. We are almost to the mountain wall when the shoreline juts in to make a cove. The tide is out, making the water level about six feet below the bank. The shore is sand mixed with craggy rocks in places. We watch small crabs scurry for cover as we spy down on their marine world. I think we could find food enough for our entire trip right here, but we need to be closer to fresh water. I see a few oysters in the rocks, holes in the sand that promise clams, and sea birds fishing. A movement in the rocks draws Evan's attention to a large crab carrying an octopus into a small cave to have dinner. He leans over to kiss me, "This is going to be a grand adventure."

We walk further around the cove and come to a rock about our height with gaping holes. What has caught both of our attention is a rope with one end run through two holes and knotted on itself. The other end is hanging free down the bank onto the wet sand.

Evan is first to speak, "It looks like a mooring rope to secure a boat coming in here at high tide."

"Evan, look at the path that leads away from the water directly into the woods towards the mountain wall. That's not an animal path, it's a people path."

"Since there's no boat here now, and the tide won't be high for six hours, let's find out what they're up to." We move cautiously down the path to the limestone wall. At the wall, the path distinctly turns to follow along the wall. We come to a few shallow caves that only go back in two or three feet. We search them thoroughly then move on down the trail. The foliage gets thicker as we go. We are pushing limbs and leaves out of our way when a clearing suddenly opens up. On one side of the open area, I can hear and see a bubbling spring. It forms a stream that heads in the direction of the ocean for fifteen feet and then seems to fan out and get lost in a marshy wetland. The path continues between the spring and the mountain wall. It seems to come to an end as we come to a pile of dead brush pushed up against the side of the rock wall.

Scott begins to announce that he has needs that are not being met. Evan looks at me, "I'm going to pull a log over by the spring for you to sit on. While you take care of Scottie, I'll see what all this dried brush is about." I'm not sure if he needs to be changed, fed, or just let loose. I take care of all three possibilities. When he's lying happily on his blanket on the ground, I turn to look for Evan. The brush has all been removed and, in its place, I see the opening of a large cave, maybe ten feet tall and the same width. Evan is staring in.

He turns and yells to me, "You've had more cave experience than me. Should I just go in with my flashlight or is there something else I should do?"

I pick up Scottie and walk over to the cave opening. "We are in viper country, cottonmouth, copperhead, diamondback rattler, and even the coral snake. It's best to use a fire stick along with your flashlight. It's even better if we do it as a twosome so we have each other's backs. I think this is a great spot for our base camp. Let's build a fire by the spring and make flaming fire sticks. Then we'll check out the cave."

We start into the cave with our backs at a 45-degree angle to each other. We each have our cell light in one hand and a flaming fire stick in the other. We are each looking from the center of the cave to our side of the wall. We are holding our fire sticks close to the ground. This would be a perfect place for a snake.

We've taken three steps inside when Evan lifts his torch high in the air screaming, "Out!". I instantly step back out of the cave. Evan takes my torch and his and douses them in the spring then taking hold of my arm urges me to run with him down the side of the wall.

We've gone about twenty yards when I finally get him to slow down. He's bent over trying to catch his breath. I yell at him, "What?"

Finally, he focuses on me, "Terry, that cave is full of dynamite!" I look at him in disbelief. "Just inside the door on my side was a pile of dynamite sticks. My torch was dropping sparks on them when I realized what I was seeing.

My mind starts working, "I think someone is still trying to destroy my concert hall."

"Do you think it's more Derksins?"

"No. I think we got all of them. That real estate man might not have been working alone. I'll bet that someone is stealing dynamite from the quarry a little at a time and stashing it here until they have enough to blow my concert hall to pieces. Let's go gather up their stash and take it back to the quarry. Maybe we can figure out how they're heisting it."

We go back into the cave this time with cell light only. The sticks of explosives are lying on a crude carrier. It's a flat piece of leather a foot wide and three feet long. On each end are handles. I think it looks like an old wood-carrying device. Evan bundles up the dynamite, and we start down the trail that leads toward the quarry. As we are leaving the cave, I hear a familiar rattling sound. I smile; I think we'll find our dinner here tonight.

A half-mile later our path leads us right to the edge of the quarry. We come to a large cave that has wire mesh over the opening. Looking closely, we can see the edge of the wire screen has been pried away from the wall and could be bent back to allow a small person to get inside. We can also see there is a box with only four sticks of explosives left in it. The main gate to this powder room is on the other side of the cave opening. If no one ever walked back here, no one would be aware of the theft.

We keep walking past the dynamite cave into the quarry. Of all the coincidences, I know the first person I see. "Hi, Terance. Checking on the building progress?"

He is surprised to the max, "Dr. Timpson, what are you doing here?"

"I own this property, remember. I'm just taking a little vacation here."

"How did you get past the security guards into the quarry?"

"We came in the back door. We would like to talk to the quarry manager." He instantly moves toward a man using a megaphone to give instructions. They both turn to come in our direction.

"Mr. Samuelson, this is Dr. Timpson and her husband, Evan. They are the owners of this property and the concert hall we're building."

Mr. Samuelson extends his hand, "I must say that I'm surprised you got past our security. What can I do for you?" Evan hands him the bundle of dynamite sticks. He looks stricken. "Where did you get this? These are special explosives that are made specifically for my use."

"We found them in a cave back by the ocean. We followed their trail to your storage room. If you'll follow us, we'll take you to the hole in your fence." We turn and both men follow quickly behind us.

"Terry, this snake is really good. How did you know there was a Diamond Back Rattler in the cave?"

"I heard him wave his tail goodbye to us as we were leaving with the dynamite this morning…Did you notice how pale Samuelson turned when you handed him the bundle?"

"I'd be downright sick if I found out someone was stealing my explosives. He got that hole patched up fast enough. What I can't figure out is why one of his patrolling guards hadn't spotted the hole in the fence."

"I guess it's his worry, not ours. I wonder how long we'll have to wait to find out who the crooks are that transferred the dynamite from the storage cave to this cave. I wonder why they didn't take it away in their boat. Makes me think they're going to use it here."

"Terry, all this crime is ruining our honeymoon. Let's put it away and not talk about it anymore tonight."

I'm awakened at the first sign of gray dawn by a whimpering baby. This is not his usual wake-up call. I listen harder and recognize another sound. It's the gobbling of a wild turkey. I think Scottie can hear him. I kiss Evan to wake him up. When he's finally awake enough to speak, I put my finger on his lips and whisper, "Our dinner's out there calling." He looks at me with a total question mark, "A wild turkey is roosting in a tree just outside the cave and calling to his girlfriend. If you use your stick sling to quiet that bird and bring him back for dinner, I'll take care of Scottie. We should be able to have a couple of hours of uninterrupted bliss.

When we finally emerge from our cave, Evan picks up the turkey looking at it strangely. "Terry, I've never killed a bird to eat before. What do we do with it? I've never eaten poultry with feathers on."

"Oh, Evan, you need to get the feathers off. You go collect a large pile of firewood, and I'll construct a scalding tank." We work as a team and soon have our bird picked clean. I show Evan how to make a spit for roasting our bird. We put him in a plastic bag and take him to the back of our cave where it's cool until we are ready to roast him. Our breakfast is leftover snake and watercress... I'm still pondering Scottie's hearing.

I'm a little disgruntled with myself that I just started cooking our turkey, and it's almost dark. Mom's plan was always to be through with the evening meal and cleaned up before dark. It makes everything so much easier. I think back over our day and don't know what we would have left out. We got to the beach at low tide and instantly started digging for clams. We also throw a dozen oysters in our bag. The tide chases us up onto the beach and the woods beckoned. On the way, we discovered a gorgeous patch of daylilies. We filled another bag with tubers. Evan looked back to the ocean and wondered how fishing would be from the rocks that jutted into the water forming our lagoon. We cut a pole and then headed back to the water. Evan cracked open one of our oysters and baited a survival hook. Within minutes he had a large flapping fish on his line. He flipped it behind him onto the grass and stared. It was 18 inches long and flat oblong. The most disturbing thing was that both eyes were close together on the top side of its head. I laughed as I explained about flounders but told him we couldn't keep the fish. We already had more food than we could use in the next eighteen hours, and we had no way to keep it from spoiling. We had learned, however, that fish could be on our menu if we wanted it.

Evan decided that since the tide was high, he would go for a quick swim. Scott and I spread a blanket and watched. Scottie is turning his head toward noises. When he does, I talk to him explaining what he's hearing. I know he doesn't understand, but soon, he'll start putting sounds with my words. A screeching seagull flies over our heads, and Scottie's head jerks up while he makes a noise like the one, I heard this morning. When an ibis flies by, he turns his head slowly as if following the wing or wind sounds. I also let him touch everything around us: grass, leaves, rocks, sticks, sand, water, clams, oysters, and even a starfish. It's so exciting to watch him develop.

I guess I wouldn't change one thing about this day, even the berry picking, so we'll just have a very late dinner.

Scott is bundled up and asleep in his carrier. I'm glad we brought the car carrier; I feel he is much safer up off the ground. Evan and I are lining up our activities for tomorrow when we both freeze. "Evan, can you hear that boat coming our direction?"

"Yes, I think it might be our answer to the dynamite." He stands and picks up his hiking staff. "I'll go check it out. You stay here by the fire with Scott. If there's danger, I will give you a sand hill crane call, and you melt into the woods with Scottie." As he disappears toward the ocean, I swaddle Scottie close to my chest to painfully wait. I keep checking the time. After about twenty minutes I hear the boat leaving. After another fifteen minutes, I begin hearing voices coming on the trail toward me, but neither of them is Evan's. I make sure that my stick sling is leaning on the log beside me.

Two images are stopped and stunned into silence when they step into the firelight. We focus on each other. They are two young men, one about twelve and the other I'm guessing near fifteen. They're hard to distinguish because their clothes and skin are black. Apparently, I'm not what they expected either. The oldest one finally musters the courage to angrily yell, "What are you doing here?"

I calmly and softly answer, "I'm camping. What are you doing here?"

Still trying to appear in charge, the same boy yells louder, "This is private property. You need to leave or else." They both pull six-inch blades out of their belts to brandish at me. I just look curiously at them.

They jump to turn around as Evan's voice booms, "No one threatens my wife with a knife." Evan quickly disarms them with his staff. "Walk over to the fire so we can get a better look at you." All their bluster is gone as they slowly come to the fire. Their eyes become riveted on the roasting turkey.

I decide to defuse the situation, "Are you hungry? It's almost done, and we have way too much meat for the two of us to eat?" The smaller of the two nods his head up and down. "There's room on either side of me for one of you to sit. Come and I'll show you how to weave a plate." Evan sits on the log opposite us on the other side of the fire. Once the plates are finished, I look and Evan and nod.

"Okay gentleman, I'm going to thank our Heavenly Father for this food. Please take off your hats and bow your heads." They quickly follow his directions, and we have a blessing on our meal.

I pull my knife out and their eyes get wide with fear. I lean forward and slice a large piece of breast meat. Balancing it between the blade and a stick, I place it on the woven mat of the younger boy. I then scoop out four day-lily tubers to add to his plate. I do the same for his brother and then for Evan and myself. We eat in absolute silence. The food vanishes from the boys' plates before I've even had my first bite.

I look at them and ask, "Would you like some more?" They both hold out their plates. I give them each a large drumstick. I hope that will appease their gaunt hunger without making them sick. Between the four of us, we finish off the bird and all the tubers, but everyone seems satisfied.

Evan sits his plate down and looks at them. They slide a little closer to me and, I put an arm around each of their shoulders. They scoot even closer.

Evan's voice has softened, "OK boys, it's time to talk about the dynamite." They both stiffen but don't move away from me. "I was by your boat when you were dropped off and heard your handler's orders. You are to get the last of the dynamite tonight. We found your stash in the cave and have given it back to the quarry people. The hole in the fence has been repaired. Would you like to tell us about your part in this? We would like to help you.

Both boys start crying and the oldest mumbles, "Yellowstone is going to kill us."

Evan continues, "We are not going to hurt you. That's not God's way. We won't let anyone kill you. We only want to help you, but you must help us understand the situation. Tell me how you got into this mess."

The older boy looks at Evan as though he's deciding if he can be trusted. Then he begins talking fast, "We ran away from home a couple of months ago to get away from our drunk dad. He killed our baby sister and hits our mom all the time. We figured we were next to be killed. We lived on the streets for a few days and got really hungry. This man offered to give us food and a place to stay if we'd come with him. He is worse than our drunk dad. We had to sleep on the cement floor, and he would throw scraps of food on the floor at times for us to eat. Said he'd turn us over to Juvie if we didn't carry out his orders exactly.

"He brought us to this island and took us to the dynamite cage. The hole wasn't there then, but he said it would be there the next time we came. He told us to take four sticks each time we came and put them in that cave." He pointed to the opening behind us. "He brought us here eight times and, we did exactly as he said. Sometimes he would pick us up the next night, but most often he leaves us here for days. We are starving to death. I think he wants to kill us, maybe starven is his plan. He did say that this was our last time and to be sure we got everything in the box. Something about caps in a sack. He also said he would be back tomorrow night at high tide." I hold them tight giving them all the love I can.

"Ok guys, I need to sleep on this one, but I promise you we'll keep you safe."

"Mister, what's your name?" The younger boy finally says.

"I'm sorry. I didn't make any introductions did I. I'm Evan and this is my wife Terry holding our son Scott. And you are?"

He answers with pride, "Mr. Evan, I'm Gabriel and my older brother is Abraham. Miss. Terry, thank you for the food. You will never know how good it tasted."

"Well, Gabe and Abe, come into the cave with me, and we'll fix a place for you to sleep. Terry, would you give me the space blanket you're carrying? If they each use one, I think it will keep them comfortable through the night. Tomorrow morning how would you both like to learn how to find real food out here and eat like kings?" I will never forget the longing in their eyes.

I sit by the fire feeding Scottie and getting him ready for bed. When I slip into the cave with my cell light, it looks like all the men are asleep. With Scottie snuggled in his bag and carrier, I kiss him and crawl in with Evan. I cuddle next to him and am surprised to feel his face wet with tears. He whispers in my ear, "Terry, this has been the most sobering night of my life."

"Evan, what's happened."

"We were all settled in our sleeping areas when Gabe asked where you were. I told them that you were feeding Scottie and getting him ready for bed. He then asked if you were going to sleep with me. I told him that you always sleep with me. Abe asked with almost fighting anger if I was going to make Miss. Terry scream and cry."

I'm shocked, "Why would Abe ask you that?"

"I asked him the same question. He told me that his dad made his mom scream and cry almost every night, especially when he was dead drunk. Sometimes she hurt so badly that she couldn't get out of bed the next morning. I then asked if their dad made them cry and scream. He told me he hit them every day. They had learned to turn to protect their heads, and they showed me the scars all over their backs. My stomach almost lost its dinner. Abe said he finally got big enough that he could run faster than his old man. One day his father caught him by surprise, threw him to the ground, and jumped on his leg. Both bones in his lower leg snapped. He got beat three or four times a day while his leg was healing. The leg didn't heal right and now he can't move as fast."

"I told them that I would never hurt Miss. Terry, a good man would never hurt his wife. I explained that Heavenly Father has sent you to me to be my wife, the mother of my children, and a special helper to me for eternity. No man of God would ever hurt his wife or his children.

"Then Gabe sent me another blow. He asked if I ever hit Miss. Terry's baby when she didn't know. I told them that Scott was as much my baby as it was hers. They looked so taken aback. We had a thorough discussion about the birds and the bees. They didn't seem to know that a woman didn't have a baby without a man's help. I let them know that a good man, or a man of God would protect his children and his wife with his life. They then told me that their dad hit their baby all the time, especially when she cried. The night they left home, Baby Sally was crying because she was hungry. She hadn't learned yet not to cry when you're hungry. Their dad was so angry that he threw her against the wall. She stopped crying or moving; she was dead. It scared them so badly that they decided to run away before he killed them."

"Oh, Evan that's horrible."

"It's beyond comprehension. We must help them. I want to help them understand that there are bad men and good men, and they need to grow up to be good, men of God. That's why I want to take troubled kids on survival expeditions. I want them to know there is a better way, and someone does care about them." We hold each other tight and sometime in the night fall asleep.

# CHAPTER 19

Even though we were up late with our new guests, Scottie is gooing again this morning with another turkey at first light. I quickly dress us both and head out of the cave. I decide we need a good breakfast first thing this morning, so Scott and I head toward the ocean. On the way, I roll over a dead log and quickly pick up a half dozen large worms. The tide is still high enough that I can fish from the rock out-cropping. This must be flounder city. Within five minutes I have four fish, all about fifteen inches long. I gut them, put them on a stick branch stringer, and head back to camp. I think the smell of the fish roasting on the coals brings the three men out of the cave.

Abe rushes to the fire, "Those smells like heaven. I don't remember a day when I had food two days in a row." Gabe is right beside him with his woven cattail plate.

Evan puts a hand on each of their shoulders, "Guys, we're getting a little ahead of ourselves. We always start the day with a family prayer." We move away from the fire and kneel. Evan motions for the boys to join us. They seem mystified but slowly kneel with us. Evan proceeds to offer our morning prayer. When he finishes, the boys watch us closely for clues of what to do next, when we turn to the fire that's cooking our food, they beat us there.

When I see that everyone has finished eating, I announce, "It's time to start working on dinner. Look around carefully and you'll see our next meal."

They all look in every direction. Evan looks especially concerned, "Terry, I don't see anything even close to making a meal. What can you see that we can't?"

I take out a paracord braided package and walk around the spring and down the other bank toward the muddy marsh. My footing begins to get slippery when I bend down and attach a slip noose to something that looks like a log or mossy rock. I tighten the loop, pull a long length out of the package, and throw it across the stream to Evan. I yell at the same time, "Pull!" Evan is almost pulled into the stream before he gains leverage to pull his direction. The boys each grab hold of the line to help him pull. Slowly, they start winning as a huge muddy thing is pulled into the water. The mud floats downstream to reveal that they are pulling on the hind leg of a large snapping turtle. Evan is laughing so hard that he can hardly keep his balance. The young men join his excitement.

When they start pulling him up their bank, I yell, "Evan, take hold of his shell behind his neck and cut off his head right behind his jaws. Keep your hands away from his mouth. He'll take your finger in one snap." Before I get around the spring and back to them, the turtle has been beheaded and is lying still. I give more directions as I get close, "Hold him up by his back legs to drain the blood, and then turn him over onto his back, belly up." I run my knife around the outside of his belly plate. "Ok Evan, take hold and pull the plate off." It comes off relatively easy, and I take out the entrails. "Now all we need to do is make turtle soup." No one has said a word.

Evan finally stammers, "Terry, how did you know this big fellow was here? I never even noticed him."

"That's because you didn't know he could be here. I saw him yesterday, but we didn't need him then. We need him today for dinner, I just kept him in cold storage…Why don't you take the boys out to the ocean and dig clams and pick oysters for lunch today? When the tide turns and is coming in, take a little swim to get cleaned up. You might also want to teach them how to make and use a stick sling. You can use pieces of this turtle's neck skin attached to paracord for rock holders." He nods his head and understands that I need to be alone for a while.

When they're out of hearing range, I call Agent Fowler. I explain the whole situation to him. "It sounds to me Terry, like we have a couple of first-class crooks setting up a couple of juveniles to take a fall. It's bad enough when they do it themselves, but it makes me fiercely angry when they destroy innocent kids. Let's catch them. Did you say that the only thing you found were sticks of dynamite? Did you find any blasting caps? They're usually little round red pieces of plastic that look like old bottle caps."

"When Evan overheard the boat guy yelling at the boys, he said to make sure they got the sack of caps, and that this was their last night."

"Tell me the name of that jerk again, Yellowrock?"

"No, it is Yellowstone, like the park, I think.

"Hang on a minute, and I'll run a MO check with his name attached… Bingo! His name comes up twice, but there was never enough evidence to get a conviction. Both times juveniles went to jail. I'll be out there this afternoon with a team. We'll come across the grass in carts not telling anyone why we're coming in." I give him directions to our camp.

"Agent Fowler, could you possibly bring a couple of sets of tan youth hunter camo clothes, a size 14 and a size 10 along with some boy's underwear the same sizes and two lightweight sleeping bags when you come?"

"Sure thing, Terry. See you this afternoon."

Scott and I are stirring the turtle soup in the turtle shell. It's been simmering on coals most of the day. I hear the posse before I see them. Agent Fowler is coming down the trail followed by three men. One I recognize, Chief Henery, Chief of Police for Sea-Side, the others must be FBI agents. I'm holding Scottie up with two hands talking and making silly noises. He reaches out with two hands to touch my face then smiles and laughs with happy sounds. When Fowler says "Hi",

Scott flips his head in their direction and makes the same sound he did when he heard the turkeys.

"Terry, this is quite the camping spot. Looks ideal to me."

"You'll never understand what a perfect survival spot this is. Evan is out teaching our two guests how to eat when they're hungry. I'm making a little turtle soup if you all would like to join us for dinner." The officers look at each other, and I can tell I just turned all their stomachs over.

Agent Fowler answers politely, "Thanks Terry, we don't want to impose. Our dinner is back at our golf cart." They probably don't have any dinner but think nothing would be better than the concoction I'm stirring up… all the more for us.

"Terry, while it's light, why don't you show us the caged dynamite cash? If they haven't communicated much, we may be able to catch them red-handed." I buckle Scott into my front carrier and head down the trail toward the quarry. The law follows. I slow down to cautiously approach the edge of the wire enclosure. Everyone stays back in some sort of cover.

Agent Fowler is close behind me, "This is where the hole was. And as you can see, it's been closed tight. That box which still has sticks of dynamite is the one the boys were supposed to take four from every night they were brought here in the boat."

"It's a long shot, but if Yellowstone thinks things are still going as planned, we may be able to catch two crooks tonight," Fowler says.

He looks at all the trees around him. Then settles on one specific skinny very tall maple tree. "Let's put the infrared camera about thirty feet up in that tree. The angle would be just right to get the best picture of the perp and what he's doing."

The men look at each other, then at Fowler, "Chief Fowler, none of us could get up in that tree. It's way too skinny, and there are no branches to hang onto. Are you going to climb?"

"Of course, I'm not climbing. We do have one agent here that is capable of ascending that tree." The men look at each other again and shake their heads. "Terry, are you up to the task?" I smile and nod my head. "Gentlemen, I would like you to meet Agent Timpson." They stare at me in disbelief. "McDonald, give Terry the camera and show her how to attach it."

I turn to the man taking the camera out of his pack. I unstrap Scottie. "I'll trade you my most precious possession for yours, for a few minutes." He hands me the camera and I put Scottie in his arms. Scott reaches to touch his face, and the man giggles. Fowler gives him a stern look. I strap the camera into Scott's carrier and use his baby blanket to do my electrician's walk up the tree. Fowler signals when I'm at the spot where he wants it attached. Once I'm down from my climb and Scott is safely back in his carrier, they test the camera and the receiving unit. The picture is coming through perfectly clear. They can even move the camera and change the focus. Now I hope our corrupt quarry worker takes the bait.

When we get back to the fire, my man and boys are there. The other three men walk past our cooking soup, but Fowler sits down to talk, "Boys, my name is Agent Fowler," Abe and Gabe bristle looking at me like I've betrayed them. Miss Terry has told me about this man called Yellowstone, and how he's using you to break the law. He is a very bad man, and I would like to ask you two if you will help us catch him.

Abe answers quickly, "He'll kill us!"

"He is never going to touch you again. You will never be close to him. All I need you to do when he comes back in his boat is to yell at him from the edge of the woods that the dynamite is all locked up and you can't get it or the caps. Do you think you could do that? Mr. Evan and I will be right there beside you to make sure you'll be safe. I even have special clothes for you to put on, so he won't be able to see you. You'll look just like Mr. Evan." He hands the camo clothes to the boys. They head instantly into the cave to put on their new outfits.

The boys strut around like peacocks in their new finery. They march right up to Agent Fowler, "Are you sure Mr. Evan will be with us?"

"Absolutely, and so will I." That statement doesn't give nearly the assurance they're looking for, but the hug Evan gives them brings satisfied smiles to their faces.

I announce the soup is done, "It's time for dinner. You're welcome to stay Agent Fowler, we have plenty."

"My dinner's waiting back at the cart, I'll meet you at the edge of the woods when we hear the motorboat coming in."

It's not long after dark when we hear the boat. My men get up to head in that direction. I give the boys each a hug and tell them how proud I am of them. I give Evan a long kiss and whisper in his ear, "I love you. You are my knight of steel and velvet. Please be careful." Scott and I follow part way down the trail so we can hear what's happening.

The silence is ominous when the boat motor is cut. It's shattered with a yell, "Hey blockheads where are you? You had better have those caps in the cave, or I'll break both your legs."

Abe's voice is slightly intimidated when he yells back, "We couldn't get them. The hole in the fence has been fixed."

We can hear Yellowstone on his cell phone. I guess criminals have access to state-of-the-art satellite phones too, "Mickey, has the hole into the demolitions cave been closed?... Well open it. Those caps have got to have the boys' prints on them. Open the hole and put the caps in the box. Wait until they've had time to take them to the cave and then come. I'll meet you there." Fowler guessed this one right.

Yelling again he shouts, "You ingrates, get back to the quarry. The hole will be open when you get there. You had better run with those caps to the cave, or I'll still break both your legs and arms." This man has moved far below the bottom of my like list.

Then I hear words that ring like music, "You are under arrest. You have the right to remain silent…"

Evan gives me a thumbs-up and takes Scottie out of my arms. "Now it's your turn to do your magic. We'll meet you at the carts."

The fires are out cold, and all our camping gear is moved back into the cave so it can't be seen. I'm hiding just outside the cave's entrance. The FBI agent who retrieved the sack of blasting caps to put in the cave and the Sea-side sheriff are hiding out here somewhere also. I've exchanged my diamond necklace for the microphone look-a-like. My target should be along any time. I'm still pondering the thought when I hear feet running down the trail next to the cliffs.

He rushes into the cave and turns on a bright flashlight. He looks around and scrapes the floor with his foot where the dynamite had been. He yells, "Where is it? These blasting caps don't do me any good without the explosives. Those sticks have to be here."

My turn, "Can I help you?"

He is so startled, that he almost falls, "Dr. Timpson, what are you doing here?"

"I own this property in case you've forgotten. I'm here camping. What are you doing here Mr. Kingman, head of quarry security?"

He focuses back on the ground with growing anxiety, "They've got to be here. I saw them myself four days ago."

"What's got to be here?"

"The dynamite, what do you think? I only have an hour before Yellowstone will be here to set off the charges. I must get everything placed." He's so panicked he's not thinking straight.

I decide to mess a little more with his mind, "Oh, that dynamite. I took it back to the quarry. It's a very dangerous thing to leave lying around. And as for Yellowstone, he's not coming to meet you. He's spilling his guts to the Feds about how all of this is your plan. He's sending you down the river of no return."

"My plan! He came to me and offered to give the marble quarry to me if I'd help him blow up your concert hall so he could buy the land dirt cheap. He was going to fix it so those brat kids would take the fall. Said he'd done it twice before... I'm out of here!" He rushes toward me with his flashlight in his hand. I kick his hand and lunge sideways into the cave opening. He tries to go around me on the other side and runs into the wall of the cave. He's out cold when Agent Fowler and Chief Henery step into the cave.

"Terry, you were fantastic as usual. Here's your diamond back. We'll take this hunk of muck off your hands. We have a chopper coming in to haul them away. What about the boys, do you want us to take them away as well?"

"Oh no, Evan promised to teach them how to survive in the wilds, and we still have four days left for their education. After that, I think I might know of a private boarding school they would be happy in."

I walk with him out of the forest and back to the golf carts. We watch the chopper land and pick up the two crooks. The boys look anxiously at us. Evan puts his arms around both of their shoulders and turns then toward the woods, "Come on fellows, we need sleep. We've got a big day tomorrow. Terry's going to show us how to lasso a pelican for dinner, and you still haven't brought down a squirrel yet." I hold Scottie cheek to cheek as we walk back to our cold camp.

I wish I could figure out how to get those turkeys to roost somewhere far away. Scottie was talking with them this morning. He almost sounds like a gobble. I take him out of the cave to get our day started. We have the fish cooked that the boys caught yesterday when they magically appear at the fire. We all go down to the cove when the tide is at its highest. I show them how to make bolas and explain how they work. We then fade back into the woods to watch for any birds coming to fish in our cove. I'm excited to find Bracken Fern still in with fiddleheads. We pick all we can find. We can eat it raw or cooked. It's kind of like eating asparagus.

Gabe's been faithfully watching the water, "Miss, Terry, a big white bird is floating on the water." It is a pelican. We slowly move toward the water keeping as much foliage between us and our prey as possible. We circle to get even closer by staying behind the rock outcropping. I tell everyone when I say start, to swing their bolas over their heads in a circle and then let them fly when I say throw. We spread out so as not to hit each other. The bird is swimming closer to shore. I let him keep coming then give the signal, "Start," We only make a few circles when I give the throw signal. Two of the bolas wrap around the head and neck of the pelican. It lets out squawks and starts swimming. I hand Scottie to Evan and make a long shallow dive into the water after our dinner. I grab a flapping wing and start swimming back to shore. I think about using my knife to take the fight out of this bird, but I don't know for sure if there's a shark nearby.

When my feet touch the rocky ground, Evan is by my side. We hurry up to the shore with our fighting ball of feathers. Evan quickly decapitates him and all his struggling ceases. Then it hits me, he doesn't have Scottie. I panic a little looking around. Abe is holding him up next to his face and Scott is laughing and patting his cheeks. I breathe deeply to calm down. We start back to camp with Evan holding our prey, I have the ferns, and Abe is still holding a happy Scott. Gabe runs ahead calling back that he will build up the fire.

We've decided to bake our pelican. He is now buried under a mound of coals. Gabe turns to Evan, "Will you help me learn how to hit a squirrel?"

I interject before Evan can answer, "It might be easier to start with rabbits. They don't move as quickly. I saw a bunch in the grass field out by our golf cart yesterday."

"Come on tiger, let's go get a rabbit. Abe, are you coming with us?"

"No, I just want to sit here by the fire for a while... Gabe, you have to throw harder if you want to get a squirrel." When they're out of earshot, Abe looks directly at me, "Gabe can't throw very hard or run very fast. I used to be able to run faster than anybody in my neighborhood until my leg got broken... Miss. Terry, can I ask you something?" I nod while I feed Scottie under the blanket draped over us.

"Mr. Evan told us that every person is made up of pieces from their mother and their father... Does that mean that when I get bigger, I will hurt my wife and kids?"

I use my free arm to pull him closer to me, "Oh Abe, definitely not. You have a Heavenly Mother and a Heavenly Father. They are the parents of your spirit body. Everyone that's living has a spirit body in addition to the one they received from human parents. That spirit body will teach you what is wrong or right if you will listen to it. You will always have a choice. If you do too many bad things, you block out the good things from your spirit. If you follow your spirit and the rules that Jesus taught, you will always do good things—

"I've watched you use your stick sling. It is very fast, and you have the natural motion for a serve in tennis…"

He interrupts me before I can go on, "I love to watch tennis. I played down at the rec courts before my leg got hurt. I just wish I knew how to do it better and my leg worked again."

"Does Gabe want to be a tennis player too?" I ask.

"No way. He wants to be a music man. He's singing and rapping all the time. He heard a recording once of a Black dude playing jazz on a piano. That's all he dreams about. His visions of fame will only live in his head, just like mine."

My attention is drawn to a large gray squirrel going up the trunk of a red oak. I point, "Hit that squirrel." He quickly loads his stick sling, stands, and fires." He served a perfect tennis ace… I need to talk to Dawn.

As I drift off to sleep, I'm almost praying that the turkeys won't wake Scottie up. It feels like I've just gotten to sleep when something wakes me with a start. I set up nearly in a panic reaching for Scottie. Evan grabs my hand, "Terry, it's all right, listen." I'm awake enough now to be aware of my surroundings. I hear the hoot of a Great Horned Owl, and seconds later I hear an almost hoot from Scottie. I can't believe this. He's trying to mimic every sound he hears. I'm never going to be able to sleep. Evan is laughing at me. Then we hear the scream of the Eastern Screech Owl. It is followed by the strangest sound I have ever heard Scott make. We both laugh.

Then I moan. "Alright, you little imitator. You're coming to bed with us, and we're both going to get some sleep even if I have to put earmuffs on you. He laughs and pats my face."

Our yellow cart is slowly making its way across the grassy acres to Dawn and Sol's new home. Our second survival honeymoon didn't turn out anything like we planned or even imagined, but we wouldn't trade it for the world. Our two new survival grads are sitting amid our gear laughing and reminiscing. One is wearing a squirrel headband with a tail hanging down the back of his head. The other is wearing a rabbit fur headband. They're not experts in survival living but left on their own, they wouldn't starve. It's late in the afternoon when we arrive at the Tune's dwelling. They must be watching for us. As we drive to the garage the door opens and we drive into park.

Dawn laughs as she greets us, "My, but aren't you five an interesting sight. Dinner's almost ready. I'll show you to your rooms so you can shower and get cleaned up." The first door she opens is where Evan, I, and Scott will be. I walk in and put Scott in the playpen that's placed by one side of the bed. Evan follows Dawn with the boys. Their ominous silence is a dead giveaway to their fears. I know he'll be back when he's sure the boys feel safe. I go to work on Scott.

All during dinner Abe can't keep his eyes off Dawn. Finally, a light seems to go on in his eyes, "I know who you are. You're part of the doubles team that beat the pros in the Open Tennis Tournament last year. You're a phenomenal tennis player."

Dawn nods her head and smiles, "Want to know who my teacher was?" She doesn't wait for his reply, "Miss. Terry."

His head snaps around to me, and I laugh out loud, "I don't know how much I helped them. I was in the hospital at the time they won. Both she and Celia are remarkably talented players."

Dawn takes advantage of the silence that follows, "Abe, Miss Terry had me set up an appointment with a bone doctor for you tomorrow to see if he can fix your leg. Are you interested?"

"Can my leg really be fixed?"

"We're hoping so. If it can, I'm wondering if you would like to stay here with Miss. Dawn and learn how to play her kind of tennis." All he can do is nod his head.

We move into the living room after dinner and Sol heads straight for the grand piano in the middle of the room. I can't tell if he knows Gabe is following in his footsteps. When Sol sits down, Gabe stands by the side of the keyboard to watch. Sol puts his hands on the keys and then turns his head in Gabe's direction, "Gabe, what would you like me to play?"

Gabe says one word, "Jazz!" Sol plays for the next five minutes to the most engaged audience I have ever seen.

Sol again turns his head in Gabe's direction, "Do you like music Gabe?"

"More than anything in the world. I want to play the piano like you do."

"You would have to practice every day with no complaints and go to school every day with no complaints. Let's see how your brother's doctor's appointment goes tomorrow. If he's staying to play tennis, I don't think he should stay here alone," Sol says.

Abe moves to stand by Gabe, "That school you're talking about, would it teach us to read? We've never been allowed to go to any school."

"Yes, we have the perfect teacher to help you learn to read."

I turn to Dawn, "Have you found a school teacher already?"

"Yes, Celia's mother is a certified K-12 teacher, and she is eager to be part of your dream, Terry. They have one daughter left at home who is doing well on the piano and the tennis court. She'll come with her mom."

Waiting is always the hardest part of being in a doctor's office. Abe, Evan, and I are trying to wait patiently. Gabe was elated to stay with Sol. I only left Dawn with one bottle of milk for Scottie. I hope this is not an all-day wait. Finally, we're ushered into an exam room, and in the next instant, Dr. Lyster appears. "Dr. Timpson, I am so glad to meet you in person. I was at the concert you gave for our town. It was stunning. I want you to know you have the support of the entire community and double my support. What can I do for you today?"

I put my hand on Abe's shoulder, "This is Abe, and he has a problem with his leg. I'm wondering if you might be able to fix it?' Abe pulls up the pant leg of his new jeans.

Dr. Lyster instantly reaches for the deformity in his leg. "Son, what happened to your leg?"

Without any pretense, he simply says, "My dad jumped on it so he could catch me and beat me every day." The doctor looks at me with concerned questioning eyes.

"The FBI is aware of his situation, and at the moment he is in my protective custody. I want to help him be normal again if it's possible."

The doctor visibly relaxes, "A quick x-ray will tell us what we need to know." He turns to his assistant, "Jim, will you take Abe into the next room and get the images we need." Abe looks a little reluctant to go alone, but Evan quickly guides him that way with his arm on his shoulder. They're back in less than five minutes. The Doc examines his leg again while we wait for the X-rays to come up on his computer. The images finally fill a large screen on the wall as well as the computer. "This is what I thought I could feel. Abe, see these two bones that are growing together, and these other two that are touching, they don't belong together. This should be easy to fix. We will just disconnect everything and then put them back where they belong." He draws lines on the X-ray to show us what needs to be done. "Abe, the big question is, do you want to go through all the pain that will come to get it fixed and will you follow my directions to stay off your leg until I give you the okay?"

"You can fix my leg so I can run fast again?"

"I can if you will follow all of my rules."

"That's a no-brainer. I went through all the pain to get it bad. I can certainly go through all of that again if it will make me better. I don't want to be a cripple my whole life."

"Good, that's settled. Let's do it at 5:00 am tomorrow. I have an opening in the operating room then." Abe punches the air with a fist of determination.

"Dr. Lyster," Evan says to get his attention. "Could you take a quick look at my stump? I started getting a sharp, pricking pain near the end yesterday afternoon. It seems to be getting worse."

The doctor looks at him questioningly, "Do you have a prosthesis?" Evan pulls up his pant leg to show him. "Man, you handle yourself well. I never even suspected." Trade Abe places on my exam table." Evan removes his foot and sits on the table. Doctor Lyster begins examining the calloused stump. Every time he touches one particular spot, Evan winces. "It feels quite strange. Let's get an x-ray and see what you've got.

How did you lose your foot anyway?" Evan explains how his missionary experience ended.

When the films come up on the screen, the doctor looks extremely puzzled. "I know there's something there, I can feel it. But the X-ray isn't picking it up. Now you have me concerned. Whatever it is needs to come out. Let's schedule you right after Abe tomorrow. We'll only need to use a local anesthetic. You'll be done before Abe's out of recovery. You might need to use crutches for a couple of days. I'll go in from the side, so I won't disturb the beautiful callous you've made on your stump."

Dr. Lyster notices that Evan is limping more when he puts his foot back on. He leaves the room and returns with crutches. Evan is happy to use them as we head back to the golf cart. He is even happier to have me drive. He takes his foot off as soon as he finds a chair by the front door. That seems to bring immediate relief. I wonder if this is something left from his gunshot injury.

Abe's in recovery and Dr. Lyster invites me to go with Evan into the OR for his brief procedure. We talk about the new concert hall and school while we wait for his local anesthetic to numb his leg. He starts the incision and stops instantly. He moves the blade slightly and tries again. This time it slices smoothly into muscle. He opens the wound to look at something. He clamps forceps on his finding and slowly pulls. The object starts coming out of Evan's leg, but the doctor must continually cut the tissue that the thing is attached to. It's about an inch long, looks like clear rigid plastic, and could pass for an extremely skinny grasshopper. Puzzled, the doc holds it up to closely examine it. His aid hands him a glass specimen bottle, and he drops it in. He examines the incision again and begins to close the cut.

The aid is holding the bottle trying to get a good look at its contents. She screams, "Dr. Lyster, it's moving and getting larger."

The doctor grabs the bottle, "I think this is a mechanical parasite that I read about last week. It's entering the biological warfare game. I need to get hold of someone in the war department."

I immediately think of Agent Fowler. I hit his speed dial button, and he answers on the first ring. "Terry, more bombing attempts?"

"No, biological warfare." I have his full attention while I explain our whole situation.

He tells me to hold for a minute. "You say you have the whole parasite intact," I tell him, yes, and it's in a sealed glass specimen bottle. "It's a heat-seeking explosive. Get it on ice if you can. There'll be a military chopper landing on the hospital roof heliport in less than five minutes. Clear everyone out of the room you're in and get someone to the roof to guide the soldiers coming in."

Dr. Lyster has been listening to our conversation. He runs through a door and returns with a metal ice chest. "We had a kidney come in thirty minutes ago for a transplant. It's been put in our cooling chamber, use this chest for the parasite. We bury the bottle in the middle of the ice chest and vacate the room just as two soldiers in full battle gear rush into the room. We point them to the door yelling that it's in the ice chest. They rush back out carrying the lethal weapon locked in the chest. The three of us stare at each other.

Doctor Lyster is the first to speak, "Dr. Timpson, are you more than a concert pianist?"

Evan burst out laughing, "Oh, she is so much more."

Since I've blown my cover, I pull out my FBI identification. He looks it over and then looks strangely at me, "Which is your first job, pianist or agent?"

"My first and foremost job is being a wife and mother. My second is being a teacher and concert pianist at Augustine University. My third is being an undercover FBI agent. If you would not mention that little detail to anyone, I would very much appreciate it."

"My lips are sealed, but by just looking at you, I would say you don't carry a gun of any kind."

Evan's still laughing, "She doesn't need to carry a gun, she's classified as a lethal weapon." I know the doctor doesn't understand, but I'm not going to explain. He hunches his shoulders and finishes bandaging Evan's cut. We leave to go to the recovery room to be with Abe. It takes most of the morning for him to wake up enough to leave the hospital. While we wait neither of us talks much, but I'm sure his brain is in overdrive just like mine is. That parasite had to have been planted when he was shot in Africa. Does he have more? Will one eventually take his life? What do we do now? Finally, I drive my two crutch hobblers back to Dawn and Sol's home and put them to bed.

After I get Scottie settled in his playpen, I slip into our bed. Evan wraps his arms around me and smothers me with a long lingering kiss. When I start to talk, he puts a finger to my lips, "Terry, I want to tell you about the most fantastic journey I've had today." I'm not sure I'd label my journey today as fantastic. He has my full attention. "When I first realized what the impact of that mechanical parasite could have on my life, I almost panicked. I could have more of those pests eating away at me. I could die any day. I might never live to hear Scottie in a concert hall. Everything could be lost. I was starting to spiral into my what-if world of unreal scenarios."

"Then I heard my dad's voice, 'You are a son of the Savior. Your life belongs to Him.' Then this vision opened in my mind. I began to understand my dad and mom. Dad had a heart condition that could take him at any time. They decided to not live in fear and panic every day but to focus instead on how they could serve the Lord best. When he was needed on the other side of the veil, the Lord would simply move him to the other side to continue his work. This parasite thing is the same. I could go any day, but if I put my life totally into the Lord's hands, He'll take me when it's my time whether that's tomorrow or fifty years from now. The most important thing we can do is to become one in our relationship so we can have eternity together."

"Your mom and dad were taken early but look at what your mom has done working from the other side of the veil. There's a beautiful home and a functional music and tennis school ready to begin this fall. The most majestic concert hall in the world will be ready for your first concert in June. All this is because of your mom's work. She's still there. We will always be there for each other. Thank you for coming back to get me." He's right; we'll make the most of the life we have ahead, together.

# CHAPTER 20

Scott has awakened me again with his babbling. I roll over to look at him in his crib. He is on his back babbling, clapping his hands, and kicking his feet. That's usually what he does when he recognizes familiar voices. I listen harder, then sit straight up in bed. It's a quick enough movement that it rouses Evan. "What?"

"Tom and Pam, and Celia and Jefferson are in the kitchen with Dawn and Sol," I say as I throw on my sweats.

Evan asks me to hand him his foot. I give him a concerned look. "The incision is higher than the prosthetic attachment, and I don't have any more pain." We both dress quickly, and I grab Scott as we rush through the door.

When we hurry through the kitchen door, all eyes turn to us, and laughter fills the room. We must look like we just fell out of bed. When the noise calms down, I ask, "What's going on? Are you all having a party without us?"

Tom makes his voice heard, "No, we're having a party because you're here."

Silence descends and all eyes turn to Dawn. "Terry, Sol, and I are going to be baptized tomorrow. Jefferson is going to baptize us. With you already here, it seemed like the perfect timing." I hand Scott off to Evan and capture Dawn in a giant bear hug. I turn and do the same to Sol. I didn't even let him know I was coming, but he seemed ready for me.

Keeping one arm around my shoulder he says, "Doc T, I couldn't get the words of my sister out of my head. It was like she was yelling the same thing at me every day 'Learn about God, get baptized, get our family baptized. When I finally listened with real intent to the teachings, it all seemed so right. We wanted all of you to be here on our special day."

There's a buzz in the kitchen as we all seem to get caught up with each other. During a lull, Celia raises her voice, "Terry, is it possible for us to see your new concert hall?"

Before I can reply, Dawn takes over, "Brunch is almost ready. Help me carry it out onto the deck picnic table and we'll go sight-seeing after we eat." I grab Scott's blanket and feed him while people are setting up for brunch outside. I first notice Abe stretched out in a lounge chair and Celia's mom is sitting beside him with a book in her hand. I catch sight of Tommy weaving in and out of legs. I can't believe he's almost a year old. Even more, I can't believe he's walking. That opens my mind to a long string of questions I need to ask Sol.

When we're seated with our loaded plates, I find myself across the table from Celia and Dawn. "I am truly sorry that Evan and I couldn't make it to the College Nationals. I would have loved to see you take away all the honors. Scottie just decided to present himself at that exact time. Evan and I have arranged our schedules so we can be at the Open. I just need to know the exact dates."

Dawn and Celia look at each other and back at me. Celia decides to answer, "We're not going to the Open."

Now everyone at the table is silent except for Pam. "Why?"

Now they are trying to hold back smiles, Dawn can't help but laugh, "We are not going because we are both pregnant." That leads to cheers and clapping. I hand Scottie off to Evan and rush around the table to hug them both.

Celia works hard to get our attention, "We were both so jealous of Pam and then Terry that we decided to just let nature run its course. Being a mother trumps being a star tennis player any day and every day. Coach Vickery knew what he was doing making me his assistant and a faculty member."

"Congratulations, you two, I mean four. That takes one event off our August calendar. We still have the Doctoral Graduation. Sol and Pam, will you both be there for sure?" I get a thumbs up from both them and their spouses.

Pam jumps ahead of me, "And all of you will be going to Carnegie with the Oratorio Choir the third week of August! No exceptions!" We all laugh and clap for Pam who will be Dr. Masters when she directs this competition.

As the meal is winding down, I share our nightly awakening experiences with Scott trying to imitate bird sounds. Then I ask Sol, "How did you and your mom cope with you waking up in the middle of the night after you learned to walk.?"

"Terry, that was a zoo. I never knew if it was day or night, so I would just get up and walk around. I started playing with all the things in the kitchen including the stove. When I started going outside at 3 am, I got locked in a closet. When I got too big for the hall closet, my sister made me a bed on the floor of her double closet. Sometimes I'd be awake all night and then sleep all day. Polly finally took pity on me and gave me my first brail lesson. She found an old windup clock and took the cover off the face. She taught me to tell time by feeling the hands on the clock very softly so as not to move them. I also learned when the house was quiet, I needed to be quiet. If I could hear people, it was okay to be up… You and Evan have a very interesting and challenging experience ahead of you. I hope you cherish every moment of it."

Our golf cart train makes its way to the top of the rise. There in all its majesty is the Sea-Side Concert Hall. It glistens in the afternoon sun. The domed copper roof is in place and the heavy wooden doors almost make it look finished. The holes with no window glass reveal its unfinished secret. Pam breaks our silent awe, "Terry, I want to see the inside."

We all look at Dawn, "I thought that you all might want to do that, so we've given all the workers the afternoon off.

Security is waiting down by the fence to let us in." We wait anxiously as the massive doors are unlocked and thrown open. We all move slowly inside. I hold my breath as we begin to move down the stone center aisle toward the raised stage. It's here, the magic is here. By the time we reach the raised stage area, everyone can hear that the acoustics are phenomenal.

The stage pulls us up to its center. Pam lifts her arms and announces, "Let's sing!"

Sol points out, "The women need a second soprano."

Pam takes care of that, "Let's sing 'The Prayer', to initiate this concert venue. Terry, you sing second." We move together, and I give them their pitches. This song has never had such a sweet sound. Tears roll down my cheeks, and I do not try to stop them. The richness of this sound buries the acoustics in the old Sea-Side Hall. When we get to the last note, Pam raises her hand in the air to direct our finish. When she closes her fist, we all stop singing but the music doesn't stop. There are three voices still ringing out the last note in full harmony. Scott is giving it all his little lungs will give. Tommy is singing in Pam's arms, while Gabe is doing his part of harmony holding Sol's hand.

I should be relaxing and sleeping, but my mind can't stop wondering if the rest of our Oratorio Competition will be as wild as our last two days. We should already be in New York. The night before our departure, the airline called to inform us that our jet scheduled to take our entire group had been grounded. The only way they could now fly us was to take us on the day of the concert in two separate jets. The first one left in the middle of the night, and the second one would just barely get us there in time for the concert. Pam and I frantically put our heads together to decide who would go on which flight. All my Master's Touch ensemble is on this flight along with a group of our strongest singers from each section and all the solos. Dr. Rich and President Drake will be on the later flight with the rest of our group. Our flight's people should be able to go through our stage setup and then get checked into our rooms in Emmerson's hotel. The latter group will have to change backstage just before the concert starts. I fear no one will arrive rested to sing their best. That one, I'll have to leave in the Lord's hands.

Our bus takes us directly to the stage door of Carnegie Hall. Owen Stirling is there to meet us, "Dr. Timpson and Dr. Masters, I'm so sorry for all your delays. You're not the only one with travel complications. Texas University arrived late yesterday, Stanford got here early this morning after traveling all night, and Kensington hasn't arrived yet. It almost feels like an unwanted hand is stirring the pot. Let's get you right on the stage for your setup."

Thank goodness, the setup goes without a hitch. Owen greets us again as we leave for the hotel. "Dr. Masters, I want to congratulate you on your new degree. I don't think it could have gone to a more deserving person. The music you compose is exquisite." Pam blushes a little as he shakes her hand. He then turns to me, "Dr. Timpson, congratulations to you on your new status of motherhood. I see very few concert pianists who take on that title. But when they do, they also take on a radiance and gentleness that their non-mother counterparts will never have. You have become even more beautiful." I'm speechless as he shakes my hand. He opens the door for us, and we all board our bus for the hotel.

Emmerson directs us to the dining room as we leave the bus. After a prayer of thanksgiving, we all attack the buffet smorgasbord. As stomachs are filled, Emmerson hands out room keys and the dining room slowly empties. Emmerson approaches me, "Dr. Timpson, we have prepared enough sack dinners that all of your people arriving on your second flight can eat at The Hall before they dress. I hope that will help a little." Pam and I both give him a hug and head to our rooms to change for the performance.

Our bus with the rest of our choir arrives just as we do at the stage door. Pam gets on the second bus and gives detailed instructions to the group. As they take their first step onto the asphalt, we hand each person their sack dinner. Most look like they're ready for bed, not for a concert. I hope their dinner will revive them. The group on our bus is directed by a host to the balcony where they will watch the pre-show and show until it's our turn to perform. Again, Augustine is the last group to sing. The rest of our group is led to our balcony when they are ready. We are at last one group as the pre-show is about to end. The balcony spot for Kensington is still empty. I start moving to find Mr. Stirling as a clause of the contract presents itself in my head. 'If a choir is not seated and ready to perform when the concert begins, it will be disqualified from the competition.' I think about all those students who have worked for a whole year for this night.

I find Owen backstage by the exit doors with Pam and the other two directors. Owen is repeating the clause of the contract, "It specifically states that they cannot compete."

Pam objects, "Think about all those students that have given their hearts to get ready for this night. There must be something that can be done. They're off the plane and on their busses to get here. Don't they just need about thirty minutes?"

I interrupt their discussion, "Mr. Stirling, what if we extend the pre-show?"

"Dr. Timpson, you saw the pre-show. They have nothing more to give, and I'm not sure the audience will take any more of them."

"What if you had a different group for about thirty minutes?"

"Dr. Timpson, are you volunteering?"

"I am! The teacher in me takes precedence over everything in advocating for students. They deserve the chance to perform."

"Dr. Timpson, thank you... You're on!"

I turn to Owen, "I'll start. Alert your sound crew and bring me a mic. Give me a signal when I just have enough time to end with 'Moonlight'" I look at Pam, "Will you send the Granddad, Solomon, and Arundel down here?"

Mr. Stirling walks onto the stage, "Ladies and gentlemen, our last group is on its way from the airport as I speak. Dr. Timpson and her troop have offered to give us a short concert to allow them to be here for the start of the competition. Please welcome on stage, Dr. Terry Masters Timpson." He extends his hand to me, and I walk onto the stage. I'm blown away by the thunderous standing ovation I am receiving. I acknowledge their appreciation and move toward the grand piano.

When I sit down, there is instant silence. I lower the mic so I can talk from the piano. "I am honored to be with you tonight. I just need a little communication with the sound booth, and we will begin." I lift my left hand and get a loud clap of thunder. My right hand brings bolts of flashing lightning. I turn to the mic again, "My first number tonight will be an original composition, 'Flash Fire'" I move my hands to the keys before the audience can respond.

If nothing else my first number wakes up the audience. The Bumblebee with Dr. Martin keeps them awake. Now it's Arundel's turn, "I would like to introduce you to one of our newest piano faculty at Augustine, Dr. Arundel Williams. She will be playing a part of Frenz Liszt's, 'La Campanella'. Dr. Williams." As we pass, I hold her arm for an instant and whisper, "Clear your head and only think about what the music has to give to your audience." She nods and moves on stage. She receives a welcome applause which she acknowledges and seats herself at the piano. She takes a deep breath, looks inside her mind, and plays the most beautiful rendition of "La Campanella" I have ever heard her play. The standing ovation she receives confirms my assessment.

I give her a well-deserved hug as she comes off stage. I move to the mic again, "I would like to introduce you to another new piano faculty at Augustine, Dr. Solomon Tune. He is being guided to the piano by his lovely wife Dawn. Dr. Solomon has been blind since birth. Dr Tune, bathe this audience in your latest jazz composition." The audience claps for him until he raises his hands to the keys. When he finishes, the audience is again on their feet clapping and cheering to show their appreciation. When the audience is seated and quiet, Sol calls me back out onto the stage, and we go through our mock challenge of playing four hands in the dark.

I can see that most of the Kensington performers are in their seats, and I finally get the signal that I have about ten minutes left. Arundel joins me at the piano for "Moonlight." I'm not at all surprised when Mom slips between us and claims the melody.

We walk off stage into a scene of panic. The OC director from Texas is crying as her students are moving onto the stage. Stirling catches sight of me and then hails me over into their conversation. "Dr. Timpson, you don't happen to have a couple of accompanists in your back pocket, do you?"

The Texas conductor sobs in my direction, "My accompanist is in the ladies' room puking her guts out. I know we will sound terrible singing a cappella, but we don't seem to have a choice."

I'm surprised when Arundel steps in front of the director, "I know the piece you're singing. I can accompany you."

That stops the sobbing, "Are you sure?"

I need to create credibility for Arundel, "Dr. Williams is a very accomplished accompanist as well as a concert pianist. I have heard her play your song. She would be perfect for you." The Texas conductor grabs Arundel by the arm and pulls her onto the stage.

"Got another accompanist up your sleeve?" Owen sheepishly asks.

I'm concerned, "What's going on? I can see one being sick but not two."

"Someone gave both accompanists a vile of fluid and told them that the Hall always provides a calming solution for the accompanists to take the edge off their butterflies. Both were so nervous that they opened the bottle and swallowed it right down. In five minutes, they were both vomiting violently."

At that moment a man breaks into our group and stands in front of Owen. "Thank you so much Mr. Stirling for delaying the start of the competition. Our students would have been so disappointed if they couldn't sing after coming all this way." He then turns his gaze in my direction, "You must be Dr. Timpson. I'll bet you've been praying your little heart out that we wouldn't make it in time and would be disqualified. Well, we're here, and we're going to oust you out of this competition one way or another."

I'm stunned. My mind swirls in a backward twist. This all sounds so familiar. Then I know where I've heard something similar before. "You sound like a Butler."

My comment catches him so off-guard that he can't say a thing. He turns and walks away.

"Mr. Stirling, I will be the accompanist for the Stanford Choir. It would help if I could look at the music before they perform. Then I could really help them."

The Stanford director grabs my arm, "Dr. Timpson, would you do that for us? That would make you compete against your own school."

"I'm not competing in either place. I'm here to help students be the best that they can be. Do you have your music?" She puts the score into my hands and hugs me. I slip behind a curtain so I can play the music in my head. But before I open the first page, I put a call into Agent Fowler. I have a feeling that things are going to get nastier before the night is over.

The Texas performance was great. Their first few measures were a little rocky until the director figured out that she was in charge. Then things changed drastically. Arundel was a masterful accompanist. The director gave her a huge bear hug before Arundel could leave the piano. They walked off stage together. When they were close enough, I could hear their conversation, "Dr. Williams, I have never been able to conduct my choir like that before. I have always needed to follow my pianists. What a difference it makes to have a genuine accompanist. What would it take to get you to come to Texas University? With you there, I think we could give Augustine competition."

Arundel laughs, "It was awesome to make your choir sound good, but I've signed a contract to stay at Augustine. Right now, my heart would never let me leave." The director gives her another hug and follows her choir back to their balcony seating.

I grab Arundel's arm, "I want you to stay right here off-stage while I accompany Stanford." I see a plain-clothed FBI-looking man close by and motion him to join us. "Candy's apple is red."

He gives me his full attention, "Red candy apples."

"Will you please stay with Dr. Williams until I finish with Stanford on stage? Don't let anyone she doesn't know even come close to her."

"Terry, what's going on?"

"Mischief by the truck full. Please stay by this FBI agent." I follow Stanford's director onto the stage.

I can almost play their piece without looking at the sheet music. I support a section when it's struggling with more of their notes and follow their director exactly. By the middle of their piece, they sound very good. The better they sound the harder they try. It is such a spiraling-up circle. By the end, they sound great. I hope some of this chaos calls attention to the fact that good choirs need accompanists not the top piano player in the school.

After receiving thanks from the Stanford director, I move off stage to grab Arundel and rush to get to Pam. I realize how easy it is to sabotage a choir. All one needs to do is disable the accompanist, the director, or the piano. I hope we're not too late to help Pam. When we enter the balcony, Pam is seated in the front row by herself, and the choir is in their designated seats ready to walk onto the stage. Dr. Rich and President Drake are in the center of the last row.

We rush into the seats on either side of Pam, "Are you okay?"

She slowly turns her head in my direction. With tears streaming down her face, she whispers, "I can't move." My heart falls into a hole. We are too late. Pam looks anxiously at me, "I shook hands with a man, and his hand stuck me with a needle." I turn Pam's hands up and see a pin in her right palm. I take a tissue from my pocket and pull it out. I also get Agent Fowler on his way to us. Pam tries to speak again, "Terry, you'll have to direct the choir from the piano. We can't let our students down. We can't let the Butler side win ever again."

Our Carnegie hosts are now standing the choir to lead them onto the stage. I stand and motion Dr. Rich and President Drake to come to me. Pam seems to be moving a little more. "Terry, my body is trying to wake up. I can now move my feet a little, but I could never direct. The choir will follow you. Take them to the top. I'll just stay right here and watch you do your magic." I explain our situation to our administration, and they both move to sit on each side of Pam. When we leave at the tail of our choir, Pam is describing her assailant to Agent Fowler. She even gives me a little wave with her fingers.

We reach the stage as the last of the Kensington students leave through the curtains. The accompanist is still at the piano staring under the lid. I grab a uniformed security guard and Arundel and rush toward the piano. When I smell smoke, I know it's too late. The security guard grabs the accompanist, and we all investigate the guts of the beautiful piano. Pieces of copper wire have been laid across the piano strings and are shorting out the electric circuits. I kick out the plug that is attached to the floor, but again it's too late.

Now Owen Stirling is by my side, "Terry, did this jerk just destroy my Concert Grand?"

"He did, and he's going to be charged with two poisonings, and attempted murder by lethal injection."

"Hey, you ain't pinning those things on me, Butler had someone else do them. I'm just the piano guy."

Owen is seething with anger, "Get this piece of garbage out of my sight before I put him through my shredder." Four security guards frog march him off stage. Owen turns to me, "What are we going to do now? I have twelve grand pianos I could roll in an instant onto this stage, but none of them have been tuned and they would need to sit for 24 hours before we could even tune them."

I don't even have to think about it, "Owen don't you have a deluxe keyboard with all the bells and whistles?"

"Terry, can you play on a keyboard?"

"I teach on one every day. Move the grand and the conductor's podium off and put the keyboard right here facing the choir with two benches."

He looks at me with deep concern, "Pam?"

"They tried to take her out, but she's going to be okay. She is not able to conduct at this point, so I'll lead them from the keyboard."

The choir and the keyboard are in place and ready at the same time. I have Arundel sit at the keyboard, but I walk around it to talk to the choir. "As you can see, we are missing a very important part of our choir. Dr. Masters can't lead you tonight, but she can see you and hear you. Evil people have tried all evening to win this competition with illegal and despicable tactics, but we will not bend to their dishonesty. Tonight, we sing for goodness and honesty and our conductor Dr. Pamula Fletcher Masters. Wave to her on the balcony and then don't let one eye stray from mine for the entire piece."

When I'm seated and ready, we are announced, "Ladies and gentlemen I am proud to present Augustine University singing an original composition by their director Dr. Pamula Masters." The audience is on their feet with an explosive ovation. I wait until they are mostly seated and bring my hands to the keyboard. When there's not a whisper in the room I nod to Arundel, and we begin the introduction.

When we finish, we all know that it is the most masterful piece we have ever performed. I am so proud of this group of students. Before the crowd even sits down, I am signaled that we may sing an encore. When I lift my hands to the keys, the audience quickly takes their seats. We are singing Pam's Hallelujah. Our singers are stronger than last year and their twelve-part harmonies swirl to the top of the Stem in clarity. It almost takes my breath away. We have overcome every obstacle thrown at us, and we have done what we came to do. Now we wait for the audience to quiet for the awards ceremony.

The stage begins to expand to hold all the choirs, but we are not moved to one end of the risers. We stand still centered in the middle. Arundel and I move to stand with our choir. I look up into the balcony and see that Pam's guard has changed to Granddad Martin on one side and Agent Fowler on the other. She looks like she has more of her movement back. Her arms are waving and giving us a thumbs up. We all wave back to her.

The fourth-place choir is announced as the students from Kensington University. A ribbon metal is placed over their head as each one walks onto the stage. To everyone's surprise, there is no trophy presentation to the school administration. Instead, the third-place school is announced, Texas University. They seem to be thrilled as they move onto the stage receiving their ribbon metals. Their administration is presented with the third-place trophy. When second place is announced the whole theater is wild with noise because that also announces that Augustine is in first place. Stanford moves onto the stage to receive their ribbon metals, and their administration graciously accepts their second-place trophy.

"We would like now to present the first-place award to Augustine University."

While they are handing out the ribbon metals, the back curtains part, and Pam is wheeled onto the stage by Grandpa Martin and Agent Fowler. Tom breaks rank and immediately scoops her up in his arms. I am so glad that we decided to leave our babies and Evan home for this trip.

Emmerson climbs onto my bus as we pull up in front of his hotel. "Dr. Timpson, we have a buffet all set up for you. That competition was the most impressive concert I have ever been to, except for maybe yours. You were there in every facet of the evening. You are a most exceptional woman."

"Thank you, Emmerson. But right now, I am a most tired and hungry woman. And I have two busloads of people just like me. Lead the way." He ushers us into his dining room which has been sectioned off with curtains again. Only this time there are more tables on our side than there are for his other guests. As our tired company starts filling their plates, I know I need to talk to Emmerson again. I find him just outside the curtains, "Emmerson, this has been one of those days… Would it be alright with you if we do a morning concert after breakfast at about tenish? Our flight doesn't leave until 4:00 pm and I know we would sound much better in the morning."

"Dr. Timpson, I wouldn't dream of having you perform tonight. After breakfast in the morning would be perfect."

Dinner is a mixture of eating and bringing everyone up to speed on all the events of the day. Dr. Rich and President Drake seem to eat in stunned silence. Pam has recovered enough that she is talking, walking, and eating with no problems, but Tom never leaves her side. I head to bed knowing that I need to meet with Agent Fowler in the morning. I can't help but wonder what's ahead as we leave this school year behind and jump into the next one in two weeks.

www.ingramcontent.com/pod-product-compliance
Lightning Source LLC
LaVergne TN
LVHW021757060526
838201LV00058B/3134